KNIGHTS OF PAST

THE TRANSFUSION SAGA
BOOK 13

STEPHANIE HUDSON

Knights of Past
The Transfusion Saga #13
Copyright © 2023 Stephanie Hudson
Published by Hudson Indie Ink
www.hudsonindieink.com

This book is licensed for your personal enjoyment only.
This book may not be re-sold or given away to other people. If you would like to share this book with another person, please purchase an additional copy for each recipient. If you're reading this book and did not purchase it, or it wasn't purchased for your use only, then please return to your favourite book retailer and purchase your own copy. Thank you for respecting the hard work of this author.
All rights reserved.
This is a work of fiction. Names, characters, places, brands, media, and incidents are either the product of the authors imagination or are used fictitiously. The author acknowledges the trademark status and trademark owners of various products referred to in this work of fiction, which have been used without permission. The publication/use of these trademarks is not authorised, associated with, or sponsored by the trademark owners.

Knights of Past/Stephanie Hudson – 1st ed.
ISBN-13 - 978-1-916562-34-9

I dedicate this book to Ireland.
Where I found comfort in its rolling green hills,
And serenity in its stunning countryside.
I found sunshine in the rain,
And wind lifting the leaves making them dance,
There is laughter and friendliness,
Smiles in the shops and music for my walks.
But most of all there is inspiration for my book,
And creative thoughts for my pages.

Thank you, Ireland, for all the words

CHAPTER 1
LOYAL PROMISES
AMELIA

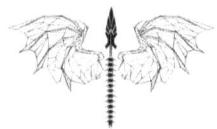

I took a deep breath and looked up as if I could still see his heavenly light, closing my eyes the moment I realized it was already long gone. With a shudder, I remembered the promise I made him the second glorious white wings had erupted from his back. Then once he had gathered his daughter's body in his arms and stood, I quickly did the same. In that moment he had looked down to me and while placing his forehead to mine, he asked,

"Wait for me."

Of course, my promise was said instantly in return,

"Always."

"Amelia!" I heard my parents both shout, making me turn in time to see them running towards me. In that moment of deep vulnerability, I ran towards them, meeting them halfway after an emotional sob tore free.

"Mum, Dad!" I shouted, seconds before throwing myself into their awaiting arms. I felt the tears soaking into my dad's

black shirt as he held my head cradled to his chest and my mum hugged me from behind. I hardly took note that my father looked barely affected by the fight with my mother. However, my mum was looking a little worse for wear with her jeans now ripped at the knees and her dark red sweater near in tatters.

"God's child," my dad breathed before I felt him tense, holding me tighter as if he was still trying to find the words. I pulled back a little so I could look up at him and with tears streaming down my face, I told him on a shuddering breath,

"I did it, Dad... I... I beat him." At this his own eyes glistened with unshed tears as the pride poured out of him. He reached up and cupped my cheek.

"That you did, my child... *you were utterly breathtaking.*" I smiled before biting my lip, and my tears started to flow more freely before I hiccupped a sob back and threw my arms around him.

"Oh, Dad!" He wrapped his own arms around me once more, this time lifting me slightly, so he could whisper,

"I was wrong, all these years. I was so wrong, and I am so sorry, baby girl... so sorry I tried to protect you... I... I was so blind... I..." I gripped him tighter before telling him,

"It's okay, Dad, I get it... I understand it." At this he lowered me down until my feet were back on the ground so he could look down at me and take my tears away with his thumbs, just like he used to do when I was a kid.

Then he told me earnestly,

"Then understand this, my child, I could not be any prouder of you, Amelia, than I am in this moment. I feel as if my pride will burst this old man's heart. Your strength, your courage, your heart and the power of your good soul... *all of it was a gift to witness.*" I grinned up at him and felt the emotions pour out of me, especially when I heard him say,

"You saved your mother, my Chosen..." He paused at this and pulled my mother to his side. And just like my own Fated had done to me, he bent his head enough to place his forehead to hers as emotions led his actions. And he wasn't the only one, as she cupped his cheek and silently told him,

'I love you.'

My father smiled at this before my mum turned to me and, like my father had done, showered me with praise.

"You saved us all, Amelia!" I swallowed hard at that, only now realising for myself what I had done. The gravity of it all. It started to hit me as my heart began to hammer in my chest.

I had killed a God.

I swallowed hard before nodding behind my parents, telling them,

"Yeah, well I had help." Then I pulled back enough to look at the army that had now all stopped. It wasn't hard to see those that had been fighting against us. Lucius' army were now shaking their heads, ridding themselves of the remnants of control from their unsure minds as all souls had now been restored to their rightful owner.

"And speaking of help," I said before pulling away from my parents. I looked overhead as I saw the McBain brothers' combined creature swooping low in the air and in their grasp was none other than Pip. I had to smile, because there she was, calling out as if she was having the time of her life,

"WHOOOOHOOO! I'M COMING, HONEYBOO!" She screamed because clearly there was one part of Hell that still had its fair amount of problems. I looked to the distance to see my uncle Adam in his other form, the greatest beast ever created, Abaddon, who was still causing havoc upon the land. He had just finished picking up a castle-sized rock and throwing it towards the cliff face, making it crumble in an avalanche of red dust. He then looked up at the sky and started roaring out at the sight of his Fated mate being flown in from above.

Yeah, it was most definitely time for Pip to take over, I could see her in their dragon-like clutches as she was already trying to strip herself of clothes. The sight made me chuckle, especially when she tossed her t-shirt in the air, as if she was at a rock concert. I knew then it wouldn't be long before Hell was back under the Devil's control, and Pip's Beast would be calm once more.

But before then, they had to get her safely to him, something that looked to be a bit of a mission, when Abaddon looked even more gripped by fury at the sight of his woman in the clutches of another Beast.

Clearly, the McBain brothers sensed this too and knew to give him a wide berth, especially when Abaddon threw another chunk of Hell's earth at them, trying to take them down.

"NOW STOP THAT! IT'S NOT NICE, POOKEY!" Pip chastised, before she was dropped at a safe height and far enough away that the McBain brothers had a chance of escaping. Now he was no longer under the same control that Mathias had on the others, Abaddon started to reduce in size with every earth-shaking stomp he made over towards his wife. His wife who was running back to him like something out of the Sound of Music as she frolicked and pranced, twirling her naked body with her hair dancing out behind her.

"Amelia?" My dad questioned, bringing me back to my own duties and making me grin back at them before saying,

"It's time for me to go and make someone else proud… *time for me to go and be their Queen.*" I made a step away from my parents but stopped when I felt my mother's hand shackle my wrist. I looked down before I raised my eyes to my mother in question, her beaming grin was the only comfort I would need in that moment. Anything just to be able to rid myself of the haunting memory of seeing her in such pain only a short time ago. Seeing such agony on someone you loved was an agony shared, especially knowing that I was the only one that had the power to stop it.

So yes, seeing her smile now was like a soothing balm to that memory.

"Then I suggest you look the part, my beautiful daughter," my mother said, before looking back to my father who grinned in agreement. Then, before I could even ask, my father's eyes started to glow a deep fiery purple, as he slowly raised his hands up. I looked down at myself to see what he was doing, only to find that my own tattered clothes were now transforming into something more fitting for my claim on Lucius' crown. Transforming into what can only be described as making me look like some warrior Princess.

I was now wearing a deep crimson colored dress that reached to the floor and was edged in a shimmering black, spiked thorn design. The front of the skirt held an embroidered Crest of my family's house, with a glistening black design that was also framed by the same pattern of thorns. The cut of the dress was both beautiful and practical with two long slits at each side of my legs reaching my hipbones. Underneath I now wore a pair of thick, leather trousers with shining black, plated armored boots that came up past the knee. A long, flowing cape of black and red attached to the high collar, one that was held there with curved plated shoulder pads and overlapping armor that reached all the way down to my wrists. Underneath, the long sleeves of the dress provided some comfort under such heavy weight. Now, after a day of wearing this bad ass outfit I had a feeling I would never complain about wearing a bra ever again!

However, despite how brutally beautiful it was, I soon realized that it had more than one point to make. I knew this when I looked down at myself once more to find the curved chest plate molded like a glove over my torso.

"Lucius's sigil?" I questioned in shock, looking back at my father who simply nodded with a grin. Lucius's sigil was engraved silver against the black, demonic armor that was so similar to that of his own, making me wonder if this had been my father's intention. To make me an extension of my Vampire King... his counterpart and leader of his Kingdom in his absence. It covered most of the space across my chest, reaching down to protect my belly, and I felt near indestructible in this thing.

Oh yes, it seemed as if my father was making a statement alright, and to all of Hell at that, signifying the bringing of our two houses together and presenting them on me, his daughter. One that with my last breath would continue to make him proud.

Now with my new power thundering in my veins, I reached out a hand behind me, calling for Lucius's sword, Caliburnus, waiting for my palm to be filled with the extra power. For every warrior needed a weapon, and I was determined to become its keeper until such time that I could return it to him.

I heard my mum mutter to my father,

"Could she be wearing any more armor?" At this he chuckled before reminding her,

"She's still my daughter, bad ass or not." I stifled a chuckle at hearing this, knowing old habits would definitely die hard with my father, no matter what he had just seen me do.

Once my transformation was complete, I walked towards Lucius's army, one that was no longer trying to kill the opposing side. A side that, now it was safe to do so, had fallen back at the commands of all of those that led them and had fought valiantly for us.

Lucius's army were an ocean of brutal, horned Demons with muscles bulging as they held Demonic looking weaponry in meaty grasps. These were mixed among some of the most terrifying creatures I had ever seen, with more fangs and pointed teeth than facial features could claim. With twisted, spiked limbs that looked more than capable of impaling their enemies and decaying skin that looked poisonous to touch. Intermingled between these powerful beings were mortal vessels that played host to a nation of vampires. Each wearing Demonic armor that looked as though it had been forged in the depths of a volcano before being cooled into plated armor shaped igneous rock.

It was chilling sight to behold, and one I steadied myself mentally against so I could do what I knew needed to be done next.

A show of strength and leadership.

So, after squashing down the urge to look back at my father for comfort, knowing this would be seen as a weakness, I approached the great army. However, what did surprise me was what came next as they all started to part down the middle, each taking a step backwards as if this had all been choreographed.

Before I could question these actions further, my eyes grew wide when I started to comprehend why. This was after I could see others making their way down the centre, making me understand why even the most terrifying looking Demons were now giving those that approached me a wide berth.

My Wraiths.

Of course, calling them mine was a bit of an exaggeration. They weren't mine as such, yet their souls were still under my control... *Under my care.* I hadn't wanted to use them in the army. I hadn't wanted to take advantage of them and do to them what their once king, the Wraith master, had done to them for all those years. But when I looked over the sea of Demons all fighting the wrong side, those that had been made to fight for a cause that was not their own, I couldn't help but fear for all the souls that would be lost.

So, I'd done something I promised myself I wouldn't do. I called forth the Wraiths and asked them to do something that in all their years of being enslaved, they had never been asked to do before. I asked them to fight a war where death would not be the outcome. I had merely wanted to create a distraction between two enemies fighting that could all lose their lives. A way to prevent pointless deaths. A way to save souls, not have them taken and used for a King's gain, just like what had been done to the Wraiths. So, knowing this, they fought for a justice, until such a time where these souls controlled by Matthias could return back to their rightful owner.

Their Vampire King.

In truth, I had thought that I would have been met with resistance, especially after vowing to them not to be like their master had by using them. However, it was as if they realized that this was not the same. That each of them could see down to the core of what was only ever to be a noble cause when I was the one asking it of them and in turn, I felt no conflict as they rose to the call of their new master.

And as for now, well here they all were, swiftly marching down the center of those that they had not long ago fought against. An unbeatable army, for nothing could kill a Wraith, which was why they were quickly given their space to make their way through.

I felt my father come and stand behind me, feeling the tension coming off him in waves at my back.

"Amelia?" He said my name in a questioning, unsure way, making me glance over my plated shoulder before telling him,

"It's alright, trust me, they will not hurt me." I then proved this by stepping forward and as I did, my father soon discovered why I was so confident. I watched as the one I had named Trevor came forward, making me grin at the sight of him. Most would have no doubt found this as an unnerving reaction to such a haunting being, but seeing him now leading the way brought me a comfort I could barely explain. One that only increased the moment he started to lower to a single knee, causing all the rest to follow, just like they had done the first time I freed them from their metal cages. Then, in what I had come to understand as the ultimate sign of their loyalty and respect, as one they all made a gesture with their hands. Ghost like fingers pointed up to the sky with phantom palms covering their faces for a few seconds before their hands all slapped to the ground at the same time, doing so in a thundering salute that echoed throughout the canyon.

"Wraiths, hear me now… your souls have been entrusted to me, and the honor you grant my own soul by answering my call to fight by my side makes me forever grateful. Your loyalty is never to be questioned and in return, I hope that my own is never to be doubted when I tell you all, I am forever in your debt. I bestow upon you my eternal vow that I will stop at nothing until I can finally discover how to release your souls back to their rightful owners. So that you may one day know what it is to gain back the pieces of the past that were stolen from you. As for this victorious day, you may return to your realm and wait for me, for I promise you with even my last breath, your day of freedom will come."

Trevor was the first to react and, like he also did that day, he placed a palm over his heart before rising to his feet. Then after nodding his head, he made a clicking sound, one that I still had no clue how to translate. But whatever the words were, their meaning became clear as, one by one, they started to float away like a wave washing the footprints from the sand.

I wondered briefly where that thought had come from, as if there was something there in my mind I couldn't yet reach. A memory that seemed to be lost and one deeply implanted yet despite this, it was also one I was not allowed to breach. I shook these strange thoughts from my mind as soon there was another heartwarming sight making its way down the center of the parted army.

"Clay! Caspian!" I shouted the second they came into view making me run towards them. Caspian grunted, which was all he was able to muster, making me smirk up at him,

"So, tell me, how's it feel to get your soul back, big man?" My comment must have worked as he granted me a rare grin. As for Clay, his return was a little warmer as he embraced me in a bear hug and said,

"Now *that,* was kick ass, little bird." I couldn't help but smirk, giving him a wink, telling him with a casual shrug of my shoulders,

"Yeah, but I didn't get to break any arms this time... so what you gonna do?" At this he boomed with laughter, but then he looked towards where the carnage of my rage had been directed the most and asked,

"And Luc?" I shook my head, before looking up at the Hellish sky and told him in a quiet, calm voice,

"He had something important to do." Clay nodded as if

understanding this and before I could say anything else on the matter, something seemed to settle within him, as if his mind was made up. Then, before I could question the look further, he started to lower to one knee, making me gasp in shock.

"My Queen!" he shouted firmly, bowing to me and making me swallow hard, whispering,

"Clay, what are you…?" This question was left unfinished and my breath was robbed from me as every single Demon behind him started to also lower to one knee. Just as the Wraiths had done. Clay then elbowed Caspian in his leg, making the big bastard grunt before he too lowered to a knee. This was before granting me a playful wink on his way down, as if his reluctance had only been in jest.

It was a sight I would never forget as long as I lived.

As far as the eye could see, legions upon legions all lowered, creating an ocean of bodies now bowing before their Queen.

"I…I…"

"You, my child, were born for this… *now it's time to embrace it,"* I heard my father whisper from behind. So, I took a deep breath and addressed my Kingdom,

"The fight has been won! Our King's enemy slain by my hand! The hand of your Vampire Queen… Now, each of you rise and bask in the glory of our victory, for it is eternally ours!" I shouted, making everyone do as I asked, now rising to their feet and crying out in their own victory because for the first time in history, it was a war with no losing side. For it was only one dark heart and one rotted soul that had lost. A newly born God had learned that even a life fueled by the heart of darkness could be extinguished by the light of the good and pure of soul. As for the army, they cheered and were soon basking in their glory, like I wanted them to.

However, it wasn't enough to drown out the sound of

clapping from behind, making me turn just as my parents did. This was only to discover that now they weren't the only family members at my back.

For there was my grandfather and with him,

My soon to be father-in-law…

The Devil.

CHAPTER 2
FAMILY CONNECTIONS

"*Lucifer,*" I uttered in awe, making him smirk. A sexy feature indeed and I couldn't help but be totally transfixed by him. I don't know why I was surprised to find Lucifer's vessel so intimidatingly handsome as really, I should have expected nothing less. He looked so regal, with defined cheekbones and a strong jawline. A long, straight nose and shoulder-length hair was currently pulled back, giving him that air of authority that a ruler like him really didn't need. His reputation was more than enough and always would be. However, it was his intense, pale, aqua blue eyes that had me enslaved to his gaze, making me too afraid to look away.

Lucifer's armor was unlike anything I had ever seen before and looked more like a blanket of screaming souls had enveloped his huge, towering body, all trying to escape him. Then with merely a click of his fingers, they had all transformed into molten metal before hardening as if cooled rapidly. Hints of horrified, skeletal faces were cemented in each overlapping plate, with the largest ones being positioned at his shoulders, knees and thighs. Their fang-filled mouths spread wide and open, crying out among decorated plates of jagged and deadly barbed metal. Spikes that looked sharp enough to cut through flesh like butter, with his chest plate mimicking a Demonic boned ribcage, as though he was wearing a metal skeleton on the outside. His gauntleted hands descended into deadly tips at the end of each metal clad finger. This sinister design matched the ends of his plated heavy boots.

This was a complete contrast to my grandfather, who was dressed more like some noble knight in gleaming gold. However, the closer he got, the more detail could be seen, and instead of looking like thousands of souls all trying to escape him, his armor was decorated with the faint outline of skeletal hands all over his body. It definitely screamed the difference between the two kings and the realms that they ruled over.

As for Lucifer, the moment it was noticed he was here in our presence, the entire army at my back lowered once more to their knees. He took no notice of this, however. He seemed to only have eyes for me, as he soon motioned me forward. I sucked back a fearful breath, making my father grab the top of my arm and quickly hold me back.

"She is fine where she is," my father said in a stern tone but again, this only managed to amuse Lucifer as his handsome but deadly grin deepened.

"You believe I wish to do her harm?" he asked, his voice as deep and commanding as one would expect from the Devil himself.

"Even if she wasn't my daughter, ask yourself, Lucifer, if your son were here right now, do you really believe he would allow his Chosen One to go anywhere near you?" my father argued.

"My son has trust issues," my grandfather, Asmodeus, muttered, as he too was clearly amused.

"And for good reason, after learning all that was kept from him," my father countered, shooting his own father a glare.

"I'm married to an Oracle, son of Asmodeus, I am as tied to the Fates as any man," Lucifer replied, making my father snap,

"Don't you mean the Fates are tied to you."

"Draven!" my mother warned, now placing a calming hand on my father's arm. Of course, I also knew it was a bad sign when Lucifer growled low in his throat and took a menacing step towards my father. Which was why I decided now was the time to intervene.

"Do you wish me harm?" I asked, feeling my father's grip tense around my arm.

"After what you have been prophesized to become, I would be a fool indeed to even attempt it after witnessing what you are capable of… for in truth, you surpassed even my greatest vision." My eyes widened in surprise when hearing this, making me reach up and gently try to uncurl my father's fingers from my arm while telling him softly,

"It's okay, Dad, I trust he won't hurt me." My father looked down at me in shock before asking, incredulously,

"Remember that you're putting that trust in the Devil, my child." I took his hand and gave it a reassuring squeeze before replying,

"No, I am putting that trust in the father of the man I love… besides, I have a feeling that he had a hand in this." I looked to my mother to see her biting her lip and realized, in that moment, that I wasn't the only one thinking the same thing. Draven looked to my mother who nodded, agreeing with my decision. He released a heavy sigh and let me go, meaning I was free to walk towards the God of Hell.

As for Lucifer, he watched me do this with great interest

as every move I made was one he took careful note of. Then, when I was close enough for my own liking, I stopped, still having to look up at him due to his colossal height. He was so big, he would have made Ragnar seem like a normal height.

"Brave girl, and it is now easy to see."

"Easy to see what?" I asked with a questioning frown.

"To see what it is he is so obsessed with and why he would go to great lengths in hiding you from me." I took a quick breath knowing he was talking about Lucius.

After this he took a few steps closer, and his long legs cut the space between us in a single heartbeat. I had never before wanted so badly to take steps back to counteract this action. But I also knew that when faced with a man such as he, the King of Kings, in this brutal realm, then gaining his respect was only going to be done with the bravery he had praised me for having.

I knew this to be true when his eyes glowed and that spark of interest in me was deepening by the second. Then I felt almost as if the entirety of Hell behind me all took a collective held breath as he reached out towards me. However, this nation's breath was released all at once when his actions ended with a tender touch and not bloodshed like everyone feared. The backs of his metal clad fingers were cold as they made their way down my cheek. But this was when he surprised me the most, for it wasn't his gentle gesture but more so the tender words that followed it.

"For so long I have waited, and now here you are. The most perfect soul created, and one I finally had a hand in." At this I heard my mother snort a laugh and forgetting herself she muttered,

"I think I would have remembered you being there." At this Lucifer grinned, and said to her,

"Oh, but I was, as you don't think I took all of the blood

of a God inside you, do you?" At this my mother gasped as her hand went to her belly as if remembering that day.

"No, I just gave it to someone else and as for Lucius, my most perfect son, well then it was Fated that when she was born, he be trusted to keep it safe for her." The moment he said this I tensed.

"What… what do you mean?" My mother gasped the question, making Lucifer smirk down at me.

"You didn't tell them?" he asked in an amused tone, making me reply with the obvious truth,

"We have all been a little busy… me especially."

"Ah yes, I must say you have made these last few weeks in Hell very interesting, although your grandfather was quite worried," Lucifer said as he looked behind him to where his friend, Asmodeus, stood and at hearing this, my grandfather winked at me.

"Amelia?" My father said my name in question, and I took a deep breath knowing there was no sense in prolonging it. The time had come for my next confession, only not exactly the God I would have thought being the one to witness it.

"Best get it over and done with, little one," Lucifer said, leaning down slightly when gifting me this advice, before jerking his handsome head towards my parents. I nodded before releasing a deep and regretful sigh just as I turned to face them.

"I wasn't born mortal like you both thought."

"What!?"

"What!?" Both my parents gasped, even though my mothers was whispered whereas my father's was hissed.

"It seems as if it were possible for even a mortal to surpass Fate's expectations," Lucifer said, not exactly helping with this, although his compliment was appreciated all the same.

"Turns out, I was the first-born vampire," I said, making my mum start shaking her head in disbelief, muttering under her breath how it wasn't possible.

"No, you were born mortal, Amelia, no one felt anything…"

I cut my father off, giving him a soft smile and told him, "It was Lucius that brought it out in me." My father's eyes went wide at this new knowledge, whereas my mother's mouth dropped open a little.

"Then why didn't we feel it? Why did we never know?" This was a good question and unfortunately, one I would have to answer in place of Lucius, as my father deserved a reply to his question.

"Go on, little Vampire, tell them… this is, after all, the best bit," Lucifer said as if he knew and had always known. But then he was married to an Oracle, and clearly not one who had lost all her powers as we had been led to believe. Not even after the prophecy had been fulfilled with my mother as was what had always been predicted to happen. Or maybe this was always Lucifer's intent, to steer others away from the potential of stealing her from him. A power he wanted to keep hidden so as to keep her safe.

As for me, I still had part of the story to tell.

"It happened when I was a baby, the only time Lucius ever saw me," I said, making my mother cry out,

"Oh God no… what did he do to you?" my mother asked, making me shake my head.

"It's not what you think, he didn't do anything to me… it was, well it was actually all me."

"You? Amelia, you were but a baby," my father argued softly.

"Yes, but I was a baby drawn to him even then, as the second he came close enough, I grew fangs and I bit him."

"What?!" my mother shouted, whereas this time my father looked simply stunned into silence.

"It's true…" I said smiling, before carrying on and being able to laugh about it now.

"I bit him through his glove and into the hand that held the Venom of God, I don't know how, but a piece of my soul got transferred into him. It was the supernatural piece of me… the part of my blood that most likely would have torn me to pieces, that would have darkened my mortal soul and left me a shadow of what I have finally become today."

"What she says is true," Lucifer added, as if knowing this outcome before it had chance to take root and guide my destiny down this dark path.

"It was the part that Lucifer had left inside you, Mum, when I was nothing more than a tiny spark of life… that was the piece Lucius took. He didn't intend for it to happen, but it was why after it did, he never came near me again. Not until the next time we saw each other, which you both know was when he saved me at sixteen years old," I said, now telling them it all and surprisingly, feeling better for it.

"A kidnapping attempt that I believe Matthias was responsible for," Lucifer added, surprising everyone this time.

"You gave her Pertinax's blood… *my unborn child!?*" My mother accused the Devil in a dark and dangerous tone, and it had to be said, she was as brave as I was to face him like that.

"I did as I was Fated to, my dear."

"Fated?!" my mum shouted, making my dad be the one to restrain her back this time.

"What your daughter says is true, had my son not taken that piece of her, she would not be the daughter standing here today, she would not have been the symbol of our victory, but instead the symbol of our defeat for she would have been the ruling force and what we would have been fighting against. Lucius saved your daughter's soul, *you all did,"* Lucifer said, surprising me with his honesty and the fact that he obvious cared.

But then, considering what the outcome may have been, was it all that surprising? Since the beginning of Hell's existence, Lucifer had ruled this dark realm and despite knowing the fable tales of the few times he had come close to losing that rule before, it had to be said, that none were as close as this had been.

Was this his way of thanking me, I wondered, as he most certainly seemed to have my back now. Along with that of his son's. Something he proved when he continued on,

"…and because of that Fate, Hell is still mine…" At this he took pause so he could go back to addressing me, obviously having said all he intended to say to my parents. Which was when I felt the back of a smooth claw at my chin, guiding my face back to his, silently demanding my attention.

"Now, I entrust you to take your rightful place as Queen and rule the Kingdom and army that is yours by birthright, as well as what will no doubt be in marriage as well. Something I am certain will happen sooner rather than later. Which, take heed, little Vampire born, for I remind you, this will make you my daughter-in-law, so I trust you to be on his throne and stay there until his return…" He tapped me twice under my chin in a teasingly gentle way before he cast his dark and foreboding gaze over to the sea of Hell's armies still kneeling at my back. Then he raised himself even taller and bellowed out across the canyon floor,

"…FOR LET IT NOW BE KNOWN TO ALL MY KINGDOM, HEED MY WORDS AND MARK THEM AS LAW, FOR NO ONE DARES STAND AGAINST MY

DAUGHTER, BE IT PUNISHABLE BY DEATH OF YOUR SOUL!" I swear I nearly choked on my own shock, as Lucifer, Overlord and King of all of Hell had just proclaimed me as his daughter and made it law that no one should ever threaten me.

I. Was. Speechless.

After this, Lucifer turned to my grandfather, a being that was clearly a good friend of his and had been grinning throughout this whole thing.

"Here's to another tale to regale our old souls with, for as always it is a pleasure having you fight by my side, my friend," Lucifer said, making my grandfather bow his head.

"As it was with you, forever, my King," Asmodeus replied, adding his respect for whom he was clearly loyal to at the end. After this Lucifer walked further past and held out his hand towards the destruction I had made. I had little time to wonder why he did this as suddenly the box that had once been the key Matthias had used, shot into his hand from beneath the rubble. I then watched as it quickly formed into that of a box again, just exactly the same one as it had been when I had first laid my eyes on it back on that Fated day.

The day that brought me Lucius.

Uncurling his impressive Demonic blood red wings, Lucifer then took off to the skies, making me watch as he flew off into the distance. I could just make out as he flew over where Pip was still 'entertaining' Abaddon, who had thankfully calmed significantly since Pip had been flown over there and dropped to his feet. In fact, shamefully, I think I could still see her little naked body dancing for him and it looked as if all she was missing was the pol... oh no, there it was, I thought, now wishing that was one part of my uncle's Demonic anatomy I wish I could scrape from my memory. I could only hope that he wouldn't start clapping as I think that might have started an earthquake, and the cliffs surrounding us already looked as if one had happened.

I released a sigh and turned back to my parents the moment my mother called my name.

"Amelia."

"Why did you never tell us?" my father asked, but then took pause and looked at my mother. "Unless this is yet another thing you knew and chose not to tell me?" he asked skeptically, making my mother growl at him and smack him with the back of her hand.

"What? No! Of course I didn't know!" she shouted angrily. This was when I started blurting it all out like I was some kid again, confessing all my childish sins to my parents and praying for them not to ground me.

"I didn't know myself until the Keepers of Three told me... who, I should probably mention, are most likely squashed right now in the temple of the Tree of Souls, but before they became grotesque piles of goo on the floor, they showed me Lucius's memories. I didn't realize at the time, but they were showing me what was manipulated by Matthias and what he wanted me to know. He needed to get me into Hell, which was what kickstarted this whole thing. Lucius tried to stop me, begged me to listen to him." At this my father took pity on me, as he framed my face with his hands and told me,

"My sweet, dear child, it was not your fault, this was your Fate, this was *your destiny* and as much as I hate to admit it, much as I did when your mother did the same, you cannot change who you are, despite how those who care for you may wish to change certain compulsive actions of yours. You are here now because you were always meant to be here," my father told me, and I have to admit, it felt good hearing it. Like having his blessing was cleansing my soul of all the remorse I felt. Because ever since I had stepped through that Tree of Souls, I had felt guilty about so many things. I blamed myself for every minute that had happened after I did the one thing that Lucius asked me not to do. But my father was right. This had been my destiny. Because Matthias wouldn't have stopped. He wouldn't have just given in and given up. Not when this was a grudge that spanned over two thousand years. A hatred and resentment that went far beyond Lucius or his brother Dariush. It was one that lay at Lucifer's feet and ironically, it was one that, in the end, he didn't have to fight.

Matthias would have continued in his quest to destroy us all. One way or another it wouldn't have stopped had I not stepped through the Tree of Souls and started this journey. So, the Keepers of Three were not wrong when they told me I was the only one who could stop this. The only one who had the power, because the infection would have kept on growing and more souls would have been lost to the roots of his rage. A dark essence Lucius had unknowingly released to the roots that lead straight to the core of his own souls.

And now it was done.

Matthias was finally where he belonged. Lucifer should have killed him long ago, and maybe that was his mistake. Or maybe, like he said, this was simply all Fated to end this way.

Either way, as I looked back towards where his body still lay, his head severed and his dark soul being no more, I felt that sense of victory warm my heart. We had won and for me now, well there was still one more thing I had left to do.

"Amelia?" my mum called my name in question when I walked away from them both and over to where the Eye of Crimson was still lying in the dirt. I reached down to pick it up and sighed when that too felt right being back in my charge.

"Fae! Be careful, don't touch it!" my mum shouted too

late, for it was back in my grasp and once more protected, as was my responsibility to do so. I was still its Keeper, and I would do right by the Fates. So, I turned back to face them and said,

"It's okay, everything will be okay now." Because I knew with everything deep inside me that it no longer had just one keeper.

No, now…

It had two.

Lucius

CHAPTER 3
PEACE AND FORGIVENESS
LUCIUS

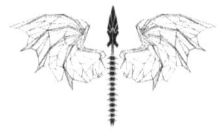

F *orgiveness.*
It was a word unspoken yet here I was.
Proof that it happened.

The sins of my reckoning forgiven. The words of damnation lost now to memory, for no longer did anything stand in my way from entering Heaven. A place I still to this day had always believed myself holy unwelcome. And yet, here I was, with my daughter's body in my arms and even though I could feel that her soul was long gone, just being here allowed me the gift of hope once more.

All I could do was hope.

As honestly, I had not a single clue as to whether this would work. I had nothing but a faith that I once believed in that had been firmly eradicated from my heart, now powerfully resurrected in my soul. For white wings in Hell had never been seen before, and that was all the sign I had needed.

This had to work.

Because the moment my Chosen One had told me who it

was that lay dying on the battlefield, I knew it in the depths of my own soul to be true.

It was, *at long last...*

My Kala.

All of this time walking the same earth together and I never knew. All this time she had been trapped. Her own body made a slave to that of my wife's, so that Dalene could continue to grow her obsession of hatred and revenge against me. Using her own daughter, *my daughter,* as a weapon against me. Her own body becoming a cruel cage she couldn't escape from. It was the cruelest of realities to accept. For it meant that she hadn't just taken Kala's first life, but she had made our daughter a slave in her second.

I had always believed the Gods hated me. I had always believed that Jesus, the man I would have given my life for, had forsaken me.

But I had been wrong. For he had done as he had promised he would. He had resurrected my daughter, and I had not been there for her. If only I'd have known, I could have done something. I could have saved her.

I could have saved her this time.

And now I was here, and the bitter irony did not escape me being the one to bring her to this white paradise. An endless pristine garden that was overflowing with white flowers of every kind known to man. A wall of flawless marble arches surrounded us and each without the grey veins of stone to blemish them. They stood like silent heavenly sentinels guarding this sacred space. A forest of trees beyond them, that look bleached of any color and leaves so delicate they looked more like woven lace flittering like butterflies in the wind. Then, there in the center of it all, was four gleaming white pillars standing at each corner of the raised dais. The raised platform held a large pale stone altar, one surrounded by blooming white roses. Of course, I knew that the white rose symbolized loyalty, purity, and innocence, making me understand why this garden existed.

I lay her down so gently, it was as if I had convinced myself she was but a doll made from the finest of glass. Lowering her breathless body down on a place I knew was waiting for her among the white bed of roses. And just like on that dreadful day, the worst of my life, the same tears fell as they did then. Yet despite my heartbreak, I grew some comfort at seeing her finally looking so peaceful. No doubt, the most peaceful she had ever been since her rebirth.

"I'm so sorry I couldn't save you… I couldn't save you the first time… *my little girl… please… please forgive me…* forgive me and find peace for this is the only place you deserve to be when finding your eternal rest," I said with tears flowing freely as I lay my head down so as my forehead was cradled in her still hands. The scars and evidence of how hard she had fought against the evil will of her mother, now long faded away. For the spells cast by a witch were lost the moment the power of life was gone.

I raised my head up, without bothering to wipe away my tears. The evidence feeling as though it would stain my skin just as her strength and bravery had once stained hers. I didn't even flinch when I felt the presence appear at my back.

For I knew who it was.

For I knew… *our time had come.*

"Tell me… she is… at peace," I stammered out, forcing the words to be heard through the thickness of my emotions.

"She is, for it is her time." The voice of Jesus struck me like the holy lance, the spear of destiny I had embedded in my vessel had just been ripped out only to be pierced into my lung.

It had been so long, I thought I would have forgotten it by

now. A foolish thought indeed, for how could I ever forget? How could I have honestly believed my faith in this man so dead that I would not have known him? When in truth...

I remembered... *Everything.*

It seemed as if two thousand years was not enough to bury such loyalty. Which was why I found the bravery to speak again,

"You kept your word."

"I did... as you kept yours." I started to shake my head at his words, making me say down at my daughter's hands,

"I thought lying was still a sin." At this he laughed and even that managed to sweep away more of the dust on my memories, revealing them so purely, it took my breath away.

"So is drinking until you fall off your stool and declaring to all you will pay for their drinks, despite us all knowing you had not a coin to your name." This ignited a strange sound from me, like a scoff that finished on a sob as my emotions were near too much to bear. Because hearing this and I knew it was my turn to laugh. Which was when I finally found enough courage to turn and face my past, and the moment I did I could not help my reaction.

I fell to my knees and lowered my head. Then I held out my hands, cupping them in front of me as I had done all those years ago when first declaring my life forfeit to his cause. Hands he had once filled with wine from his own cup, before raising them to drink from. And for the second time in my life, I begged for the life of my child.

"I have no right... I know I do not. I had forsaken my faith the moment it was tested too far for me to be able to live with. I know this. I have always known this. You were my brother, my father, and my friend..."

"And you felt as if I had abandoned you... as if I had forsaken you, my brother, my child, my friend," he said, making me look up at him, seeing him finally just the same as I had that day. A face even lips or mind or fear could not describe. A face that had haunted my dreams for so long, it felt as if just looking at him now was penance for my sins... *my atonement.*

"I did," I said as tears continued to run freely before he placed a hand on my shoulder.

"Then we were both wrong... ask it of me once more, Judas."

"Please... please, my Lord, please I beg of you, grant me back the soul of my daughter... *at the very least... let me... say goodbye this time."* Jesus bowed his head the once, and told me,

"I did this once before, as it was your choice to make, however, this time... *it is hers..."*

I turned my head when he gestured behind me and gasped the moment I saw my daughter draw in her first heavenly breath. I was up on my feet and gathering her in my arms in the time it took for my heart to be faster.

"I will give you two a moment alone." I looked behind me to see that he was no longer there, and we were in fact now alone.

"Father?"

The glorious second I heard her voice, a shuddered breath escaped me. I then held her tighter to me for a moment before pulling back and cupping her face. Her beautiful face, one that still belonged to that of my little girl. Now a grown woman, with eyes that remained the same, eyes that at one time may have looked as black as the soul that had taken her from me... *but not now.*

No, now they were the bright and vibrant hazel I remembered them to be. Those swirls of amber framing the irises that I used to adore seeing in the Jerusalem sunrise. She had always been an early riser and it had always been our time. Her sun-kissed skin had once matched my own, along with that little dip in her left cheek. Brown hair with its streaks of blonde from playing outside for endless hours, and it warmed my heart to see it once again paint the strands like the sun was still with us.

"Kala, my beautiful girl... my beautiful daughter... I am here, *I am here now.*" At this she grabbed on to me and hugged me back, holding on for dear life as she too started crying.

"For so long... I dreamed of this moment for so long!" she told me, now sobbing her heart out, and I too did not have the power to stop the tears, not hers nor my own.

Minutes past, but then again, it could have been hours for everything felt right finally having her in my arms. Yet despite this, I knew that our time was limited and there was a lifetime of things I still had left to say. So, I pulled back gently and in turn, she moved so as we were both sitting on the altar.

"I want you to know... no, no, I *need* you to know... I tried everything. I didn't know... I didn't know Jesus had brought you back... if I'd have known...*Gods...*" She covered my hand with hers, giving it a squeeze before telling me,

"I know you didn't know about me. They tried to make me hate you. For a long time, they made me believe that you had abandoned me. That you had abandoned both of us, my mother and me, all so as you may live a life as a Vampire King. That you chose power over us." At this I sucked in a sharp breath, taking her hands in mine so as I could raise them to my lips to kiss before assuring her,

"No, my child... never, never would I have left you, not for all the world offered at my feet. It was in my bitter heartbreak at losing you that I chose my next life, but never before." At this she gave me a teary, wide-eyed, tender look as my words clearly meant something to her.

"I know… I know this now as I soon learned the truth. Because after Dalene, my mother took possession of my body, I was plagued by the truth of her bitter thoughts. The truth of her memories. I knew it all." I gave her hands a squeeze, trying to ease her of her thoughts as I continued to listen to all she had to tell me. The pain in her voice was so crushing, it was as if each word endured was a fresh new crack inflicted upon my heart.

"I knew then that I had been nothing more than a pawn in their game for revenge against you. That every word spoken before that point had been a lie. I saw the memory of you in her own eyes, the devastation in your heartbreak when you realized that she had killed me. I knew then everything that they had said, every single word about you, had been a lie. One with the sole purpose of luring me deeper into their game of revenge. Because after she took host in my body, well nothing could hide the truth… that… that you did in fact… *love me.*" The moment she said this I pulled her into me and let her cry freely on my shoulder.

"Oh, my daughter, I loved you more than anyone else in the world… you were the single most beautiful thing I ever did in my life. You made me want to be a better man, Kala," I told her, for it was true. Because before Amelia had come along, I had never loved another more and never thought myself possible of ever loving again.

I loosened my hold on her so that I could wipe away her tears, just as I used to do when faced with a three-year-old little girl who had just fallen down and scraped her knee.

"I'm so sorry I failed you. I never should have left you with her… I never should have trusted her. Trusted that she loved you as much as I did, as any mother should love her child." Once again she took my hand in hers and squeezed, giving me even greater strength.

"I don't blame you. I only blame those that were truly responsible for your demise and in the end, for my own," she told me, and I found myself holding my breath as I asked,

"And now?"

"I fear that Earth has no place for me." And there it was, one of my greatest fears in this conversation now spoken aloud. I shook my head gently and told her,

"That's not true, Kala, for your place is with me, your place is and always will be in my world, finally by my side and forever under my protection, just as it always should have been." At this she shook her head, and I felt the pain and rejection like a lash against my soul. But I knew that Jesus was right, this was her choice… *not mine.*

So many choices had been denied to her all her life and I was not about to do the same. No matter how much it pained me to let her go.

"I have seen so much pain and destruction, in all honesty I have never known anything other. Not until those memories were given to me by my mother… the only gift she ever gave me, no matter how unintentional it was seeing as I had to steal them from her. But until then, I had never known laughter, love, all the things you gave to me as a child. In truth, Father, those memories were what kept me going." I closed my eyes at this as I let her words sooth my soul, healing the pain enough to bare it. I released a held breath and told her,

"Then allow me to give you more of them, please… *come with me,"* I told her as fresh tears rolled down her cheeks and my own.

"My soul is fractured, broken and needs fixing. I know

that and I fear there is only one place that it could finally happen. I am not saying never, but I am saying not now, for I am not ready." I swallowed down my regret that the time she spoke of wasn't now and that what little of it we did have, was far too soon to come to an end.

"I just need time, and if the Gods are good enough to grant it to me, then this will not be goodbye… it will only be, until then." I nodded my head once, then twice, holding back my selfish need to beg, as she was right. She had to be ready.

"They do say that time heals all wounds," I said, trying to offer comfort in what I knew was a difficult decision she just had to make.

"Is it true?" she asked of me and I turned to face her. Then with the backs of my fingers I took even more tears away, before telling her,

"Two thousand years I have waited for this moment, but I believe yes, time has the power to grant many things and if it is time you need, then it is time I will give you, my child. For it will be worth every moment spent waiting for you knowing that you are now at peace." Her eyes closed as her emotions overwhelmed her.

"Thank you for understanding," she told me, making me reply in kind,

"Thank you, Kala."

"For what?" she asked, clearly surprised.

"For teaching me what it is to love another." At this she threw her arms around me and whispered a sound I never thought I would ever be blessed enough to hear again,

"Oh Dad!" I held her so tightly I knew its reason was because I didn't ever want to let go of this feeling. But then when she needed to draw breath, I pulled back and the smile she granted me felt like another gift. That was until her words followed, for she playfully nudged my arm and said,

"I like her, she seems nice, and she loves you, so very much." At this I granted her a small grin in return.

"She is and she does, and when the time is right, I just know that she will welcome you with open arms."

"You really think so?" she asked in a hopeful tone that melted my heart, happy to hear how much she wanted this.

"I am certain of this as I am of taking my next breath." I then pretended to hold my breath, making her eyes widen before I let it out in a rush of air, making her laugh. Then she playfully nudged my arm again.

"I'm not used to being teased."

"Then I look forward to being the father that teaches you many things, child… but most of all, the lesson to laugh and to smile," I said, running the back of my finger along her grinning lips.

"And I will look forward to it too, every minute I am here." This is when I made her a vow.

"We will have our time, Kala, I know this. For it has been my greatest wish."

My spoken wish was then granted by the gift of another, when she told me all I needed to hear…

"It is my wish too, Father."

CHAPTER 4
HOLY REQUESTS

H oly Requests

After this Kala, looked behind her and when she focused on the open doorway that just appeared, I felt every muscle in my body tense knowing what it meant. It was one that was framed by an intricate arch of delicate golden roses. Of course, I knew what this symbolised also, as it was sign of Jesus' joyous resurrection. It meant reverence and affection, but it was also a symbol of crossing over and entering your next journey in the Afterlife.

One I selfishly didn't want her to take.

But one I knew she would take regardless, when she told me softly,

"It's time." I started to shake my head, admittedly telling her,

"I don't want you to go." She granted me a small smile as I could see my words had meant a lot to her.

"I never knew it was possible to gain a lifetime in a day," she told me, making my breath catch in my throat. Then she took my hand and lifted it to her lips, granting me a kiss on the back of my palm before holding it then cupped to her cheek.

"I am happy knowing that I am finally loved wherever I am meant to be, and that you too are loved where you were always destined to be. And until it is our time, we won't say goodbye, for this isn't the end…" She paused, now looking up at me with those big, beautiful hazel eyes, eyes now simmering with unshed tears, just like she did as a child. Then she finished her vow,

"… it is only the beginning."

After this we both stood and she took my hand, and I forced myself to walk with her towards the doorway. But that was when it suddenly hit me, the realization nearly making me stagger in my step.

This exit wasn't for her.

It was for me.

It was her symbol reverence and affection for me. She had created it and I lowered my head as the weight of that knowledge nearly brought me to my knees. But I didn't want to leave without granting her a gift of my own. So, I plucked one of the golden roses from the arch, holding it by the stem before her. Then with a thought I rolled my palm just above the perfect bloom and turned it to clear obsidian, making it now look like black glass.

"What does it mean?" she asked as she reached out and took it into her grasp, looking down at it in awe.

"It is my gift to you… it symbolizes power, strength, and

most of all, my hope... *it is a piece of me."* She looked so touched by this and whispered gently through fresh tears,

"Thank you, Father... I will treasure it always." At this I ran the back of my finger down her cheek, smiling down at her.

"You are most welcome, my child," I told her, knowing that I couldn't prolong this any longer, but as I turned ready to leave she grabbed my arm. Then she utterly amazed me with what came next. For she cupped both her hands to her chest, my rose held firmly between them and closed her eyes. I didn't have long to question why, as a blue light started to glow between her hands and I frowned in silent wonder at what she was about to gift me in return.

"For your sacrifice you were granted your wish to bring me here yourself. To speak with me one more time and give me the choice of where my soul remains. For the time being, I have chosen to remain here, but I was also granted a wish for my own sacrifice made. For wanting to protect a very different world than this, to protect it against the hatred that wanted to consume it. I give that wish to you now, for I know there is one other soul you would have wished to have saved." At this she handed over the glowing blue light with one hand, keeping her rose firmly in the other. My eyes widened as realization hit me as to what this could mean.

Could it be truly possible?

"I... I don't know what to say," I whispered in awe and dreamlike disbelief.

"Say not goodbye, but only farewell... *for our time will come."* At this I looked away from the glow in her palm, and before taking it, I used my own hands to frame her face. Then I leaned down so as I could grant her a tender kiss on her forehead.

"Then farewell, my daughter… *until our time.*" I felt my tears drip down my face and soak into her skin, sealing this vow with the strength of my emotions. By the time I pulled away, I saw the same emotions glistening in her eyes before falling from the weight of them. Then I took the glow into my own hands, holding it to my chest as I stepped away. And with each step I took closer to the doorway at my back, I then watched as another appeared behind her, knowing that she was in God's hands.

My once mentor.

My eternal friend.

The man I had always intended to follow into the Afterlife no matter what the outcome. I just didn't expect it to take me over two thousand years to get there. So, with little else to say, I parted with only this,

"Goodbye, my old friend." And with that, Jesus Christ nodded behind me and for the first time, acknowledged me not as the man he used to know…

But now as the King I had always been destined to become.

"We will meet again, Lucius Septimius, but until then, I will keep the souls you cherish safe." I nodded my thanks before allowing myself the bitter indulgence of seeing my daughter for the last few precious moment before this Demon King was made to leave Heaven. And I may have left a soul I loved behind, but I was also taking away another I cared for. That, and the eternal gift of my daughter's face now smiling at me. Something that finally had the power to replace the haunting memory of her lying dead in my arms. A wound I can honestly say, I had never once believed capable of being healed.

I had never been happier to have been proven wrong. So as darkness enveloped me, I welcomed it as I looked down at the blue glow in my hands, knowing what this meant.

It was also why I was not surprised when I found myself back in the Temple of the Tree of Souls. The destruction from the battle that had ensued here still remained, yet one thing had changed. The roots leading to the Tree of Souls we're now free of the infected hatred that had once consumed them.

I walked over to the body that still lay as if asleep, waiting for its master's return. I took in a deep breath as I knelt down next to Ruto, an angelic soul that had been with me for the last eight hundred years.

"I once gifted you my soul's blood, now your soul is that of the gift from my daughter. Rise again, child of my blood, and once more breathe life into this mortal realm." This was when I opened my hands over his heart and allowed his soul to seep back into that of his vessel. I then watched as he finally took a breath and I myself closed my eyes, this time thanking only one God in particular, for he had granted my daughter's selfless wish.

"My... Lord?" Ruto questioned the moment he came to, now sitting up before looking around the broken space. So I stood, and told him,

"You may have lost the fight, my second, but thankfully we did not lose the war." Then I offered him my hand which he took without question.

"How is it that I'm here?" At this I looked up, a symbolic gesture even my own kind could not overcome, for Heaven was not to the skies like many would believe. It was merely a realm like any other, however one thing could be certain... *it was a realm we all looked up to.*

For the light of good usually came from above not from below.

"It seems that even after having my blood in you, the heavenly Gods do not forsake those touched by Hell as we once thought," I told him as I pulled him to his feet, before then turning to the temple that was the symbol of my birthright. It was mine once more, and no longer a vessel of hatred. So, knowing this, I closed my eyes and set about righting the wrongs of the rotted soul of my blood kin. Now bringing back the former glory of the Temple, one without the rot of its tainted Keeper. This meant that by the time I had opened my eyes, it was once more as it had been when first created by the Gods of Fate for me.

"And what now, what is to become of us now, my Lord, what comes next?" I looked towards the portal back into Hell and only one face made it to my mind's eye. For I knew what I was about to do. But as for Ruto, I told him to make his way back to the surface for in all honesty, the moment I had seen my daughter dying on the battlefield I had thought of little else. Nothing more than trying the only thing left I knew was capable of saving her. But now as I thought about it, I was faced with all I had left behind in that moment. The moment after we had won the war,

Seconds after my Chosen One had defeated a God.

I had asked her to wait for me but in all honesty, I had no idea how long I had been gone or what I would find when I went back there. Time worked differently in each realm and up until today, Heaven had been one that I had never stepped foot in before, naturally, for obvious reasons. So, as I looked up to the top of the tree of souls, I released a relieved breath to find the crimson rose still safely blooming there. Now knowing it always would, for the eternity I prayed to the Gods to have with my Chosen.

Only then did I answer him.

"Now it is time I go and claim my Queen."

The moment I landed back to the same spot I had left my Queen, I was not surprised to find the battlefield empty and desolate. I was, however, disappointed. Because it meant that with my short time in Heaven it had transpired into something significantly longer here. Even though I knew the threat of Matthias was now long gone and from this moment onwards, would be nothing more than a turning point in Hell's history. Nothing more than a battle fought and won to add to the long list of battles before it, I still couldn't help but worry about her.

But then again, no matter how powerful my Chosen One had obviously become, and despite the fact that it was now blindingly obvious that she was a mortal no more, it didn't matter. For I knew that this feeling of anxiety would never leave me when we were apart. No, too much had happened between us and the bitter memories of her dying in my arms would haunt me for the rest of my life.

I was, however, at the very least, comforted to know that she was surrounded by my own people once more. After Amelia had saved my life and forced my hand upon the Eye of Crimson, I had felt whole again, as every soul ever connected to me returned all at once. But it was a weight that I was no longer burdened to hold by myself. For I also had felt each of those souls share that connection with Amelia… *their new Queen*. Now each of us were forever Fated to hold within us a piece of our Kingdom. Meaning that they would all embrace Amelia as their Queen and their loyalty would be shared between us just as they did when following me as their King.

It was a comforting thought, but admittedly not as comforting as the feeling of her in my arms, held there against me so that I may once more breathe her in.

"You're back!" I heard my brother say, and I turned

quickly on the spot to find him sitting casually against a broken piece of a boulder. One, if I recall, had broken when Keira had thrown her husband into it and not a memory I would likely forget... *nor would Dom I can imagine.*

"Dariush?"

"Who else did you expect?" he said, and the moment my face replied for me, he added,

"Ah yes, but of course, well trust me, given the opportunity she would have stayed, but I didn't think you wanted me to allow her to set up camp and sleep in this barren wasteland as she waited for you." No, I would have not wanted that. But this wasn't something that I needed to say for he already knew. Therefore, also knowing what I would now want, he snapped shut the book he had been reading, and pushed himself from the boulder he had been using as a seat. Then after dusting himself off, he walked towards me. I met him halfway and the emotions of the day dictated my actions as I pulled him in for a hug.

"My brother." I could tell he was caught off guard, for his body tensed before finally relaxing into the rare show of emotion.

"Brother." His tone of voice said it all, the relief was easy to hear just as mine was.

"And what of the hex?" I questioned, knowing this was the reason he had become unconscious, missing the battle and no doubt still furious at the thought. Especially when he had been forced by our brother into creating a portal so as he could get to Keira. In fact, I knew that it had been his efforts to fight back against the summoning Hex that had caused him to lose consciousness for so long.

Hence, for once, why he didn't look smug and I soon knew why when he told me,

"The Hex disappeared when the one who cast it passed on."

"Amelia told you?" I summarized in a somber tone.

"She did, and I'm sorry for your loss, my Šeš," he said, using the Sumerian term for brother.

"As am I…" I paused at this and looked up, telling him what my daughter had not long ago told me,

"Although not all is lost, for we will have our time." He clasped a hand to my shoulder and with that gentle squeeze, I felt his unspoken comfort.

"Speaking of Amelia… tell me, where is my Queen, Dariush?" At this he smirked, before replying with the shocking truth,

"Where do you think she is?" Then before I had a chance to tell him to stop fucking around, he dropped the biggest bombshell of all. One I should not have been surprised to hear, not considering this was Amelia we were talking about.

A woman who had the canny ability to continually rock me to my core, and I would never stop loving that fact.

"Why, she is where a Queen should be…" He paused again before whispering with glee at knowing of my surprise when finally telling me…

"…Sitting upon your throne."

CHAPTER 5
IF THE CROWN FITS
AMELIA

Two days.

That's how long I waited. At least that's how long I think I waited because, in all honestly, it felt like much longer. But I also knew that time worked differently here, so for what may have seemed like only minutes for him, was most likely hours for me. Yet, I also knew how important this moment was for him, as I still couldn't even imagine the pain he had endured all these years. The immeasurable heartache that must be experienced when a parent loses a child.

It was no wonder that when my mother told me this, told me of what I knew Lucius hadn't had the strength to, well I had cried. I had cried so hard, with every tear weighted like an anvil lifted from my soul. Each one filled with so many different emotions it felt as if my heart had fractured for him.

The bitterness of injustice.

The heartbreak of unmeasurable loss.

But more than anything else, the burning hot hatred I had felt for the two responsible. It had been nearly enough to consume me whole. Which made me understand why the man

Judas had renounced his faith at the end of it all. And why he had seemingly easily endured all the pain and agony he had done at the hands of Lucifer just to be turned into the powerful being he was today.

Because he had already endured all the pain he could as a mortal.

But it also made me realize why King Lucius had become who he was today. How that hard shell had formed around his heart that had only started to crack when being faced with his Fate.

When finally meeting his Chosen One… Me.

Meaning, I could understand why he didn't tell me, as the Gods only knew how hard that conversation would have been to endure. How difficult it would have been to speak of and, for once, I hadn't been paranoid or hurt by my mother knowing this before me. No, if anything, I had been thankful, just to spare him the pain of reliving it. Because sometimes the hardest things to say were made even harder when you were forced to tell those you care about the most.

So, I endured this time apart and so as I could make him proud upon his return, I took my rightful place on his throne. Of course, it did help when my father walked in behind me like a badass when entering the throne room. Quickly snarling like a wild beast when they didn't automatically all fall to their knees. Although it had to be said that in the days since the battle, word had spread far and wide and people now knew they had an extra ruler to fear. Because Lucius was right, in a place like Hell, respect came in the form of fear. It was a twisted form of loyalty at best, but who was I to dispute, not only in my father's world, but that of Lucius's who had ruled this realm in Hell since his rebirth? These were his people, as Demonic and scary looking as they were. Which meant they were also now my people.

So, with the grateful guidance of my father, and the welcomed instructions from Dariush, a man I was glad to see gained consciousness quickly after the battle, *I took to the throne.*

As for Lucius's brother, well once I was safely situated upon the throne, he had been keen to get back to the battlefield, knowing this was where Lucius would most likely return to. In truth I had been wanting to wait there myself, but my father made the point that if I was ever to gain the respect of Lucius's Kingdom, then now was my time to act. Now was the time to carve my place firmly within this Realm.

But then I hadn't been on my own, even after my parents had left me to it. This despite my mum worrying about leaving me and clearly being reluctant to do so. No, because I now had my own council standing by my side and giving me strength when facing the unknown. In fact, I had just been saying goodbye to my parents at the time, when something unexpected had happened…

∽

Two turns of the Hellish sky ago…

"Mum, I will be fine," I said, despite not exactly feeling a hundred percent confident in this statement. It was at this point that Dariush stepped up behind me, placed his hands to my shoulders and assured them,

"She won't be alone." My mother nodded a few times, and I could see her trying to hold back her tears, something she did not accomplish when I pulled her to me and hugged her. The room gasped, clearly not used to this display, making me put my foot down addressing the room,

"What? Have you not seen one badass woman hugging another badass woman before!?" At this my father smirked and there were a few chuckles among the crowd.

"You sure you're going to be okay?" she asked me, making sure to be quiet this time, and it was my father's turn to answer, now stepping up behind her and wrapping his arms around her.

"She won't be alone, my love." It was at this point that there was a ruckus coming from behind them, before I heard the voices of three men I would recognize anywhere,

"Aye, lik' th' lassie said, she won't be alone."

"Trice!" I shouted as my parents parted, turning to watch as three unmistakable sights walked down the center. For there were three battle clad warriors striding across the throne room, dominating any space they were in and only stopping once in front of me. This was so as that they could each drop to a knee, each swinging their weapons around in front of them.

"My Queen," Trice said, bowing his head before raising it enough to wink at me, making me giggle.

"Erh, Fae, you know these men?" my mum asked in an unsure voice that made me grin, one that was so big, it made my cheeks ache. Then I looked to my mother before telling her,

"Oh yeah, we go way back… isn't that right, boys?" They each rose back to their feet, but this time it was Griff who answered first, quickly followed by Vern.

"Oh aye, lass."

"I wid say so."

"Way back," Trice added with a playful smirk, something that made my dad growl a little. I bit my lip and rolled my eyes at Trice, making him chuckle before I turned to face my parents ready to make introductions.

"Mum, Dad, I would like to introduce you both to the infamous McBain brothers." My mum just grinned back but my dad, well clearly he had heard of them, as shock showed in his expression.

"You aided my daughter here?" I laughed at my dad's question before telling them,

"Let's just say they saved my life a few times." My dad shot me a look before then granting his whole attention on the three men in front of him. Then the King of Kings and ruler of the mortal realm stepped up to these three misfits and held out his hand,

"Then I owe you a great debt indeed."

"That's nae needed, as 'twas a pleasure 'n' a debt that haes bin paid wi' oor souls intact." As Trice said this, he looked to me, making me gasp with realization at what he was saying. Lucius had returned their souls just like he had vowed to. I couldn't help but feel the tears rise up, before I rounded my parents and ran to him. Then I hugged Trice to me, surprising everyone else in the room yet again. I vaguely heard Dariush mutter,

"Good job my brother isn't here, or I fear those souls wouldn't have lasted." I ignored this sneer, despite knowing that he was right, I wouldn't have been able to get away with hugging my friend like this in front of Lucius. Of course, there was nothing in it more than friendship for me, but then again, it wasn't my feelings that Lucius would have worried about.

Although with the way the room reacted, I wondered if I was to get away with this embrace without the whole realm talking about it, as it looked as if Hell was not immune to gossip.

"What? Never seen a badass girl hug a badass Scottish warrior before?! Seriously, I'm going to make hugging mandatory in this realm," I shouted, and all three of my Scottish warriors laughed, even when my father rolled his eyes and my mum chuckled. As for Lucius's brother, well I just ignored his groan of disapproval.

"No?" I questioned, looking back at him and making him chuckle this time.

"Hug a Demon day, I personally think it has a nice ring to it," my mother agreed, making me laugh. As for my dad, he simply tucked her closer to his side and looked down at her with adoring eyes, before whispering something in her ear. And well, with the way she blushed, I most definitely didn't want to know what it had been.

But then it soon turned out that the McBain brothers weren't the only ones who were happy to see me, as suddenly a woman appeared with wild navy-blue hair and white tips, shouting my name,

"Amelia!"

"Nero!" I shouted back, embracing her after I prepared myself for her throwing her body at me.

"Seriously, just how long was our daughter in Hell for?" I heard my mother mutter before my father answered in a dry tone,

"Only our daughter could be in Hell for few weeks before befriending half of it." I smirked at this.

"Mum, Dad, this is…"

"Let me guess, Nero, is it?" my mother said with a smirk, whereas my father asked,

"Another person who saved your life perhaps?" At this I looked sheepish and said,

"We might have been through some stuff together."

"Oh yeah, out running the HellHounds chasing us through the ruins of Tartarus were really fun." My mother's face dropped, as well as my father's, who looked slightly horrified before commenting dryly,

"I see the number of people I owe a life debt to is growing by the minute."

"Good job we have a house here," my mother commented wryly, making my dad wink down at her.

"Yeah, about that, there may also be some more people in the elemental realms that could do with a handshake," I added because, well, if we were sharing and all…

"Elemental realms?" my mother questioned, making me laugh when my dad said,

"Keep reminding you, sweetheart, we do have a very well stocked library, wife of mine."

"Yeah, didn't you used to be a librarian, Mum?" At this my mum blushed before gripping my dad by the collar of his jacket and pulling him closer before hissing,

"Yes, and I also remember what happens every time you find me in said library." At this I covered my ears and did the typical daughter sex talk freak out,

"La, la, la, la, soooo not listening!" The McBain brothers chuckled obviously, before Vern commented,

"I am starting tae see whaur she gets it from."

"Shut it, ginger, anyway what happened to posh Vern…? I miss him," I mocked.

"He fucked aff, thankfully… and don't ye dare git any ideas, lass!" he said, aiming his narrow gaze at Nero and wagging a finger her way.

"Well, I miss him," I said, making Nero hold up her hand and say,

"Chill your tail, Wyvern… I learned my lesson… besides, I have such a thing for the French accent." Then she winked at him when he growled her way. A sound that even I could tell was without malice, making me wonder... what, if anything, was going on with these two?

"Well, I think it's clear to see that our daughter is in safe hands," my father said before turning to address everyone.

"I cannot thank you all enough for aiding our little Queen here in her quest," he said, teasing me.

"Hey, less of the little, old man," I said when he ruffled my hair, making me mutter,

"Trying to look like a bad ass here." It was at this point that he cupped his large hand at the back of my neck and pulled me forward as he leaned down to say,

"I think beheading a God on the battlefield already set that badass status in stone, my daughter, no matter how little you may be." I gave him a wry smile.

"Annoying, isn't it? I get little everything, little one, little vixen, little Queen, little wife... now ask him if size matters." My father growled at this, but it was definitely on a more playful side, and one that made everyone within ear shot chuckle.

"Yeah, Mum, definitely not going to do that," I commented dryly, making Lucius's brother laugh behind me.

After this, I said goodbye to my parents before watching as Dariush led them away into his office, no doubt creating them a portal back to the mortal realm and doing so away from prying eyes. It was also a place that, at this moment, held the Crimson Eye locked away in a vault that was hidden behind the wall.

I would have liked to have placed it back where it belonged, but without Lucius being here, well, there was no way to get into his private quarters. And let's just say, I wasn't trying my luck by sticking my hand inside that creepy ass door of his. So, this made his intimidating tower of doom off the cards.

It had also been after we had locked away the Crimson Eye that Lucius's brother realized that after everything I had been through, a much needed bath and sleep was to me, a glorious idea. As, well, I may have been wearing a pretty kick ass warrior dress, (thanks, Dad) but that didn't take away from the fact that I still looked like crap. Which meant that once my parents were long gone, Dariush showed me to a room I could do all of these things in. Needless to say, I nearly wept for joy.

But then one look back at the door towards the throne room and he could guess where my worries lay.

"All will be fine, Amelia, after all, I have spent more years on that throne than not. Now rest…" He paused before looking me up and down so as he could add,

"I will also have our servants run you a bath." I laughed before looking down at myself, saying,

"That bad huh?"

"For Hell, no not at all, but for my brother, well, I can imagine scenting a certain Cockatrice on you will be the very last thing he will want to come back to. Unless you want your first moments reacquainted to be of the murderous kind?" I rolled my bottom lip in between my teeth before saying,

"You may have a good point." At this he stepped forward, kissing my forehead before telling me in a cocky tone,

"I usually do, my soon to be sister." I smirked up at him hearing this as it warmed my soul to see how deeply he had chosen to accept me into his brother's life. Oh, and let's not forget, taking his place on that throne, as that was quite a biggie.

"Thanks, Dariush… *my soon to be brother,"* I added with a wink after he had made his way to the door and was looking back at me. In response to this, he bowed his head respectfully as if my words had meant something to him as much as his own had meant to me. Then he left me to my own devices, starting with taking a look in the full-length mirror, seeing all the armor I still wore and asking myself,

"Now how the Hell am I going to get out of this stuff?"

Thankfully, my sanity was soon saved and shortly after this my silent prayers were answered as Nero knocked on the door. This was to find me jumping up and down, twisting as I did as if this would help in ridding me of this chest plate.

"Oh, forget killing a God and chopping his head off, now this is the bad ass look you should have been going for... what do you call it, the dance of death?" she commented with a smirk, now leaning against the door frame, crossing her arms and ankles casually.

"Jeez, would you look at that, comedians made it to Hell after all." She laughed at this, now pushing off the frame and kicking the door closed. Oh, and thank the Gods she did as she was now coming to my aid.

"You know I will need your help getting all this shit back on... right?"

"Just call me your fairy Godmother... speaking of which, I thought you could do with some of my fairy dust by now." She said lifting up a little leather pouch and waving it at me. Which was when I realized, my eyesight was still fine.

"That's strange, my eyes seem fine," I told her after narrowing them as if to test my vision further.

"Umm, perhaps you don't need it anymore."

"Like Peter Parker when he becomes Spiderman?" I asked, making her scrunch up her beautiful face, causing the tattooed white line and blue symbols down the center of her chin to crinkle.

"Who?" At this my mouth dropped open in disbelief.

"Seriously? You don't know who Spiderman is?" I asked in a horrified tone.

"Is he like some creepy Demon with eight legs or something?" she asked, making me jerk back in shock.

"Well, he is this super… you know what, so not important right now," I said, deciding it was one mortal conversation that could most likely wait. Especially when the door opened and I saw a line of servants enter, the same girls I recognized as being the ones who had assisted me when I had first been brought here. Each of them, were also carrying steaming urns on their shoulders, no doubt ready to fill the copper bath that I could see was situated behind a papery thin screen that looked beyond pointless. What was it made from, tissue paper?

The rest of the room was more like something out of a medieval castle, with what was known as a tester bed clearly being the focal point of the room. It had four thick posts that were highly decorative carved black wood, with a carved canopy supported high above the on a frame. On closer inspection, the carvings all depicted scenes of Hell with souls rising from a river of fire. Which didn't exactly surprise me in Lucius's realm, not considering it was named the Kingdom of Death.

I mean, what else was it supposed to be, garden scenes and ladies frolicking in meadows? No, I didn't think so. As for the rest of the room, it was decorated in much the same way, with furniture to match the bed and walls of stone that were adorned with tapestries of Hellish battle scenes. Ones, it had to be noted, that were not that dissimilar than the one I had not long ago witnessed and played an integral role in. Unsurprisingly in a place like this, if there was any theme of color to speak of, it was black and red. With all the fabrics used in the place being the color of blood with black brocade thorns. Strangely, the room actually matched my dress. Umm… wonder if that had been on purpose?

As for the bath, just the smell of hot water and whatever oils they had used, and I was near breaking my nails just to get the battle element to this dress off me quicker. Thankfully Nero sensed this desperate need in me to be clean and battered my hands away so as she could do the job herself. Then once I was alone and, thank the Gods, naked, I sank down into the bath with Nero promising to come back later after I had gotten some rest. I swear the sound I made, anyone else would have thought I wasn't alone and someone else was in here helping me bathe.

I knew Lucius was in Heaven, but this right here, well it felt as if I was right there with him. A thought that made me warmer than the water I was now bathing in. Gods, but I missed him and it hadn't even been a whole day yet. In fact, once I had finished with the bath, doing so only when the water went cold, I had thought I would have trouble sleeping. But once my head hit the pillow, this turned out not to be the case at all.

Ironic, seeing as I slept like the dead in this Kingdom of Death.

In fact, it was only the smell of food that started to rouse me from my sleep and as I opened my eyes, I found Nero circling what looked like a bowl of stew in front of me. She was also wafting the steam from it towards my face.

"Yep, I knew that would do it." She sniggered as soon as I quickly sat up and looked near wild in my desperation for food, practically snatching the bowl from her.

"I'm glad you like it, it's..." This was when I held up my spoon and said,

"I'm going to stop you right there and tell you I really don't want to know."

"You don't?"

"That depends, do you have a shit load of Demonic cow

farmers around Hell that I don't yet know about?" At this she smirked and commented,

"Point made, human... although, that term isn't really applicable anymore, is it."

"Yeah, well applicable or not, if you tell me these floating balls of meat once belonged on a Demon named Jeff, I will freak, and we are talking the vomit variety freak-out here." At this she burst out laughing and I soon joined her.

But that had been two days ago and like she did every morning, she came and helped me to get redressed in all my 'Queeny get up' so as I was ready for my day on the throne. My Queeny get up had been missing one thing before that first day, something Dariush had been sure to hand me before taking my place on the throne for the first time.

Needless to say, I was shocked but managed not to embarrass myself in front of 'Lucius's court' on my first day. So, I simply accepted it with what I hoped was a regal nod of my head.

Which meant that I was now looking like the Queen I hoped Lucius would be proud of finding sitting on his throne when he returned. And speaking of a King finally returning, the second I finally heard those massive doors open at the end, I just couldn't help myself. Not when they were now being pushed open by the man himself awarding me with the delicious sight of my Vampire King in all his dark and foreboding glory.

So, what did my cocky ass do? I swung my legs up and over the horn covered armrest, looking as casual as possible as I twirled in my hands, the one other thing Dariush had add to my warrior Queen outfit...

Lucius's Crown of Obsidian.

CHAPTER 6
A ROYAL WELCOME
LUCIUS

The moment my brother created a portal just outside my castle I stormed my way through it, now with only one destination in mind... *My Chosen One.*

Fuck, but I was almost shaking in my need to get to her quicker.

This was even more so after discovering from Dariush what my little Queen had been up to since my abrupt departure and well, in truth, I wasn't surprised.

However, what I was...

Was fucking proud.

I was also insanely impatient to get to her, hence why I was soon using both hands to push open the colossal doors to my throne room with even greater purpose. And fuck me but what I treat I was awarded with.

Fucking perfection!

Just the sight of her now sitting, lounging in my throne, one that made her look fucking tiny, dressed like some warrior Queen, well it had me near biting my fucking lip. Gods, but I didn't know whether to laugh or release my wings just so as I could get to her quicker so as I could beg her for mercy. Especially as she twirled my Crown of Obsidian around in her hand, one I barely fucking wore but now only wanted to see a smaller version of the same crown sitting upon her head.

In the end, I did a combination of these things. Oh, and how I couldn't keep the smirk off my face as I strode down the length of the room. Doing so now to the echoing sound as my kingdom all lowered to their knees in sight of their King.

But my interest was solely on her, my cocky little Queen who was letting that confident mask slip as soon as she saw me. Naturally, I took in the sight with satisfaction. Especially, when seeing the way she started to squirm in my throne at the intense, heated look I was giving her.

However, this look quickly turned to one of fearful uncertainty when I brought forth my sword, one I could feel had been stored away in my brother's office. I wondered briefly who it had been who had retrieved it for me… my guess was on my little warrior woman. Of course, that same bravery I knew was deeply engrained in her soul, slipped a little more the moment I made my sword ignite with a roll of my wrist as I approached. Even her little mouth opened as I saw my name escape on a breathy whisper from perfect kissable lips… lips I planned on dominating the first chance I got.

But then I surprised her further, as the moment I reached the bottom of the steps, I lowered to one knee and swung my sword forward directly in front of me, holding both hands at the hilt. Then I only needed to say one more thing,

"My Queen."

At this she released a held breath before she dropped the crown, making the echoing sound of it hitting the floor a backdrop to the chorus I focused on, which was the glorious sound of her gasping my name,

"Lucius!" Then she was up out of the throne and because I knew what was coming, I let my sword join the sound as it clattered to the floor. I caught her as she ran at me, jumping into my arms, and making me instantly breathe her in as my soul finally centered around my heart.

"Amelia." I uttered her name as I buried my head into her neck, holding her up so as we could easily reach each other. As if she too needed to breath me in. I kept my hand to the back of her head, holding her to me until I could stand it no longer.

I had to kiss her.

"Baby…" I didn't get out anything more before she crushed her lips to mine, meaning that gentle hand soon fisted in her hair as I consumed her lips, getting lost in our connection. Gods, but just the feel of her back in my arms again was like taking your first breath after you felt yourself drowning. The relief was immeasurable. In fact, it was only when I heard my brother clear his throat behind me that I realized we didn't just have an audience here, but we had my entire fucking court!

No, not mine…

Ours.

For now, we both ruled, and clearly, Amelia had taken this charge seriously and embraced this new position of hers with ease. Like I said, *I was so fucking proud!*

Seconds later, just as her body started to quake in my arms, I felt the dampness on my skin from her tears as emotions overwhelmed her. And in all honesty, I couldn't say that she was the only one, for my own nearly crippled me. In fact, I believe if I hadn't had her in my arms, then I would have, for the second time in minutes, dropped to my knees in relief. Because after everything we'd been through, the turbulent push and pull that seemed to have been the bitter flavor of our life these past weeks, this was finally the sweet we had both been craving to taste.

"Is it really over... *can we finally breathe?*" she asked, pulling back, and fuck me, but seeing the tears in her eyes was another thing that nearly brought me to my knees. Deep blue oceans shimmering with a thousand emotions for me to find just under the surface.

She was spectacular.

A Goddess.

And she was all mine.

"Only if every breath I take holds the scent of you," I told her softly, making her close her eyes as another sob shook through her body and tears escaped beneath her long black lashes.

"Oh Lucius," she breathed before crushing her lips to mine, once more transporting me back to Heaven. I vaguely heard my brother try one more time to remind me that we weren't alone but with Amelia in my arms, I found myself unable to care who witnessed our reunion.

All of Hell be damned.

Because I knew now that our story held power here. There would be no more playing the part of Demonic King with a cold dead heart. There were no more chains to hold, no more mortal slaves to collar, no more acting on this Hellish stage... *not for us.*

Because I knew with what happened here with my Chosen One destined to defeat a God, it was a tale that would span the ages. It was a story set in stone and forged in the pits of Hell for all to know. One that would spread like soul weed and reach every ear from whispered Demonic lips. For my Queen had carved her place in history and, soon, every single being would know the strength and power she held at her core.

Even the Devil.

It was why I no longer cared for the act I had once played. Because I no longer had to worry for her life, as my woman could more than hold her own. She was the storm, and I was only one of many blessed to stand in its eye and bask in the glorious destruction she had brought upon Hell when fighting back against its enemy.

She had saved my Kingdom and now, *everyone knew it.* Meaning now, no one would ever dare to stand against us. So, I didn't give a shit who saw this side of me, for I would have laid my head at her feet if that was what it took to show her how grateful I was for all that was her.

As it stood, I knew a far more gratifying way to do this, hence why I soon swept her up in my arms, promptly taking her off her feet so as I could get to my destination quicker.

"We are not to be disturbed," I told my brother, who rolled his eyes the second he saw where I was headed and muttered,

"It just had to be my office, didn't it."

"Erm, maybe we should…"

"Get there quicker? I agree," I interrupted before Amelia could finish her suggestion, now laughing when I held her tighter and started to run. But then just before I could kick open my brother's office door, she lifted herself up enough to tell me,

"You know it turns out being Queen here comes with some perks." At this I paused, raising a brow down at her playful expression. Then she whispered with a comical wag of her brows,

"They gave me a bed." I smirked at this.

"Then my brother is blessed with luck this day, for a bed does sound even better than his desk."

"That's what I thought, handsome," she said with a wink

before leading the way and, unfortunately, getting us lost... *twice.*

"I swear it was around here somewhere," she mumbled with a fingertip being nibbled in her mouth, making me groan.

"Amelia," I grumbled, and I swear I was going to end up fucking her here in the hallway if she didn't have mercy on me and my raging cock.

"Hey, it's not my fault all of your castle looks the same! I need bloody GPS in this place!" she complained before I said,

"Fuck it!" then I kicked open the nearest door, not giving a fuck what was in it. However, the second she saw inside she let out a cute little,

"Oh my!" I smirked down at her before she frowned back up at me and warned,

"I don't share, Vampy." I nearly laughed at this but instead growled down at her,

"Neither do I!" Then I looked back up at what was obviously my brother's Harem and the sea of beauties I didn't give a fuck about seeing and roared my next order, making them go screaming out the room,

"LEAVE NOW!"

"Yep, that will do it," Amelia muttered, clearly amused by the sight of all of the Demon girls each rushing out the room and leaving little to the imagination as most were practically naked. I swear I was shaking my head, muttering,

"Dariush, you horny fucker you."

"Yeah, I'll say, jeez, where did he find them all, Hell's version of Tinder?"

"Hell's version of what...? You know what, don't answer that, important thing is, we found a bed and that's all I care about." At this she made a show of leaning her head against my chest, battering her lashes up at me and saying,

"Wow, that's so romantic, baby." I tried not to grin at her teasing, but it was too hard to accomplish in that moment. She was too fucking funny for her own good.

"You want romance, we are in a ballroom full of beds, sweetheart, so hurry up and pick one so as I can romance us enough until we both pass out!" At this she threw her head back and started laughing and the sight was so fucking beautiful, I could wait no longer. Something she knew when I released my wings and flew us both across the room and to a spot I thought was perfect for one reason and one reason only.

It was a cage.

Actually, it was a bed with a gold gilded cage around it, so one made even better in my opinion.

"Lucius!" she shouted my name in shock at my abrupt actions, but I just smirked at the idea of getting her inside that cage and locking the fucking door. In fact, I was quickly starting to see the appeal for Adam whenever he decided he needed to lock up Pip in one.

This time instead of just kicking in the door and rendering the point of the cage useless, I opened the door with a thought. Then once inside, I let her feet find the soft fur floor that surrounded the bed that consisted of a large nest of sunset-colored cushions at the center. The theme of the Harem was clearly a nod back to his origins as it looked like some sex themed ancient Persian temple in here.

Speaking of sex themed…

"Wait, Lucius, we need to talk about what happened… with Kala," Amelia said the moment I put her on her feet, and she started backing away as I stalked her across the hundreds of cushions. Of course, I knew why she said this, caring for my feelings and wanting to do what was right by needing to see if I wanted to talk first about all that had happened.

However, I most certainly did not.

No, right now, all I wanted to do was make love to my woman like a man obsessed who had been starved of that obsession for way too long.

No, what I needed…

All I needed…

Was her.

CHAPTER 7
CAGED BEAST
AMELIA

Lucius continued to stalk towards me, only stopping once he had backed me all the way up until I felt the bars of the cage at my back. Then he gripped those same bars high above my head and lowered his forehead to mine before whispering my name in a pained way,

"My Amelia." This was in response to what I had asked him about his time in Heaven, making it clear it was something he didn't want to talk about. I knew that without him even saying it, as his eyes started to seep into crimson fire before his words followed,

"Not yet… I need you… I just need to be with you… *I fucking crave you."* I sucked in a quick breath at the growl of this last statement before he unexpectedly raised up both his hands. I questioned why he did this for a single heartbeat before it suddenly dawned on me. Because I now realized how this was going to be different from all other times before.

"You have no idea how many times I have wished… *been near fucking desperate…* to get to feel every inch of you with both my hands and now… *well now, you get to see just what we have both been missing out on,"* he said as he used them to run his leather-free hands down to my own, before shackling my wrists with his fingers and raising them up above me. Just the feel of finally being skin to skin with both of his hands had me shivering in anticipation at the picture he painted in my mind.

I soon found myself glad I had decided to forgo the metal gloves my father had made me. Because well, let's just say that after the first day wearing them, I couldn't scratch myself without making it look like I had pissed off a very angry cat.

Which meant my own hands were now free for Lucius to hold above me, entwining his fingers with mine as he lowered his head and purposely kept himself from kissing my lips. I knew he was teasing me, his bad boy smirk said it all, especially when he got what he wanted when I was forced to arch my neck all the way back just so our lips would meet. However, he was clearly still in a mind to tease me. I knew this when he started simply licking the seam of my lips before they opened as if he had just whispered the magic words, *open sesame*.

I swear I was like some sex-starved hussy by the time he finally gave me mercy, for his tongue was soon dipping inside and dueling with mine. A connection that quickly thrust me into some needy sex realm, like I was suddenly like a bitch in heat trying to get free just so I could bury my fist in his hair. In fact, I knew I was stronger now as I started to push back against his hold, making him pull back and raise a brow down at me.

"Ah but I almost forgot. You are not my breakable little mortal any longer, are you?"

"No, I am not... *so what you going to do about it, Vampire?"* I challenged, making him grin down at me the same time his eyes flashed an even deadlier shade of red, as if

I was now looking into twin moons soaked in blood. That was when his entire body started to change before me, growing in size as well as giving me that unrestrained version of himself, and soon I was faced with…

His Demon.

I sucked in a sharp breath in fright, making him smirk as if my reaction only fed this side of him. My eyes widened as I took in all those rippling muscles that were slowly being revealed as he made his clothes evaporate. Like this, he was even bigger than he usually was and had muscles in places I didn't even know existed. Lines, groves, and crevices of hard flesh I just wanted to map with my tongue, a thought that had me near panting.

The black network of veins started to pulsate beneath his pale skin, making him look truly Demonic, and I watched in shock as they started to branch out around his blazing red eyes. It was like staring into the darkness and find a single fire burning. He looked sinister and utterly terrifying, and he knew it, as he lowered his head further, challenging me right back when this time, it was his Demon that spoke.

"Scared, little queen?"

At this I decided to show him who it was he was messing with, even though I had to try my best to mask how truly intimidated I was. So, despite still having my wrists held in his Demonic clutches above me, hands that were now tipped with deadly claws and were considerably bigger than what they usually were, I reached up on my tiptoes. Then, as best as I could, I got in his face and showed him what I was made of.

"Bring it, Vampy!" I snarled back, making him grant me a menacing grin, his fangs lengthening at the sight. Then he nudged the side of my cheek with his nose before speaking straight into my cheek.

"Good girl," he praised before I felt something traveling up his arms and over my skin, like thick, slithering, liquid snakes. I then looked up above me, trying to see what it was he was doing until I felt whatever it was begin to harden over my flesh. Once it was done, he obviously felt free enough to remove his hold on me, clearly assured that I was going nowhere. His dark essence had formed over my hands, encasing them and locking them to the bars above, and it took me back to when he had restrained me the last time when finding me in his Demonic bed chamber. Clearly having me tied up was a big kink for Lucius and well, my only complaint was that, like this, I couldn't touch him as I craved to do.

After this he was able to take a leisurely step back, now smirking at his handy work and just to be sure, I tugged hard hoping my strength was enough to impress him as I freed myself. However, this didn't happen, and he was clearly satisfied by the sight of my failure. I knew this when he snarled down at me, in a dark yet surprisingly playful tone,

"You are not that strong yet, little Queen of mine... not when your soul still knows who its master is." I gasped at this, and he deepened his grin, morphing it into one of pure satisfaction.

"But, just in case..." he said before turning around and awarding me the lip biting sight of his well-developed behind. A muscular ass so mouth-watering, I actually whimpered. I even felt my hands tense around my unearthly restraints as I imagined kneading the muscular dips at the sides of his cheeks before running my hands down those strong, thick thighs.

Just the sheer bodily strength of him had my mouth going dry as a sexual shiver rippled through my body. Then I watched as he purposely closed the cage door, the sound of my imprisonment making me shiver again. I swallowed even harder after I watched him ripping a thorned length of metal free, one that had been curled around the bars for decoration. I then watched, open-mouthed, as he twisted it around the door, locking it firmly and making a show of the fact I was now caged. Although the moment he looked back at me, he clearly liked what he saw, as he said,

"Now that look suits you, although…" he paused, cocking his head to the side a little before stalking back to me, the evidence of his arousal now standing upright and proud… *and oh so lickable.*

"…As proud as I am to see you wearing my sigil…" he said, tapping the tip of his blackened claw against my chest plate, before continuing, "…You are wearing far too many clothes for my liking. And if you believe this strong enough to keep your body from me, well… *you're wrong, my little bird."* As he spoke, he raised up that same Demonic hand, letting me now watch as his claw started glowing as if it had just been dipped into the flaming river of Phlegethon.

"W-w-what are you?" I stammered when he brough it closer and just as I jerked away, he gripped the chest plate by the neck and yanked me back firmly to him. I found my back needing to arch as much as it would allow with my hands tied over my head.

"Don't move now, little one." Then he used that molten claw to cut down the centre of my chest plate as if it was made of paper mâché not metal. I gasped as he cut though his own sigil, one he had not long ago shown appreciation for.

"Lucius, my dad… he made…" At hearing this, he used his dangerously sharp tipped thumb against my lips, still keeping his hold on the chest plate by its collar, before hushing me,

"Ssshh now… don't you worry, my pet… for next time

you wear my sigil, it will be one of my own making. Not Daddy's... so continue to be a good girl for me now and stay quiet for me." I forced down the anxious lump that was most definitely coated with arousal. One that only acted as fuel, for when it landed in my belly it only managed to ignite the flames of my desire, especially when he watched my neck with great interest.

It was as if he could imagine his cock there, pushing in my mouth, past my lips before being suddenly thrust down my throat. As if the thought was making him salivate and desperate to feel those hard struggling swallows for himself rippling along his shaft.

Or was that thought just all me holding on to this fantasy?

He continued to rid me of my armour, piece by piece, and I had to say, he was a lot more efficient at it than I or Nero, as it was all gone with seconds. Then once I was held prisoner in front him in nothing but my dress, he took the time to scan down the length of me once more.

"Like what you see, Demon?" I braved the question, trying to sound more confident than I felt and making him grin more to himself this time when hearing my question. Then he ran the backs of his claws up my belly, ones now cold and no longer holding the dangerous scolding heat he had needed to cut through metal. He continued going, up and up, tantalizingly slow, until he was soon skimming between my breasts. He started plucking at the strained material between them, like some dangerous game he was playing, and one where he won from getting off when watching me squirm.

Only then did he answer me,

"I do indeed... but I much prefer... *what's beneath it more!"* he growled before suddenly tearing his claws down my dress, being careful enough not to mark the skin beneath. Then when the rest of my dress was torn from me, including taking his time to rid me of even my sleeves, he took another step back. Oh, and if I thought I was squirming under his heated gaze before, then now, it felt as if my skin were on fire with it!

He looked as if he wanted to fucking eat me!

"Fucking beautiful," he growled, before using his hand on my ass so as he could tug the lower part of me to his impressive cock, one that looked like it was weeping at just the thought of burying himself deep within me. In fact, I could tell he was trying to savor this moment, by taking things at a slower pace, despite the painful hold he had on my ass, something that made me whimper when his claw pricked the skin.

His evil grin said it all.

"Mmm, I fucking love that sound coming from your lips… *now give me more, woman!*" he demanded, before lunging toward my breast, gripping it in a brutal hold and lifting it up and sucking my nipple with a rough pull of his lips, biting it hard. I cried out again at the delicious pain that ignited an arousal coiling tighter in my sex, making it flutter on its own accord. Then when I didn't think I could take any more, he sank his fangs in deep around my breast, now drinking what little blood he could get there, making me cry out again as my orgasm hit with a violent crashing wave.

He pulled back once my shuddering had subsided, now with my blood staining his fangs red as he grinned down at me, before shocking me further.

"Now I am going to do something to you I have always craved to do."

"Wh-what are you…" I stammered.

"I am going to cover this fuckable… delectable… tasty

little body of yours in my claiming bites... I am going to mark every inch as mine, with blood and fangs... I fucking own you!" he declared with a sinister growl of words that had me shaking.

"Y-y-your...?" He raised a hand to my neck, using the pad of his thumb to caress down from my chin to my jawline.

"I am going to sink my fangs all over your flesh, make you come endlessly with every owning bite I make, and you know what, little Queen of mine...?" He paused, now fixating on my trembling lips when I forced out the word,

"W-w-what-t?"

Then he placed his forehead to mine and snarled in a Demonic tone,

"I am going to enjoy every fucking second... every second I get to make you my blood slut... now be a good girl and..."

"...Bleed for me, Baby Girl."

CHAPTER 8
BLOOD FEAST

"*Bleed for me, Baby Girl.*"

Once he said this, he then he lowered his head and bit hard into my other breast, feasting on it and making me cry out as another orgasm was forcibly torn from me. His dirty words playing out in my mind only managed to impact my release with even greater force.

It. Was. So. Fucking. Hot!

He licked at the holes he made in my flesh, sealing them closed, but not before he had first let my blood drip purposely down my breasts. Then he slowly lowered to his knees in front of me, gripping my sides hard enough to leave finger marks like extra claims on my skin. He tugged the next part of his meal closer, biting into my side with the tips of his claws before making me come for the third time. I howled out as if he was turning me into a beast, causing my knees to weaken this time. However, just like the first two bites, he let me bleed before sealing the skin, now painting my body with long lines of crimson. This was before moving along to the next place, making him groan in pleasure every time he bit me.

"Lucius, please... I can't... can't come... again... ahhh!" I pleaded just before he bit into my ass, digging his claws in until pain bloomed into an arousal awakening, just like it always did. However, he didn't manage to break the skin with anything but his fangs, only licking the holes once I felt enough of my blood trickling down.

But then of course, he ignored this plea for mercy, as if he was too far gone in his own blood-soaked mission. Too far gone in his pleasure and the deep-rooted need he felt to mark me as his... *all over.* I knew this when he simply moved back to the front of my body, leaving my ass for now and instead paying my thighs attention. He lifted my legs up and situated himself between them. I braced myself for the next release, as I knew the following bite was coming and wasn't shocked when he bit down on the inside of my thigh.

Honestly, this man was trying to kill me, death by orgasm!

"AAHHH!" I screamed again, my body shaking with each release growing in its intensity, more so than the last. He did the same to the other leg, doing so fast enough that this time, two orgasms erupted out of me, one after the other in quick succession. This was when finally, he licked up my blood-soaked legs and decided he was now going for gold... straight for my pussy. A calculating move, and one he took his time in doing, making sure to first look up at me. I heard his growl, gaining my attention enough to do as he wanted, which was look down at him. Then, once he had my wide eyes focused solely on him, he decided to make a show of the next part. Starting off by licking his bloody lips before dipping his face in between my legs, making me hold myself tense once more.

"Lucius," I breathlessly called his name.

"You can beg me all you want, little Queen, for nothing

can sate this insatiable appetite I have for you… *nothing*… for your begging only drives me on to push you deeper… which is why for all your sins at trying to stop me, you will be punished…" he told me in between stopping to lick up my leg, making the lower part of his face even more bloody.

"Punished?" I questioned quietly, making his eyes heat up and glow deeper at the sound.

"I want this to be the biggest one yet, I want this cum to rip its way through you… *I want you to feel fucking consumed by it!"* he snarled into my leg, licking over the place he had bitten me, purposely nicking the skin with his fang to create a sting.

"Now… *hold on, little Queen… it's about to get rough,"* he warned, and suddenly both my legs were grabbed in a bruising hold before he tossed them over his shoulders. Then he latched on around my small, aching bundle of nerves, making me scream. He began biting and sucking my clit into his mouth, taking not only my blood with every draw, but also my now abused and throbbing pussy.

"AAHH AHHH AHHHH, LUCIUS, PLEASE… FUCK!" I screamed even louder this time, making him chuckle against the abused flesh. Seconds after he pulled his fangs from me, refusing to seal the wound before he was ready, my sex was soaked in blood, as if this was the place he wanted to coat in red liquid the most.

"I think we can let this one drain for a bit," he commented darkly, before he rose back to his full height, finding me panting and totally spent, despite knowing that he was far from finished with me. I knew this when he fisted my hair, using the dominant hold on me to yank my head back from where it had fallen forward, as I had little strength left to hold it up.

"What a fucking beautiful blood slave you make me, *my*

love... my life... my soul's keeper... just fucking look at you, now painted in my favourite colour... now look at the beauty I possess... *look, Amelia!"* he ordered the moment my eyes fluttered closed, and I snapped them back open at the dark command.

I did as he asked to see he was right, I was now painted crimson and knowing what he was, *what we both now were*, it was... *unbelievably hot.*

"Ah, but there's that fire I fucking love!" he snarled against my cheek, before dipping his head and speaking his next words against my pulsating neck,

"Now time for dessert."

Before I could question anything more in my mind, he suddenly sank his fangs into my neck, and I came screaming his name again. A sound so powerful, so raw, so beautifully pained, I even made the bars on the cage shake with the force of it all.

"LUCIUS!"

Once I had come apart yet again, now limp in his hold for how much blood he had consumed, he forced his fangs from my neck, making sure to seal the holes this time given that he didn't want me to bleed out. But then he pulled back and opened his mouth, growling like some wild, unrestrained beast. His snarl caused his mouth to open, and my eyes widened in shock as I could see my own blood pooled in his lower jaw. There was so much blood that the moment he dipped his chin down so his eyes could burn into mine, it seeped over his bottom teeth, dripping down between us and landing all over my heaving breasts.

It was so fucking hot, but was only made even more so when that fist of his tightened in my hair again as he claimed my lips, letting me taste my own blood, sucking it from his tongue like candy. I then felt his hands all over my body, rubbing the blood into my skin, trying to paint every inch. He then spat onto his hand after growling at his palm and started rubbing the bloody mound of my sex with it to seal the holes he had left open. I had never seen Lucius so wild and unrestrained before. So, blood-thirsty and sex-craved, making me realise all this time he had been holding himself back with me, for fear of scaring me or hurting me. But now I was stronger, he wasn't holding himself back any longer. Not now I would heal on my own and the bruises he made would be gone like a whisper of dirty words forgotten after the act.

It was clear that Lucius was far from being done with me. I knew this when he picked up my legs and wrapped them around his back, just above his ass. Then, after leaving bloody handprints on the back of my thighs, he framed my face, so he could look down at me tenderly. An act almost as shocking as smearing my own blood on my face with his gentle hold.

"Fucking addicted… my Fated Queen… my Chosen One… *My Amelia.*" As he said this, he growled every word but when Lucius' voice shone through at the end just when he lowered his forehead to mine, I couldn't help but close my eyes against the intensity of it all. Then with my head tipped back with his hands still framing my face, he whispered four words.

"I love you… Amelia…" My name came from his lips softly, and ended with the sound of me crying out as he suddenly thrust up inside of me. As soon as I cried out in pleasure, he captured the sound in his kiss.

He reached down and with my ass cheeks held firmly in each hand, he fucked me in earnest. If I hadn't been now changed into my Vampire side, I can honestly say, I might not have been able to take it. As it stood, I could not only take it, but I relished in every long, painful feel of him as he bottomed out inside of me, getting off on knowing that he now filled every part of me with every single thrust.

Not surprising then when minutes later, I shattered around him, coming hard enough that I finally broke away from his restraints at my wrists with the force of it. This was at the same time he found his own release as he held me so tightly I feared to breathe, only to discover that I couldn't. He hammered my body down over his cock one last time, and I would have shattered like glass around him if it was any harder. I felt him empty himself into me at the same time he roared to the ceiling,

"RAWWWWAAAHHHHH!" This time, the force his release shook the cage around us so violently that it started to twist inwardly as though some giant hand was crushing it in its palm. And as for me, well I only had the power to barely hold on, before finally succumbing to my body's limits, as I now slumped over him and seconds later…

Darkness took over.

~

"Drink, my love… *drink, my sweet girl."* I heard Lucius's voice through the fog, at the same time feeling something wet dripping against my lips. The smell then hit me and suddenly my hands were up around his wrist like a flash. In fact, it was so fast that I didn't know I had even moved until I felt his wrist in my hands, now holding it desperately to my mouth and drinking him down like his blood was the elixir of life!

But to a Vampire, I guess it kind of was, despite us not needing blood to survive. Gods, but if I thought I liked his blood before, well now it was like drinking down liquified Heaven… a fucking drug from above, or should I say, from exactly where we were. After all, we couldn't have been further from Heaven right now if we tried. But as for Lucius and his blood, well simply put...

He was fucking delicious!

Lucius actually chuckled at my eagerness and I felt him stroking my hair back, making me soon realise that I was now lying down as he must have lowered us both to the cushions.

"Easy, Pet, as you will soon find I only have so much to offer," he said in an amused tone. However, despite hearing this I just couldn't seem to stop. This lack of enthusiasm to let him go made him laugh again before I felt his finger reach inside the corner of my mouth and physically extract my fangs from his flesh.

"Good?" he asked when I started licking my lips and trying to reach for his wrist again. However, he knew to keep it out of reach and brought it to his own bloody lips to lick, now sealing the holes I had made.

"It's... it's... amazing. *Like seriously addictive.*" At this he smirked.

"I am glad to hear it, little one," he said happily before adding, "And nice to know I am no longer alone in my addiction... one I think I made even more obvious this time." I laughed when I looked down at myself and found I was still mostly covered in my own blood.

"I look like a giant sex steak."

"Mmm... and speaking of meals, well it looks like I am yet to finish off my own."

"Lucius?" I questioned before he dipped his head down to my breasts and started to lick me clean. I swear the man was trying to turn me sexually insane as his tongue felt incredible against my skin!

Naturally this took a while, and the teasing kisses, sucks, and long intense licks up the length of me were enough to have me begging him for even more sexual relief. This despite not long ago experiencing more orgasms than I have ever had before. But what can I say…? It was just what this man did to me!

"Hmmm… I always did like to save the best 'til last," he said after humming to himself and dipping once more in between my legs, taking even more care down there as he started to lick every inch of me clean. All the evidence of our union now becoming his meal, as he tasted not only my release, but also his own. All of which was now combined with my blood, making him growl against me, causing sweet vibrations on my clit. However, when he added to this pleasure by thrusting two fingers up inside of me, I came undone and cried out, my voice now hoarse from screaming so much. Lucius then rose up above me and sternly ordered,

"Open." I did as I was told, getting off on his demanding tone, just as much as I did when he slipped two fingers inside my mouth making me gag on him, his eyes heating at the sight.

"We taste so fucking good together," he whispered by my ear, still making me moan around his fingers.

"So, fucking good… *that I want more."* He growled this time and before I could even think of what was coming next, he thrust back up inside me with his cock and this time when he fucked me…

I got to hold on for dear life.

∾

"Well, it looks like we destroyed another room," I said, lifting my head up from where I was still panting into his shoulder. I felt Lucius chuckle all around me, including inside where he was blissfully still seated thanks to his impressive ability to stay hard.

"What can I say, must be our MO after being apart."

"Yeah, about that, I'm starting to think we need a special room for those times just in case, maybe with a reinforced bed and padded walls," I retorted, making him pull back and say my name in gentle reprimand,

"Amelia."

"What?"

"Do you really think I will ever allow us to be apart again?" I gave him a wry look and said,

"Okay, so the little collar with a bell on it was cute for fantasyland but really, Lucius, what you gonna do, add a matching lead and take me up to the winter garden whenever I need to go potty?" I joked, making him smirk.

"Watching you piss on my bushes isn't really a kink I'm into, Pet, but the collar, oh yeah, now that I can totally get on board with." I rolled my eyes at him making him raise a brow before I warned,

"Oh no, don't get ideas, you have punished me enough, Mr Bitey!"

"Mr Bitey?" he asked, making me look down at myself, sweep an arm over my naked body and say,

"If the shoe fits, my bloodthirsty man." He smirked before telling me,

"Sweetheart, you tell me not to get any ideas when I still have my cock inside you, so ask yourself, just what do you think all my ideas are centred around right about now?"

"Umm, relieved that I'm not playing Whack a Mole?"

"Excuse me?" he asked, making me laugh and because doing so tightened up my core, he groaned as he felt it around his cock… one I was currently teasing him about hitting it with a big rubber hammer as soon as it dared show its head.

"Okay, so fine, you have a good point but still, I think we can let the eye rolling thing slide now."

"Oh, I don't think so, after all... *I have been keeping count,"* he teased before kissing my nose seconds after nipping at it with his teeth.

"Oh goodie, I will order the inflatable ass donut from Amazon then as soon as we are home," I commented dryly, making him throw his head back and howl with laughter.

"My funny girl," he hummed after cupping the back of my head and holding me to him for a hug. And I had to say, I just loved these moments when he did this. It was like a physical reaction to express just how much he loved my quirky little moments.

"Speaking of Amazon..." I asked, making him chuckle.

"Were we?"

"Well not really, no, but say I did want to order stuff, now where would I say... I don't know... put in as my address?" I asked, twirling a strand of his hair around my finger and focusing on that rather than his knowing expression.

"Subtle," he commented, making me grin.

"I know right, and oh so smooth," I said winking at him.

"So, time for us to just rip the lid off that ultimate can of worms then?" he asked, making me smirk.

"I guess it's that time, yes... I mean, we did just save Hell and all, so I guess moving in together is the next logical step," I teased again, making him grin before playing along.

"Well, I do still have your picture of Spock on my wall, so having a logical conversation goes hand in hand with that." At this I slapped a hand to his oh so dreamy muscular chest and said,

"Oh, now that was what I call smooth and hey, were you researching Spock while I was away?"

"Let's get this straight, sweetheart, you weren't away, *you ran away,* big fucking difference," he growled, making me pout.

"Okay, so just how many decades am I facing with that being used against me, huh?" I asked, now feeling even stranger remembering that we were having a whole conversation with his cock still a hard weighty length inside me. I felt like sneezing just to see what would happen. Would he shoot right out or would his badassness even manage to withstand that natural bodily function?

"Mmm, let me see, how about a year for every day of Hell you put me through?" he replied, bringing my focus back to our strange conversation.

"Mmm, how about a blow job for every one instead?" I countered, making him instantly reply,

"Deal."

"Wow, didn't even need to think about that one, did you?" I commented wryly, making him grin before leaning down and whispering in my ear,

"Why would I when I am the one winning?"

"Hey, who said anything about winning?" I asked, trying to look serious but failing as I could feel the amusement written all over my face.

"Your lips around my cock, trust me, sweetheart, *I am most definitely winning."* I couldn't help it, but I burst into a fit of giggles after this and in return, Lucius gave me a warm look as if he couldn't get enough of it.

"Speaking of winning… just where might we be conducting our next victorious act of lovemaking, as no offence, but I'm starting to leak all over your brother's harem cushions and as much as I wasn't bothered about being all leaky three minutes ago, now, well I am in need of a bed… oh God, no, in need of a shower and a toothbrush… oh and a real toilet and not just some glorified bucket… wait, scrap that… a cheeseburger and some fries… oh Gods, and please get me some donuts!" At this he burst out laughing, holding me through his hilarity before telling me softly,

"Alright, sweetheart, I can take a hint…" he said, cradling my head to his chest before kissing my forehead and whispering the most beautiful words down at me…

"Let's go home."

CHAPTER 9
HOME

Home

The moment Lucius spoke about going home, I threw myself over him making him laugh. But then we both looked down at ourselves and the complete mess we both were in, prompting me to say,

"Maybe we should get clean first." At this he simply looked smug before stretching out, making a show of folding his arms and interlocking his fingers behind his head. I swear the delicious bulge of his biceps made me nearly lose focus altogether. Then he released a contented sigh and teased,

"Get to it, woman." At this I shook my head a little, confused as to what he could mean. However, the moment he nodded down his body and said,

"I am waiting, Pet." This was when I finally put two and

two together. (Damn his distracting muscles) As soon as I did, I made a sound of outrage that he looked oh so very pleased about.

"Why this is a harem after all," he argued with a grin.

"And?" I snapped, folding my arms and playing along with his game.

"I think you will find it is where most adoring females spend their time worshipping their master," he said looking around at the large space that yes, did seem dedicated to just that. There were raised dais everywhere, covered in a sea of reds, pinks, oranges and yellows, making me wonder if I had missed a sign on the door called, 'Sunsex Blvd.'

Of course, the area we had been occupying most definitely now looked a little worse for wear. Almost all the cushions around our general area were ripped and torn, with deep claws marks spewing feathered guts. Blood and sweat stained silk and as for the cage, well that was now a mangled mess. Even the ceiling above us had precarious looking cracks marring the once fancy painted plaster.

Yet despite this, it didn't stop me from grabbing the nearest pillow and smacking Lucius in the face with it in retaliation for this comment. However, seeing as it was one of the 'less fortunate' ones, I couldn't stop my hands from flying to my face as I tried not to burst out laughing the second it exploded into a cloud of feathers around his face.

As for the man now covered in white plumage, he simply puffed out a frustrated breath, causing the smaller feathers around his lips to take flight, now dancing around him. Then I watched him rise slowly, now with a dangerously determined look on his face making me raise up my hands in surrender,

"Now, now, Lucius, you started this, remember?" I said, unable to keep the playful grin off my face as I started shifting backwards as if waiting for him to strike any minute. His movements were so predatory, a nervous giggle rose up as I started to move back quicker.

"That I did, Pet, that I did," he said, now pushing to his feet and as he did, he had another cushion in his hand.

"And now… it's time I… finish it!" he shouted before launching the feathered projectile at me the moment I tried to run. I screamed in a ridiculously girly way and momentarily wondered if we were the first people to have a pillow fight in Hell. I dodged his thrown cushion, ducking in time and picking up my own, cockily shouting,

"HA! You missed!" Then I threw my own, which he dodged with ease as he simple tipped slightly to the side and let it sail right by him. So, this was when I decided to take him totally off guard, as I dropped quickly into a roll and with my body tucked in tight, I made it over to where he was standing. Then I swept out his legs from under him, making him go down hard onto the mound of pillows. After this I quickly jumped on him, grabbed the nearest cushion and hit in square in the chest before saying,

"I won! Victory is mi… oomph!" This victory cry ended when I was hit from both sides at once. Lucius had grabbed two cushions and wacked me with them both, sandwich style. They instantly tore surrounding me in a cloud of fluffy white flowers that parted for him when he sat up to growl playfully over my lips,

"Victory is mine!" Then he kissed me, and soon I found myself writhing beneath him as he made sweet tender love to me. And this time, there were no bars to contain our passion, only…

A crushed bed of feathers.

After this third round of sex, where we managed to destroy even more of Dariush's Persian style sex club, Lucius carried me off to an area that looked sectioned off. It was also one I hadn't noticed before, which wasn't exactly surprising seeing as I had been a little busy to focus on anything other than Lucius mastering my body. Gods, but I felt like an instrument that only he could play.

Although I most definitely focused the moment I saw the mosaic tiled pool that looked like it was being fed by some kind of hot spring.

"I really don't want to know how you knew this was here," I commented dryly, making him smirk before adding with even more smug confidence,

"I could scent the water."

"Um, yeah I'm sure you could," I replied in a disbelieving tone.

"And whatever could you mean by that comment, I wonder?" He asked once he stepped us both into the hot water, making me moan the second it enveloped my skin like a warm blanket.

"So are you trying to tell me this is the first time you have been in this room…? Actually, don't answer that! I don't want to know," I said, putting space between us and holding up my hands dramatically, making him look strangely pleased. But then he reached out and took one of those hands and started to draw me back to him, now raising my fingers to his lips so as he could nibble on them.

"Amelia." The smouldering purr of my name said this way made me shiver, despite the heat that surrounded me. Of course, what he was now doing only managed to add to that heat, especially when he used his hold on me to suddenly tug me back into his arms. However, the moment I looked down,

too embarrassed by my show of insecurity, I felt him tip my head back with a gentle tap under my chin with his bent finger. Then after cupping my face to hold my gaze, he told me softly,

"I can honestly say that such a room holds no appeal to me nor any other, not unless… *you are in it."*

Then he kissed me.

～

"Well, we certainly know how to make our mark on a room," I commented as soon as we were ready to leave, something that didn't happen quickly seeing as we took advantage of what the pool had to offer. Which basically meant we could get as dirty as we wanted this time. Although it had to be said that this part of the room didn't exactly go unscathed by the act, making me wince at the sight of all those broken tiles that surrounded the pool.

However, when I mentioned to Lucius about 'healing' the room he simply laughed the idea away and went back to the preferred task of drying me. This was before he conjured up a new outfit for me, one this time that was free of amor.

"Oh, you are good," I praised, making him grin back at me. And I certainly shared in that grin when looking down and taking in the sight of myself wearing clothes I finally recognized. Just the feel of my comfy grey leggings, high top, black converse sneakers, and one of my off the shoulder black sweater was making me feel more human by the second, and this certainly wasn't a bad thing. Because despite having changed physically since coming into Hell, I knew at heart I would always be mortal, and I liked that I would never lose that part of myself. And by dressing me this way, I had to say, I think Lucius liked it too. Something that seemed to be confirmed when I saw the warm look in his eyes when scanning the length of me.

"I do try, Love," he replied before sweeping an arm down himself and in place of naked skin, was now a handsome dark-navy suit that brought out the hints of blue in his gorgeous eyes. The crisp white shirt beneath the form fitting jacket and suit waistcoat was left open at the collar without its tie, just as I knew Lucius preferred it.

"You look ready for a date," I commented with my own smirk tugging at my lips. This made him reach out his left hand to me and again, it was nice to see it without its glove.

"Then would you do me the honor of being my date? As right now, I only have one destination in mind." I laughed at this and took his hand, letting him pull me from the room. However, just as he opened the door he looked back at the feathered carnage, a knowing grin transforming his already handsome face to one that was off-the-chart's panty melting.

It was like he seemed almost smug at the thought that we had left his brother's harem in such a mess. As always, I was embarrassed by the idea and wanted to make a quick getaway before his brother realized. Although this hope was dashed the moment we met Dariush in the hallway leading back to his office. Lucius approached him, then he put a hand on his shoulder and declared with cocky arrogance,

"We found your harem and I am not sorry."

"Lucius!" I hissed after my mouth dropped.

"Subtle as always, brother," Dariush muttered, and at this Lucius grinned but then again, I think it was more to do with my own reaction than that of his brother's as that grin was soon solely focused on me.

"Can I also assume that being now dressed this way, you

are ready to depart?" his brother asked, making Lucius nod before confirming with words,

"We are, for I am eager to get Amelia home." Dariush nodded as if he understood this and held his arm out towards his office door, telling us we should go inside.

"Wait! I haven't said goodbye to Nero!" I shouted as Lucius led me into the room so as we could have some privacy when Dariush sent us home. As for the McBain brothers, I had already said my teary goodbyes to them on the second day when sitting my bored ass on Lucius's throne waiting for him to come back. Now they were free men they were eager to get back to what I imagined it was they did best… drinking, fighting, bounty hunting and well, I didn't want to think of the other thing.

But as for Nero, she had stayed with me, and thank the Gods she had or it would have made my time waiting near unbearable.

"Don't worry, my sweet, she will join us soon in the mortal realm," Lucius assured me.

"Wait! She will? Has she agreed to join your council?" Lucius smiled at my enthusiastic tone.

"She has, but she is needed here a little longer so as she can… how did she put it, 'tie up the loose ends of her Hellish life'." I chuckled at this. It was weird to think of her closing the doors to her shop and sticking up a big *For Sale* sign, making me wonder who its next owner would be.

"Are you ready?" Lucius asked, once again offering me his hand to take, something I did without a second thought. Because now I was more than ready for this next chapter of our lives together to begin. Which is why the moment Dariush created a portal for us, I squeezed his hand tightly and told Lucius,

"Absolutely…" Then I let out a relieved sigh and whispered the exact same words he had said to me…

"…Let's go home."

CHAPTER 10
CURSED TO DREAM

As soon as I was faced with Dariush's portal, I found myself more than looking forward to finally going home. Although where that home would end up being was still a conversation Lucius and I needed to have. Of course, I knew that we would be moving in together, that was most definitely a moot point after all we had been through. And it was like he had said, the ultimate can of worms had already been opened.

But knowing this still didn't prevent me from having a million questions about how this was all going to work. Technically I was already moved in, as Lucius had already pointed out that my precious picture of Spock was still decorating his wall. Yet after everything that had happened, I realized all the little things didn't really matter anymore.

We had just spent weeks in Hell looking for each other, fighting tooth and nail at every turn, only to find one another, and then be cruelly ripped apart once more. It had been a constant battle to just stay in each other's arms. So, I had to question if wherever we lived, did it really matter as long as we were together?

But I also had to confess how I felt the moment we stepped through the portal, and I realized where we were... back in Lucius's mountain castle, standing in his unique living space. It was as if I could finally breathe easy for the first time since I had left my home realm.

Being fully mortal when I step through the first time, I had wondered how I would feel stepping back, no longer the same girl as when I had left. These past few days I had felt different, but over time, it was something I was beginning to get used to.

However, the moment Lucius had stepped back into that throne room it was as if the last puzzle-piece of my altered-self had just slotted into place, creating a clearer picture of what I had needed all this time. Of what my soul had been missing.

Everything within me suddenly felt right. I could breathe easier, despite the heaviness of added power weighing on my mortal-born vessel, making the weight feel lighter. Everything cleared, as if my creator had suddenly clicked their fingers and my body had responded by handing the hardest parts back to Lucius to care for. This new power that had been placed upon me, Lucius had literally lifted the burden, but then again I was not surprised. He had carried a piece of my soul with him all of this time, and it was as if my body recognized its keeper.

Being with Lucius really was the true meaning of the statement often made when you told yourself that you have finally found your soul mate. Which was why I totally understood why he pulled me close and breathed me in the moment he finally got me alone in his private living space. As if trying to merge the scent of the mountain around us with that of my own body, painting a picture in his mind. A memory he treasured of the time we had both spent here together.

A time before I ran away from him.

"I'm not going anywhere, Lucius," I said in an amused tone, trying to lighten the mood as I could feel his arms tighten around me in a possessive way. However, it was when I said this that he pulled back so as he could look down at me.

"No. You. Are. Not," he said, his tone emphasizing each word like it was law. So, knowing there was only one way to get him to stop worrying, I wrapped my arms around him and hugged him to me. Then after seconds waiting for him to relax in my hold, I reached up on my tip toes and asked,

"Does someone need a plate full of my awesome chilli fries?" At this he threw his head back and laughed so loud, it now echoed throughout the whole cavern, making me grip on to his jacket tighter. Then I raised a hand up to cup his cheek and asked,

"You okay, honey?" His eyes warmed at that and after taking a quick look around and squeezing me tight, he told me affectionately,

"I am now."

∽

"I thought Dariush could only take one person through a portal, and didn't you say something about blood?" I asked as it suddenly occurred to me. This was after we had consumed my promised chilli fries, (thank you, full pantry and well stocked freezer room) and we were now sitting all snuggled up on his couch. But of course, we had already had the difficult conversation about what had happened once he left the battlefield. Yet I also felt hope, just like he did, that Kala would one day want to join our world, but agreed that a time of peace was what she needed in order to heal. Naturally, I had also been shocked to hear that Kala wasn't the only being he had managed to make peace with. Lucius had even laughed at how I tried to play it cool with this piece of an atom-sized bombshell he just casually dropped on me. Going so far as nearly choking on a fry and needing Lucius to pat me on the back to aid its decent to my belly.

"I share the same blood with Dariush, as now do you, which means he will always be able to take both of us through his portals." I grinned at this and made the joke,

"Well in that case, I will just toss away my passport now." He chuckled at this and reminded me,

"I think you will find that difficult to do seeing as it is still in my possession."

"Wait, you have my passport?" I asked in surprise.

"That depends, which one are you referring to? The one with the name Amelia Faith Draven, or the fake one you ever so adorably named Lia Earhart, for naturally, I have both." I tensed at this.

"And there it is, the first run away snipe since being back here. Congratulations, Lucius, you lasted all of two hours before reminding me of my flighty misdemeanour," I said grumbling, and he pulled me closer to him.

"Maybe I am just using it as a way to remind you of something else... a deal we made perhaps," he whispered before looking down at his crotch and the definite hard on I found straining against his suit pants. I wondered why he didn't pick a more comfortable outfit seeing as we were relaxing in his home.

At the very least he had rid himself free of the jacket and rolled up his sleeves when he helped me chop up the ingredients for our dinner earlier. I had enjoyed the normality of it all, as I seriously couldn't remember the last time I had actually cooked or when we had done something so mundane together.

"Erh, I think you will find the deal is for blow jobs before the fact not after you have made some judgey comment and then you get one as a reward," I pointed out, making him counter,

"Then should I come up with a cock sucking schedule and fix it to the fridge, as I am more than flexible to do so… tell me, my Amelia, do you happen to have any Star Trek magnets lying around?" His teasing made me burst into a fit of giggles, something he looked pleased with.

"Unfortunately not, no," I said, still laughing and something that only continued when he replied,

"Pity… having it chiselled in stone will have to do."

"You're funny," I commented, making him grin.

"I am glad you think so, something that is vastly easier to do when you bring such light into my laugh."

"Aww, that's nice… hey, does this mean I get time off the cock sucking schedule?" At this he frowned comically before shouting as if horrified by the idea,

"Absolutely not!"

Again I started giggling before another question about Dariush and his portals popped in my head.

"So, these portals…"

"Oh good, we are back to that and not on my owed oral pleasure," Lucius interrupted dryly, making me pause long enough to frown.

"I just wondered if he can he create them anywhere?" I asked.

"He does have certain limitations, it's true, but there are not many, especially not where his powers are vastly stronger, which is most likely why he prefers Hell to the mortal realm. Creating portals there comes more naturally to him than anywhere else. I can imagine it's as easy as breathing for him," Lucius replied, being surprisingly forthcoming about it all.

"Well, it's not like blood rock is without its magic, not now we're home," I added, wagging my eyebrows in what I knew was a comical way as it made him laugh.

"Why, Miss Draven, what an insatiable creature you are," Lucius replied with a knowing grin.

But then I paused to really take in the space, and what I saw made my heart ache. Because I had to say that being back here for the first time since leaving all that time ago, it was as if not a single thing had changed. I even found myself getting up from the couch and walking over to where my geek collection was still proudly displayed. In fact, my shrine to geekism seemed to be still very much a part of his everyday life. He hadn't packed a single thing of mine, but instead chose to continue to surround himself by the reminder that I was still there somewhere in the world. Like I said, the sight warmed my heart. Of course, why I was surprised, I didn't know. Not after giving me a glimpse of what it could still look like when he had saved me from the Wraith Master's void. One he had manipulated and created into something safe and comforting.

A comfort that still surrounded me now as I took in the room that had been exactly as it was before I left, and it was nice to be able to walk over to what had been my gift to him. A Lego creation of his private space which was now displayed proudly in a glass box, one that had clearly been made for it, even after my departure.

I couldn't help but run my finger along it, grinning with happiness. I felt him come up to stand behind me and shift my hair off the back of my neck, making me shiver at his touch. Of course, it was also a lot cooler inside his mountain home and took some getting used to once again.

"Are you cold?" Lucius asked as if sensing my thoughts, doing so with his lips against what was now becoming pebbled skin, as he quickly felt the answer to that question himself.

"Well, I'm not in Hell anymore," I answered, teasing him.

"Ah yes, that myth, one that, by now, you surely understand as being nothing more than time told fable… well, unless you're in my father's realm of course," he added this last part on a chuckle.

"Why, does it have a central heating system?" At this he laughed again before muttering against my neck,

"Point taken, love." This was said before he suddenly swept me up into his arms, released his wings, and flew me towards his bedroom, all to the sound of my echoing gasp.

Then as he walked us both towards his bed, he told me,

"Fuck central heating… *I know a far better way to warm you up.*"

That he most certainly did…
Twice.

∽

I knew the moment I'd fallen asleep, because once more, I was back in this Hellish, barren land, one I thought I had forever left behind me. However, looking up to the castle now, one I had once been mentally trapped inside, it looked like all hope for it to have been erased from my memory was fruitless.

I even looked behind me, half expecting to find all those poor souls being made to fight over and over again. Just like I had been forced to watch when I was locked in this land. A sight that only confirmed what the strength of a dark, twisted mind full of greed and insanity combined truly had the power to do.

Destroy.

It could bring an entire nation to its knees as all that was left was endless death to be relived over and over again. All of this by the hands of one man.

This may have been the first of my dreams, but I knew it wouldn't be the last. Not when I realized the true horror of my future, for I would forever still be linked to this place. Linked despite the Wraith Master's demise. Despite the dark heart that I'd had no other choice but to consume, I had been a fool to naively believe that would have been enough to break away completely. To believe that my connection had solely been with the imprisoned Wraiths themselves and not this Hellish land and its long dead Master.

Because deep down I knew that it was an internal link that could only be broken in one way. I should have recognized that the moment I entered the prison. A place the Wraith Master had locked them to, and despite liberating them from these glass cages, I knew they were still not free.

Yes, they had willingly fought for me in the War of Souls. But I wanted more than anything else in the world to keep my promise to them. The promise that I would one day set them free. Which was why I knew I would be forever plagued with these nightmares as a reminder for the rest of my life. Each night until the day came when I could finally fulfil that promise… *that vow.*

I felt a rumbling beneath my feet like thousands of horses all charging in the same direction, and their destination seemed to be me. I turned just in time to see the looming storm clouds in the distance, a grey, ominous wave, blowing closer and closer toward me. A thick fog was also rolling in seemingly from nowhere, making the ground beneath my feet disappear. It started to rumble with greater depth, and I then felt myself started to sink into something I couldn't see.

That horrifying feeling that I was now being consumed by something lurking in the fog made me start to panic. My pulse hammered against my skin and my pounding heart created a sharp pain within my chest.

I tried to lift up my legs, but it was as if trying to remove my feet from thick mud. Yet I looked down to find no such thing as the disturbances in the fog from my twisting body showed nothing but cracked desert land. Nothing made sense. This feeling, this sinking dread that had gripped me, didn't make sense.

Nothing did.

Nothing until the fog finally began to roll away from me and when the sinking feeling was up to my knees, only then did I see the cause. Only then did I see what I was actually sinking into.

It was death.

The remains of thousands of warriors were now all around me. I was knee-deep in bodily remains, making me scream out in horror! Surrounded now by the evidence of what the Wraith Master's army had been forced to kill, despite the injustice of this dead army's first victory. For nothing could kill a ghost. Because that was all, essentially, the Wraith was. A moving Phantom, haunting in not only its appearance but more so with its engrained memory to kill.

You could lash out at it with everything you had, continuing to do so until your last breath, but each swipe of your blade would do nothing. No weapons could kill it. It was the ultimate army when it was commanded.

And for me, I was sinking and drowning in the memory of the horrific things that the army had been made to do. It was like a reminder to be forever tortured with. Not only reliving the horrifying crimes they committed, but now to be drowned in the evidence of it. It was more than my mind could bare!

It was as if the Wraith Master's curse had now been transferred to me. However, the difference was, witnessing such death at the hands of his men wasn't punishment enough for a King who commanded them. For he felt no guilt. No, his punishment had been to remember the darkest moment of his life. The true scars he had self-inflicted upon his soul.

He had been made to relive the heinous act of killing his family and eating their hearts over and over again. And now I was forever cursed with reliving the sins of what was now my army.

So, as I started to sink down, trying in vain to claw my way out, gripping onto rotting flesh and bleached bones baked by the sun, it felt as if nothing had the power to save me.

Because now this was my curse.

A curse even Lucius couldn't save me from.

CHAPTER 11
DATING THE AFTERMATH

This first time this happened, I woke up screaming the moment the sea of corpses beneath my feet had consumed me whole. Naturally, Lucius had woken with me, and I soon found myself gasping for air wrapped in his arms. I then had the painful experience of having to describe to him what my nightmare had been.

"We will fix this," had been his firm reply, obviously suffering with me as I knew he struggled, for how could he possibly hope to combat my dreams? How could he save me from myself?

After this, there was nothing more to do but to hold me close, and thankfully it was enough to ward off any more bad dreams for the rest of the night. But just how long would his comfort last when it was my mind we were battling against? I just didn't know.

I also had to admit that it felt like a bitter end to what should've been a happy ever after. The sour taste that was left in my mouth knowing that we hadn't even been awarded a single night together without the next thing to rear its ugly head and plague our future.

But despite knowing this, I also knew that I couldn't dwell on it for too long. After all, Lucius and I had a life to start living.

And speaking of that life…

"Where are we going?" I asked after we both found ourselves dressed for the day and breakfast had been consumed. It also had to be said that nothing could've prevented the moan of pleasure that came from me at the first taste of my blessed cereal. Oh, course Lucius had laughed at this, and continued to look at me as if he found the whole thing endearing.

But I felt like I had missed everything! Even as I was brushing my teeth, I was looking at my toothbrush like it was some magical ancient relic. This morning had felt like a gift. But then wasn't that always the case when the little things you took for granted every single day were suddenly taken from you? And now, here I was, basking in the feeling of being truly clean after another shower, my hair washed and brushed to a high shine and tied back into a ponytail. Even my hair tie was the stuff of beauty, making me hum happily as I lifted my thick hair and secured it up with such ease, I made a joyous,

"Waala!" sound.

As for what I was wearing, well the theme of the day was comfort, comfort, comfort! Meaning I was once again wearing my comfy yoga pants, grinning to myself, especially when Lucius moaned after I caught him looking at my ass.

Added to this was another comfy wide neck sweater that hung off one shoulder, with a tank top underneath and a bra that actually fit me. Honestly, it all felt like Heaven. Gods, but just having normal underwear on again was a blessing.

As for Lucius, he was looking a little more casual, now

wearing a pair of dark grey jeans, and a dark burgundy T-shirt that molded deliciously to his muscular torso. I was still getting used to the sight of him without a glove on his left hand and found myself touching it at every opportunity, making him smile whenever I did. I had never known him without the glove, so I was still getting used to the feel of both his bare hands on my naked skin.

"Still getting used to it?" he asked after offering it for me to take, after about the hundredth time of me touching it or playing with his fingers. A comment that enticed me to lift up his hand and lay a soft tender kiss to his palm. Then I looked up at him, making sure to purposely flutter my eyelashes as I asked him back,

"Are you?"

He omitted a little growl before using his other hand to curl at my hip, so as he could tug me forward.

"I will never tire of touching you," he said before kissing me, and for long, blissful moments, I forgot where we were headed and more importantly, I forgot where we had come from.

I forgot everything other than Lucius.

∽

We soon made our way through his mountain castle, and I quickly recognized where we were headed, making me pull back on his hand and ask him,

"I understand duty doesn't stop, Lucius, so if you need to do this alone, I will understand." The look he gave me in return was a curious one before I felt gentle fingertips stroke down my cheek, caressing my jaw line before he then used those fingers to tip my chin up, so as I could look up at him.

"Your place is by my side, Amelia, which means I will never have to do this alone... *ever again.*" I couldn't help but bite my lip at this, seeing as giving into the urge to bite my fingertips was taken from me, as he was too close for me to wiggle my hand up and reach.

However, instead of kissing me senseless, like he did last time, he simply placed a kiss against my forehead before gripping my hand tighter in his. Then he led me into his office where I knew his council was now waiting for us.

And how did I know this...?

Because I could feel them.

I could detect their heartbeats and hear their muted voices when a mortal would've been too far away to hear anything. The added power to my senses that bombarded my mind should have freaked me out. Should have overwhelmed me. But for some reason it was almost as if my body had just simply accepted it. It was as though it had simply embraced this change like it was as easy as breathing.

What shouldn't have been natural had simply became natural overnight. My body felt stronger, my senses heightened, and it was as if subconsciously, I had always known a piece of me was missing. Yet a slither of it had obviously remained enough for it to be awakened, just like it had when facing off the witch in my father's vault. Like it had always just been waiting for me to summon it, and let it be released into the world. It was like the faintest of melodies that had been singing in my blood and now, it had turned into a chorus.

It was calm and soothing like a comforting blanket, the envelope to me against the chill. Of course, Lucius had been concerned at first, admitting to me that he had been anxious after leaving me from the battlefield. But then I had also been relieved to know he trusted me to do this. To know that I was with family and I hadn't dealt with it all alone.

Besides, in that moment he had needed to make the decision to leave and it had been the right choice. Which is why I had encouraged it. His first wife had been jealous of their daughter, and the love that he had for her, whereas as I only wanted him to embrace it. I was happy that he trusted my heart in this. So, in the end, I had simply placed my hand on his cheek and told him not to worry. That I had managed just fine and the proof of that, well it was finding me sitting on his throne like a badass and not to have found me falling apart.

So leaving these thoughts behind we walked into his office together, and the first thing I did was shout the name of someone I believed was long lost and I would never ever see again…

"Ruto!" I knew he wasn't expecting my reaction to him. Which made it all the funnier when utter shock and awkwardness took over his features, and that normally calm, hard, exterior softened as I threw myself in his arms.

"Break any arms lately?" he asked after first clearing his throat, making me realise that emotions and expressing them was clearly not his strong point.

"No, but I did chop off the head of the guy who killed you." At this, he ruffled my hair and said,

"Please tell me you did it with a dagger." I winked at him and replied,

"Does a bloody big sword count?"

"Little bird, if it's sharp and pointy, it always counts." I couldn't help but laugh, realising that this was probably the longest conversation we'd never had. But then my eyes went to Clay, and then to Caspian, who had both nearly lost their lives in an attempt to save mine. I then went to them both, with Clay embracing my hug as I knew he would.

"Hey, girl," he said in that deep baritone voice of his, as well as patting me on the back. I then turned to Caspian and he quickly held up his hands, taking a step back and telling me,

"I'm good." I laughed at this and would have replied with a funny comeback, but then Leissa stepped from behind him and she was the next one to receive a hug. Like always she was dressed in an immaculate 1950s pencil skirt dress, looking like some sexy pin up girl. Her hair pinned in big barrel rolls with deep red shiny lips to match the color of her outfit. However, her stiletto heels and little lace gloves were black.

It had been so long since we had seen each other that we instantly started chatting. However, this was when Lucius obviously hit his limit and staked his claim on me once more. He did this by placing his hands on my shoulders and pulling me back firmly into his embrace.

I could help but turn my head and grin up at him, knowing he needed this connection between us as much as I did. However, I also knew that, with time, things would settle between us. But for now, our constant touch was healing old wounds that had been inflicted by being constantly forced apart for so long.

After this Lucius motioned for us all to sit and the meeting to start when he led me to his chair and sat down, promptly pulling me into his lap. Luckily the comfy leather seat was big enough for the both of us to sit in, or this would have felt and looked more awkward than I would have liked.

As for the meeting, what was discussed was mainly about the aftermath of the war. Lucius wanted to know of the casualties, most of which were of the oldest turned vampires.

These were the first leaves to have fallen from the Tree of Souls, each one turning Roque. Some had managed to be contained but unfortunately, for most of these poor souls, there had been little choice other than to end their lives.

A thick folder waited like a tome of the death on his desk, and I knew that it pained him with the knowledge that each one contained the name of someone he had turned all that time ago.

Thankfully, because of the outcome of the war, that list wasn't any bigger and every single person in this room knew it could've been a lot worse. Yet this still didn't make it any easier for him. I was just glad that all those souls had now been returned to him and well, partly to me too.

There still felt like an immeasurable amount of stuff we had left to discuss, left to deal with. But I knew it would all come in time, so I didn't rush it... despite this going against my personality, somebody like me, who thrived on asking questions and gaining information like it was candy to a sugar addict. But for once, I was trying to be patient in this department. Then again, one look at Lucius and I don't think I was the only one trying to be patient. Especially as he was forced to listen to the fallout of his people and what they had been made to endure at the hands of his brother's hatred.

Hatred that turned into a Hellish infection.

Because it had been the result of the Devil's imprisonment of his villainous son, Matthias, after his attack on the woman he loved. His own Chosen One, the Oracle, Pythia. It was this imprisonment that drained him of his power and that hatred had filled the roots of soul weed that kept him locked in his sarcophagus. And as for Lucius, it had been unknowingly his sacrifice that had released that power into the roots of Tree of Souls, taking thirty years for it to reach those he had sired.

As for the rest of the meeting, once the lives of his people had been discussed, talk turned to more lighthearted matters. This included the grand reopening of Transfusion. Strangely enough, I had to admit that I missed the place. I was looking forward to walking back through its doors under more certain circumstances. The last time I was there, I was still confused about Lucius in regard to our relationship.

But then the place also held so many wonderful memories for me, erasing those of my first experience quite quickly. It was the first place Lucius had kissed me. The first place we ever made love and he claimed my virginity. We were here the first time he admitted to me how he felt about me. Which meant that at its core, it was the place that held so many of my firsts, and I couldn't help but feel an affinity with the place.

So yes, I was definitely looking forward to getting back there. Something that I realized would be happening in only two days' time. It was also nice to hear that my own aunt Sophia had a hand in redecorating the place as with everything else going on at the time, I very much doubt this was something Lucius had been interested in undertaking himself.

According to Lucius, my aunt had received only one stipulation, and I couldn't help but chuckle when I heard it relayed back to me.

Purple was banned.

This of course was my family's colour, with purple being used to represent the King of Kings throughout history. Of course, he wasn't the only royal to apply this colour to his statues. No, purple being known as a royal colour started with ancient monarchies. This was because the colour was difficult to produce, and when I say difficult, I mean if uck and ick had a baby, then purple would be the outcome.

To produce it, dye-makers had to crack open a snail's shell, extract a purple-producing mucus and if that wasn't bad enough, then then exposed it to sunlight for a precise amount of time, the smell of which was utterly disgusting. It also took as many as two hundred and fifty thousand mollusks to get just one ounce of usable dye. Hence why it was so expensive and available only to upper society.

But hey, that didn't make it any more appealing for Lucius, as there was only one colour that was to be associated with the Vampire King. A colour that would now forever ignite a certain hot memory within my mind… a thought that would make me shudder after being made to wear my own blood painted on my skin.

Now as the meeting went on, it soon became clear to all when Lucius wanted it to draw to an end, as clearly, he had more important things on his mind. So, one by one, they started to leave, and Liessa gave him knowing look making me wonder what Lucius was up to now. A question that grew when she stopped and told him softly,

"Everything is ready as you ordered, my Lord." He bowed his head silently, telling her that he understood without words, and I waited until she had closed the door behind her before asking,

"So, are you going to tell me what all that was about?" The question came with a raised brow of my own, an expression usually saved for the men in my life. However, Lucius just looked amused by this before giving me very little in the way of an answer.

"I might have something planned," he replied with a knowing grin.

"And these plans of yours, do they include your girlfriend?" I questioned, now walking my fingers up his neck until I could tug slightly on his hair.

"Perhaps," was his one worded answer and again, it gave me nothing.

"Why, Mr Septimus, are you planning a date?" I asked, almost giddy with the thought of it. As let's just say that since Lucius and I had been together, most of what very few dates we'd had were cut short in explosive ways.

"I think we are long due one, don't you?" he admitted, his thoughts clearly mirroring my own. And oh, but I couldn't agree more, hence why I kissed his cheek before suddenly making my way out of his lap.

"And just where do you think you're going?" he asked, being needy and obviously not happy by my sudden retreat.

"Why to get ready of course, you don't expect me to turn up to this date in yoga pants and a sweater, do you?" I teased back, looking over my shoulder. To which his reply came in the form of tipping his body closer to the armrest and leaning his head to the side so as to purposely look at my ass. Then he replied with a growl of heated words,

"Sweetheart, with how hot you look in those fucking pants, I'm tempted to make all of our dates in my training room, just so I can recreate all the fun I had when getting you out of them the first time." His comment made me blush, as I remembered the time he spoke of, when he ever so skilfully got me out of my pants.

Which was when I decided to tease him as I turned and then placed both my palms to his desk. Then I leaned forward, now purposely giving him a glimpse of my cleavage, as my sweater draped down low. This giving him more than an ample view, and one he most certainly didn't miss. Then I told him,

"You might like the pants, but the dress I have in mind, it's far easier to get into, especially when..." I paused so as I could make my way to the door and after tossing my hair back, making the ponytail swing, I told him,

"...I don't wear any underwear." Then I walked out of his office to the sound of him groaning and muttering to himself.

"Fuck me, but I am a…"

"...Lucky bastard indeed."

CHAPTER 12
OTHERS LIVES

Standing here, looking at myself in the mirror, I saw a sight I had almost forgotten I could achieve. The last time I faced Lucius looking even close to this, had been the night of his ball, one thrown for his birthday. A beautiful night that had ended on a sour note to say the least. Especially considering it had been the start of the death of his people, for it marked the day of the infected rot upon the Tree of Souls.

All that aside and firmly in the past, I glanced back at myself in the mirror again, now spinning as the dress flowed around me. It also turned out that my sassy comeback about the dress I was going to tease him with for our date, ended up being a moot point. As when I made my way back to what I was starting to think of as our place at the centre of his mountain, I found Liessa there are waiting for me. Oh and she also had with her a big white box that didn't take a 'know it all scholar' to guess what it held.

It seemed as if Lucius had been planning for this night and it was going to be far from a simple date. In fact, the moment that Liessa showed me the dress I was expected to wear, I had to question if there was another ball I was to attend. It also turned out that my underwear comment wasn't going to apply, not when Lucius had obviously had ideas about that aspect as well. A good job really, considering the thick red corset underneath was needed just to kept my boobs in place. The dress was an off the shoulder design that dipped into a deep sweetheart neckline and was meant to show off hints of the black beaded lace trim that framed the edges of the corset. Or so Liessa assured me when I asked after she helped me get into the huge thing.

As for the top part of the blood red dress, this was a full bodice covered in floral, applique embroidery lace that was a finished in a tear shape with the point leading down the front of the skirt. Swaths of delicate red organza trimmed with a satin boarder cascaded in folds over heavy red shimmering taffeta beneath, giving the skirt its body. And what lay hidden beneath this were black stockings edged with red lace and panties that matched the red and black corset.

A pair of satin stiletto heels thankfully added enough height that the skirt of the dress wasn't tripping me up. Although with how clumsy I could be, then it was most likely that the shoes were enough to achieve me falling on my ass without the aid of extra fabric. But hey, with the amount of material around me, then I guess my landing would be soft, so there was that plus.

"So erm... this date..." I had asked when Liessa was doing my hair and makeup, making her simply wag her lace covered finger at me.

"All will be revealed soon, Sweetpea, now hold still or I will burn you with this curling wand, and Luc would be so pissed," she said, now forced to wind the same piece back around the heated curler for a second time. Which meant that by the time I was finished, my hair was pinned high on the back of my head in elaborate twists before allowing the ends to cascade down in bouncy curls. As for my makeup, this was done in an elegant, yet smoky style, that made my eyes look bigger and the red at my lips just made them look sinful.

"Don't worry, it's kiss proof," she told me with a wink once she was finished. Again, I had tried to get any clues out of her, but she just laughed at all my attempts. In fact, the only thing that gave away that I was not attending another ball, was that Liessa was dressed exactly the same as she had been for the meeting in Lucius's office. Of course, she most definitely seemed to enjoy my attempts at gaining information from her. But then, that was Liessa for you, she always had a mischievous edge to her.

I remember one of the first things she said to me, about hoping I would cause trouble like the last human did, which obviously turned out to be my mother. But as time went on, I really started to like Liessa and her quirky ways. I was just glad that her husband had survived and was now back with her with his soul fully intact.

He had fulfilled his duty and saved me when my life was in danger back in the temple of the Tree of Souls. I almost shuddered as I remembered that utter devastation and feeling of heartbreak when I believed that I had lost all three of Lucius's councilmembers men during that fight.

I was still amazed that we had managed to get Ruto back and to know that he owed the gift of a second life to Kala was even more heart-warming. But I was still astonished that we had all gone through all that we had without losing a single being we cared for. It made me reflect on what he told me about Kala's decision to stay in Heaven, and after all she had been through, well, I couldn't exactly say that I blamed her.

I did, however, hope that in time she would come to realise the potential life that she could have here with us should she choose to come back to the mortal realm, I so wanted that for Lucius. He deserved it. He deserved nothing less and I was just happy that he'd finally found the peace he had been searching for all these thousands of years.

"Are you ready?" Liessa asked, jarring me out of these thoughts and I was no longer focusing on my reflection in the mirror.

"Am I ready for the unknown…? Sure, why not," I answered with a nod, knowing now that she was the one who would escort me to where this secret date of Lucius's was being held. And I was more than glad for it as I was still learning the tunnel system in Lucius's mountain castle known as, Blutfelsen, which of course translated to…

Blood Rock.

I did however, recognise the grand entrance to the ballroom making me look at Liessa and say,

"But I didn't think we were… *oh my!*" This question soon ended on a whispered breath as the dark double doors swung open and revealed the most perfect sight in the world. Again, I couldn't help but gasp when I saw not only that the room had been utterly transformed into some romantic fantasy land, but mainly who now stood at the centre of it all.

Lucius.

My King.

As for the ballroom, it was now glittering with thousands upon thousands of fairy light twinkling delicately around stone pillars. They also framed each side of the grand staircase, wrapped around every inch of the iron railings, transforming the brutal thorns and spikes into something beautiful. Then surrounding the edges of the dance floor were hundreds of lit white pillar candles all in different sizes. But all of this romantic beauty was nothing but a soft glow casting its warm light on the only one who held my attention.

The utter perfection that was Lucius, who was standing in the middle of that dance floor, holding in his hand…

A single red rose.

Nothing else mattered to me in that moment. In fact, I didn't even register that Liessa had left, closing the door behind me. But then again with Lucius in my sights, I didn't think there was much else I would noticed. Not with such a man now beckoning me forward, holding out his hand and prompting me to walk down the stairs and quickly fill it with my own.

As for the way he was dressed, well I wasn't surprised to find that we matched in colour. However, whereas his suit was mostly black, the hints of red to match my dress were striking. His waistcoat was black and red brocade, that matched the collar of his suit jacket. His tie was the deepest of crimson and his shirt was black. This had a thin red line of piping down the edge, matching the red cuffs I could see peeking out from the sleeves of his jacket.

He was utterly magnificent and he stole my heart with every breath I took. Lucius's grin was infectious as he felt my hand now in his and I couldn't help but smile up at him.

"You look so beautiful… just breathtaking, my Amelia," he said, making me blush.

"You look very handsome yourself, Mr Septimus," I replied, and again that bad boy grin of his tugged at the corner of his lips. But before I said anything more, he suddenly snapped the head of a rose from its long stem, reached out, and tucked the flower into my hair. He said nothing to this but simply gave me a warm smile in response to my own tender expression.

Then he took a step back so as he could bow before me like a gentleman.

"May I have this dance, m'lady?" he asked, now holding

out a hand for me, and I couldn't help the tips of my fingers finding their way into my mouth. Then I told him in a shy voice,

"It would be my honour, My Lord." He smirked at this before those fingers tightened around my hand a second after I placed it in his own.

He then nodded to the shadows I could see in the corner of the ballroom, before beautiful music started to play. But this wasn't all, as stunning lyrics added to them as a man's voice started to sing.

"I chose this song because its words express my heart to its fullest," he told me, and I swear as I listened to every one, tears started to fill my eyes, even as we danced around the candle lit dance floor.

Words like,

'I'm the luckiest man alive, I'm so lucky I'm terrified'

I gasped before the emotional moment continued when he sang out,

'I lay at night, I wonder why you're by my side, I can't deny, I'm the luckiest man alive.'

This made me reach out and lay my hand at his cheek, making me whisper during the song,

"Because I love you." At this he swallowed hard, and I could tell the same emotions were affecting him just as they were me, making him place his forehead to mine as we continued to sway to the beautiful melody. But as the words continued to flow over us, I realized just how deep the lyrics went.

'Lying next to you, what the Hell did I do, I must have done something right, in my other lives, lying face to face, after all my mistakes, I must have done something right in my other lives.'

"Oh Lucius," I whispered before kissing him through the next verse, lyrics so apt, he felt the tears for himself as they landed on his cheeks.

'Maybe I saved the world, maybe I paid my debts, maybe I gave it all, maybe I did my best, maybe I saved someone, maybe they saved me too. Maybe I just survived in my other lives.'

By the time, the song came to an end, we had both stopped dancing, now standing in the centre of the room, locked in each other's embrace. Even more tears escaped my lashes and rolled freely down my cheeks, and for Lucius, he watched every single one before using his thumbs to swipe them gently away.

"Why do you cry, my Queen?" he asked me in a soft, tender voice. One that would have lulled me into telling him anything.

"The song... It was so... so beautiful, I can't... can't believe that's how you feel," I told him, trying to push past my emotions to do so.

"You're in my arms, and with the knowledge of an eternity to finally have you in them each night, then how can I not feel like the luckiest man in the world?" I swallowed hard, trying to stop the tears but failing, causing him to simply take more of them away before my own words could follow.

"I can't... can't believe you did... did all this for me," I told him, cupping his cheek and glancing around the magical room.

"I have something to confess, Amelia," he told me, and I couldn't help but tense, something that made him chuckle before assuring me,

"Don't fret, it is not bad."

"Then does it need to be given the title, confession?" I asked, making him tap me on the nose and say,

"It is merely a technicality."

"A technicality?" I asked, making him sigh before telling me,

"The night you rang me, on the ship... the night you were..."

"Far too drunk and missing you?" I filled in, making him give me an affectionate smile in return.

"You made me promise that I would not look into your mind, do you remember?"

"I do," I answered, quickly seeing where this was going.

"I may have promised not to do so after that night... but..."

"It's okay, Lucius, this was so long ago, I don't see..." He quickly cut me off.

"You saw a couple dancing, you told me that you miss dancing with me and well... I promised myself that if I ever got you back, that I would take every single opportunity to make up for the past... past mistakes," he said, adding this last part as if pained by the past he spoke of.

"Lucius, I..." Once again, he didn't let me finish as he continued on with what did now seem like a confession.

"I have made so many mistakes when it comes to loving you, Amelia, and now, I make you this vow, for I will atone for every single one of them. To atone for every opportunity I chose to ignore, those missed chances to ask you to dance with me. Every single ball, every event your father hosted, every one that pained me as I decided foolishly to hide in the shadows and simply watch you, knowing how you were just waiting for me to take your hand…" I gasped at this when he closed his eyes as if the memory truly did pain him.

"You… you were there?" I questioned quietly.

"At every one," he answered, now opening his eyes as the music continued, only this time without the singer.

"I never saw you," I told him, still stunned by this revelation.

"As I intended," he said, making me swallow hard before asking the ultimate question.

"I don't understand, what is it you're getting at here, Lucius? Why bring all this up now?"

"Every single one, I would watch you from afar, hidden in the shadows feeling unworthy just being in your presence." I started shaking my head at this, quickly telling him,

"Unworthy? No, Lucius… *never.*"

"At the time I was disgraced by what I had done to you, and I tried to keep my distance. I would watch you, that dreamy look on your face, as if you could imagine yourself there among the rest dancing. I know that if I had seen even one man approaching, I would've lost all control. So I forbid anybody from asking you to dance, and in doing so I deprived you of the memory," he confessed, making me suck in a startled breath.

"What?" I whispered.

"I robbed you of the feeling of belonging. I was selfish, as I knew that if I could not have you, then no man ever would. The only person I allowed to dance with you was your father, and he believed that nobody approached you because of him. But then that is the advantage of being able to access any mind and manipulate it."

"Why are you telling me all of this, Lucius?" I asked, still confused where he was taking this and not sure how I felt about him bringing up the past like this.

"Because I want you to know that my only regret is not that I prevented anybody from dancing with you. *It was that I never had the courage to ask you myself.*" At this my heart melted and I finally understood why this moment meant so much to him. Why he had wanted to dance with me on the rooftop, our first date. Why this moment was so significant now... *or did I?*

"Oh, Lucius, that was the past and I... *Oh Gods...*" This quickly ended as my breath left me in a whisper before my heart began hammering in my chest. Because Lucius had started to lower to one knee, and I felt as if I had suddenly forgotten how to breathe. This even more so when he reached inside his pocket and pulled out a red velvet ring box. Then once looking up at me, he flipped it open and I gasped the moment I saw it. It was a stunning black band of delicate vines, with leaves and thorns that held tiny black diamonds. All of which, entwined a stunning, glittering blood red diamond at its centre, and one that had been cut into an exquisite rose shape. I gasped at the sight, knowing that this ring also represented a piece of my soul that Lucius had claimed that day.

But then he started to speak and my watery gaze flicked from the magnificent ring to the beautiful man in front of me now down on one knee.

"Amelia Faith Draven, I vow that from this day on to always be the man at your side, the one who takes your hand and leads you to the dancefloor. For I will strive every day to be the man you deserve, as nothing else matters to me more in this world than loving you. I would rather die and have my soul perish than to spend second of this life without you in it… So I ask of you, my sweet, little scholar, My Sun, My Queen, and My Love… *My Forevermore… will you marry me?"*

The moment I heard this I quickly fell to my knees in front of him, cupped his face, and placed my forehead to his before telling him the only words that ever needed to be said.

The only important words left in my heart.

The words of my soul.

"I would marry you today, tomorrow, and every day after." Then I kissed him and whispered over his lips…

"Yes, Lucius, I will marry you."

CHAPTER 13
A BLANKET OF CRIMSON

That night, I found myself more than thankful for the beautiful living dream that was becoming Lucius's fiancé and that it wasn't tainted by any nightmares. As for the rest of our perfect date, it was spent dancing, laughing, and teasing each other, basically being wrapped up in our own little beautiful world. In fact, we only stopped dancing when my stomach would not cease its rumbling, much to Lucius's amusement.

This is when he led me over to a table that had been decorated with domes of silver upon a black table cloth. Then once removed, I instantly burst out laughing.

"Cheese!" I shouted before folding myself at the stomach as I couldn't contain the laughter anymore.

"Oh, but that isn't all or the end to your food oddity," he said before lifting the last dome and revealing a small mountain of doughnuts, some of which were topped with bits of crispy bacon. Again, I couldn't help but laugh, despite still knowing how thoughtful this all was.

"Well I have to hand it to you, honey, you really have

thought of everything," I said before putting a hand to the back of his neck and pulling him into me, so as I could kiss him before whispering,

"It's perfect." At this he squeezed my sides at the same time his eyes heated, this time an amber colour like the burning sun before settling down again. Then he held out a chair for me to take, and it was like we were now in the most lavish gothic restaurant that had been all but abandoned. But as I took my seat, I couldn't hold back from telling him,

"Honestly, Lucius, this is one of the best nights of my life."

"What… even better than the time mercenaries tried to kill us or the night of cheese, long island ice teas, and dancing." I groaned at this and dramatically put a hand to my forehead as I pleaded,

"Please don't mention the dancing."

"Oh, but how could I not? After all, I remember enjoying the drunk dancing immensely, especially when you threw your underwear at me. That part was definitely fun," he teased, making me roll my eyes and the second I did, he raised up another finger, reminding me that he was still counting. In fact, he teased me even more when he leaned across the table and asked,

"Tell me, Pet, how much do you really want to roll your eyes at me?" At this I burst out laughing, and then pretended to see something suddenly over his shoulder. Naturally, he took the bait and the I second he looked, I rolled my eyes. However, Lucius being Lucius, he caught me doing this just in time, now knowing exactly what I was up to.

As for the night, it continued like this, with our teasing banter making me smirk and grin like some insanely happy girl, who well… just got engaged to the man she utterly adored and loved. This thought caused me to continuedly look down at the ring on my finger, making me wonder if I would ever get used to seeing it there. If there would ever be a time that I wouldn't look at it and smile to myself.

"Do you like it?" Lucius finally asked, after catching me looking at it yet again.

"It's perfect, I honestly could not have chosen better myself."

"I agree, only that its perfection is only achieved now it is on your hand." I blushed at this, whispering a small,

"Thank you."

"You never need thank me for speaking the truth, sweetheart, but I will take your blushes all the same," he replied, deepening that blush and just because I needed something else to say before turning shy once more, I added,

"And my finger bites."

"But of course, no matter how distracting I find them as it only reminds me of what that talented mouth of yours is capable of."

"Well, it's not singing, that's for sure," I teased, making him laugh.

"Are you sure? I could get them to play a song of your choosing?" he asked, turning slightly toward where the musicians still played, without the singer as I gathered Lucius didn't want anything to interrupt our conversation.

"Umm... I think not, after all, I have only just ensnarled myself a fiancé, and I don't want to scare him off before the big day," I joked.

"Ensnarled, you say... mmm, well you most definitely ensnarled my heart so I would say there is little chance of me becoming a flight risk... before the big day," he said, adding this last part in a tone I couldn't quite detect. I was also very tempted to ask when this wedding of ours would take place, but I didn't want to ruin the moment by putting any pressure on him.

There weren't many that could claim they had all the time in the world and it be true. But for a couple who now faced an eternity together, well then, we really did, so what was the rush?

No, for now, well I just wanted to enjoy the moment.

Yet despite making this decision to play it cool, I couldn't help but ask him as we walked back hand in hand to our private space,

"So just out of curiosity, how long have you wanted to ask me that question?"

"You mean, how in the Gods did you ever discover you liked bacon on donuts?" he teased, making me tug at his hand and mouth,

'Ha, ha.'

Then he raised my hand so he could look down at my ring, using his thumb to roll it slightly from side to side, his features warm and tender as if he loved seeing it finally there on my finger.

"I have wished to see my ring grace your finger ever since I asked you that question the first time," he told me, now reminding me of back when I had stolen a shitty bike and rode past his Lamborghini with a very obvious clue spray painted on my back letting him know it was me. Of course, how could I ever forget his reaction to this, as the first thing he had done had been to practically tear himself out of the car before asking me to marry him. Something at the time I had believed to be nothing more than one of those 'caught up in the moment' things.

Now I knew differently.

Which is why because of this confession, we didn't end up making it to the bedroom. Not before I was trying to rip his clothes off his body, ending up with us having sex against one of the statues on the way there. It was raw and passionate and I loved every minute of it. Although I couldn't help but chuckle when he started complaining about my dress having too many 'fucking layers!'

Something that wasn't a problem when he finally had it gathered up around my waist as neither of us could wait for the time consuming, 'getting naked' part. No, this thankfully came later, and after our frenzied sex against what looked like between the legs of a stone gargoyle. I swear I didn't know if I should have been concerned with my dirty mind, especially considering I found myself even more turned on by finding a stone cock and balls above me at the same time as the very real thing pounding into me as I came screaming his name. His own roar of release actually managed to crack the poor stone bastard!

However, after this sex-crazed moment was out of our system, Lucius carried me back to our room and took the time to get me out of my dress before laying me on our bed. Then once there, he made sweet, tender love to me as I wore nothing but my corset this time. One that may have started on my body but at one point did end up ripped to shreds on the floor.

Oh yes, life was good, and one I knew would only keep getting better, especially when I now looked at the future where I would soon be known as…

Mrs Amelia Septimus.

∾

The next day started very much in the same way as the previous one, although this was thankfully without the shadows of a nightmare still luring and clinging to the corners of my mind like old cobwebs.

Yet it also had to be said, another difference from the day before started to show itself and this time, it was with Lucius. I didn't know why but he seemed almost anxious about something. Of course, I had asked him about it, but he simply told me that he had something important on his mind, however, after today and if all went well, then he would never have to worry again.

Naturally, this explanation didn't help. As in… NOT. AT. ALL. No, in fact, it just made me worry even more. I mean of course, I tried to get him to expand on this strange comment. But he simply hooked a hand around my neck, pulled me in for a kiss and whispered in my ear,

"All in good time, Sweetheart."

Then he told me that he needed to see to some things and suggested I have a nice long bath as he would be back shortly. I decided that after all the delicious sexual abuse my body had lovingly endured, this wasn't a bad idea. Although, I had to admit that with the extra strength I now had, I did find that I could last much longer than before and well, Lucius most definitely knew this and used it to his advantage.

After my bath, and finally having the freedom to shave now that I wasn't sharing the water with a hungry vampire, I got out of the stone bath and dried myself off. I then rubbed lotion all over my body, feeling so much better that everything was smooth again as I was starting to look beyond spiky. The scent of shea butter absorbed into my skin and I had to admit, it had been a while since I had pampered myself.

I then walked up the steps back to our bedroom, wearing

nothing but a towel wrapped around me. This was something that I nearly dropped when I saw something waiting for me on the bed. It was a red summer dress, that was maxi length, with lines of lace ruffles down the skirt that added more fabric as it reached the floor. The top part had a delicate, pretty lace overlaying the soft fabric underneath and this wrapped around my chest and tied at the back in a lace bow. The sleeves were bell shaped and floaty around the tops of my arms, ending in a trim of the same lace at my elbows. And like I said, it was different but also, strangely familiar. However, I couldn't put my finger on it. I looked around half expecting Lucius to walk out of the walk-in closet or something but when I called his name, there was no answer.

I looked back at the dress, again feeling as if I had seen it somewhere once before, but I couldn't place when, barely able to reach for its memory. Well, clearly it was there spread out on the bedsheets for a reason, so taking the hint, I put it on after first finding underwear.

This time I went for a simple but pretty matching white lace set. It couldn't be seen under the dress anyway so I didn't think it needed to match the colour I was wearing this time. Then given the style of the dress, I gathered half my hair up in twists and secured it with enough pins that were left over from last night's hair style, that I knew it would take a tornado to loosen it. It was also still curled from Liessa's handy work, and having no need to wash it when taking my bath, I decided to keep them. This meant that it now flowed down my back in big loose curls that added to the style of the dress.

Then as I was just smoothing the soft fabric down my belly as I looked at myself in the mirror, I smiled as it was obvious that Lucius had yet even more surprise plans for me. Honestly, it made me feel giddy with excitement just to see what our next date would be and perhaps it was a celebration of our recent engagement.

But then that's when it hit me what tonight was.

"But of course!" I said feeling foolish, as it was the reopening of Transfusion and now looking down at the red crimson colour of my dress, I suddenly realised why he had chosen it. However, I had to confess that the simple red ballet style shoes without a heel did make me question where he was taking me first.

Perhaps he wished to celebrate our engagement with another picnic? After all, the dress was certainly cute and simple enough in its style to imagine me out in the countryside somewhere, sat upon the blanket with Lucius by my side. But then the very last thing I ever expected to find when walking out the bedroom was Lucius's brother now standing there looking dashing in a black suit. Even his hair was tied back, and I had to say, it suited him as it made his strong jawline even more prominent and his handsome face less rugged.

"Dariush?" I said his name in question, wondering what he could possibly be doing here? Hence why I quickly asked,

"What are you doing here?" His reply to this was to first grin down at me but before he could answer, I did it for him,

"Oh of course, you're here for the Transfusion party!" I shouted, making him bow his head and say,

"That I am, but first, my brother insisted I retrieve you for him as he has something planned for you."

"Another surprise?" I asked with wide eyes now even more excited by the picnic idea I had guessed.

"So, I ask of you, Amelia, will you trust me after everything we have been through?" he said, making me frown down at the hand he held out for me to take. But then it was like he said, after all we had been through, why wouldn't I trust him? So, I nodded and said,

"But of course." Then I placed my hand in his and watched as he turned side on so as he could create a portal with his free hand.

"Wait, why do we need a…" I never got to finish as he walked us both straight through the distorted space and Lucius had been right, creating it had looked as easy as breathing. I couldn't help but hold my breath, wondering even more so in those few seconds we passed through, what the Hell was going on.

However, the moment I stepped over to the other side, that same breath I had been holding was suddenly stolen from me by the incredible sight that met me now.

"I… I…" What I was, *was breathless!*

A crimson field of poppies.

That was the magnificent sight that filled my now watery gaze as tears soon found their way down my cheeks. For I would never forget a sight so beautiful, and one that Lucius had shared with me plucked straight from his own mortal memories. That was when I remembered what he had called this place,

'Anemone coronaria, Lily of the Field,' he had told me, but that hadn't been all, for I had asked him what it meant and suddenly things started to slot into place,

'Anemone, anemos, is the Greek name and in mythology, Anemone was the name of the daughter of the winds. Now, in Latin it is known as Coronaria, Corona, meaning crown… But do you want to know my favourite?' he had asked, and this was when I had found out why his daughter was named Kala.

But that hadn't been all…

'In Hebrew, the name of the flower is called Kalanit, this is related to the Hebrew word for a bride...'

This memory made me gasp, covering my mouth with my hands as I looked at all the thousands of poppies that surrounded us now knowing how much this all meant to Lucius. How significant this was to him and more than anything else, what it symbolized.

What it now symbolized for me.

And just like last night, there he was, now standing there in a field of crimson, waiting for me wearing a light grey, three-piece suit with black velvet buttons to match the black shirt and black tie he wore beneath it. A single poppy and leaf pinned to the collar that matched the bouquet of them tied together with a thick black ribbon and now held firmly in his hand by his side.

The affectionate look he gave me before scanning down the length of my body made me also look down at myself, making me gasp. Because now I was no longer wearing red, but white, and the second it changed I suddenly knew why I had reconised it.

It had been the same one Lucius had summoned me to wear when we were here the first time. Meaning this memory hadn't just been a tender moment shared between us, but something much more. For Lucius it had been a hope, a wish, and a desire that this day would one day be real, that it would one day be...

A dream come true.

I could barely breathe, barely keep the tears from constantly flowing, but then Lucius simply held out his hand to me just like he had done last night. And that was all I had needed to see to make me move. In fact, I nearly stumbled in my steps just to get to him quicker. Thankfully I remained on my feet, and the moment I was within reach, he pulled me to his side.

Then, as his brother took his place in front of us both I had to ask, my voice nearly breaking for fear it could shatter the dream,

"Lucius, what... is this?" After this he cupped my cheek and told me tenderly,

"This is today... This is tomorrow... and this is our..."

"Happy every day after."

CHAPTER 14
ETERNAL VOWS

"*This is today... This is tomorrow... and this is our... Happy every day after.*" I sucked back another stolen breath as he repeated the answer I had given him when he asked me to marry him. Which was when this all became clearer by the second what was going on, and it wasn't just my hope blooming inside my chest like some dream I would suddenly wake from.

For, this, right now, it was...

Our wedding day.

And it was utter perfection.

"Lucius, is this..." These whispered words broke away as I couldn't finish them. Not with the emotions overflowing as more tears fell. Because he wanted to marry me... *right here, right now!* Lucius simply wrapped an arm around me and answered,

"The happiest day of my life... Yes, Amelia, it will be, but only if you say yes." At this I threw my arms around him and whispered into the skin at his neck,

"It's perfect... you're perfect."

"Only with you, my Love," he whispered before easing me back so as he could kiss me. A sweet and loving kiss that was over too soon but I knew why when he asked his brother,

"Could you give us a moment?" Dariush nodded and stepped away, giving us some privacy and, the moment he did, Lucius cupped my cheek with a single hand, for the bouquet of poppies still remained in the other. Then after he had taken away my tears of happiness with his thumb, he told me,

"Amelia, you have to know before we do this that for me, nothing else matters but you and I… now if you want the big day, I can give you that, baby, but right here and now, in this place, one so sacred to my heart, I honestly need…" He paused when I placed my forehead to his and cupped his own cheek before telling him,

"All I need is you." At this we both closed our eyes and soon I wasn't the only one with emotions feeding their tears, for the next time they opened, I could see the shimmering fall of a single tear from steel blue eyes.

"You know not what this means to me, Amelia," he told me, making my heart ache even more for this man.

"Yes, Lucius… *yes, I do, for it means the very same to me,*" I replied, making him grin down at me.

"Then are you ready to become mine?" he asked, and like yesterday, I gave him my answer,

"Today, tomorrow, and always." His own reply was another tender kiss before then nodding to his brother and prompting him to retake his place and begin. Then he handed me the bouquet, which I took with a beaming smile.

"They are beautiful."

"Not as beautiful as my exquisite bride," Lucius replied, making me blush.

KNIGHTS OF PAST

"So just to check, am I doing this in Sumerian, Latin or…"

"English will be fine, Sés," Lucius answered with a smirk before taking my hand in his.

"Ready?" Lucius asked, making me nod quickly, although my ridiculously happy grin was answer enough.

"Then repeat after me, I, Lucius Septimus, take thee, Amelia Faith Draven to be my wedded Wife, to have and to hold from this day forward, for better for worse, for richer, for poorer, in sickness and in health, to love and to cherish, 'til death of our souls do us part, according to the Fated Gods holy ordinance, and thereto I plight thee to be forever your Soul's Keeper," Dariush said, and I swear as Lucius turned to face me, ready to say those same vows, I couldn't breathe.

"I, Lucius Septimus, take thee, Amelia Faith Draven to be my wedded Wife, to have and to hold from this day forward, for better for worse, for richer, for poorer, in sickness and in health, to love and to cherish, 'til death of our souls do us part, according to the Fated Gods holy ordinance, and thereto I plight thee to be forever your Soul's Keeper." I finally gasped a much need breath of relief, making Lucius chuckle. Then I turned back to Dariush to listen as he asked me to repeat his words next. Ones I said with so much love and promise, they were near bursting from me,

"I, Amelia Faith Draven take thee, Lucius Septimus, to be my wedded Husband, to have and to hold from this day forward, for better for worse, for richer, for poorer, in sickness and in health, to love, and cherish, 'til death us do part, according to the Fated Gods holy ordinance; and thereto I give thee my Soul to my eternal Keeper."

"And now for the rings," Dariush said, pulling a red velvet pouch from his pocket as he had obviously been charged with being the ring bearer also. He then pulled on a black ribbon where two rings entwined with the satin length were revealed from the bag. He then untied the knot and pulled free the smaller of the two before handing it to Lucius.

"Repeat after me, Brother… With this Ring, I thee wed, with my body I thee worship, and with all my worldly goods I thee endow. In the name of Soul's creator and the Fated Gods that will. Amen." Lucius took my hand in his, and removed my engagement ring, ready to slip my wedding band over my finger. It was one that looked as if it was designed to match perfectly the engagement ring and was a twisted vine of thorns encrusted with tiny black diamonds.

"With this Ring, I thee wed, with my body I thee worship, and with all my worldly goods I thee endow. In the name of Soul's creator and the Fated Gods that will. Amen," he said before slipping it over my knuckle until it was perfectly in place. To which he then added my engagement ring, and the design meant that the two became one, as it slotted into place.

"It's beautiful," I whispered, making him grin down at me.

"Now for the rest of your vow, Amelia," Dariush said, handing me Lucius's own wedding band, and graciously holding my flowers for me. I then took Lucius's strong hand into my own and held the black band over the end of his finger. It was matching my own in that the same black thorny vine design was etched into the thicker band and a single red diamond was set flat into the obsidian stone. Dariush then spoke the same words he had for Lucius to repeat, making me do the same.

"With this Ring, I thee wed, with my body I thee worship, and with all my worldly goods I thee endow. In the name of Soul's creator and the Fated Gods that will. Amen." After this

I pushed the ring down until it was seated firmly on his finger, encouraging Dariush to hand me back my flowers and say,

"Then it is with my greatest pleasure to pronounce you both husband and wife, you may ki… kiss the bride." Dariush ended this in a laugh as Lucius hadn't even waited for him to say that last sentence before he gathered me up in his hold, tipped me over his arm, and kissed me deeply and passionately. In fact, it felt so perfect it could have graced the pages of any fairytale's,

Happy ever after.

But then after he pulled back, I decided to give him my own version and tossed my poppies up in the air for Dariush to catch. Then I gathered up my skirts enough so as I could jump up at Lucius, forcing him back a step as he caught me. After this I put my bent arms to his shoulders, so as I could use my forearms to frame the back of his head as he lifted me up so as I could reach his lips with ease. Then he started turning us both as we laughed between blissfully happy kisses.

"Congratulations to you both," Dariush said when we had finally contained ourselves enough to stop kissing. Lucius placed a hand at his brother's shoulder, squeezing it in thanks.

"Thank you for performing the ceremony," he replied, but as for me, I pulled Dariush in for a hug and said,

"Yeah, thanks, my new big brother." At this he groaned in a teasing way, making me elbow him in the belly.

"Oh, just you wait until it's your turn… you did catch the bouquet after all." I winked at him when he looked at me in horror, making me giggle. But then I turned back to my new husband and grabbed his hands

"I can't stop shaking, it just feels like a dream," I said,

looking down at our wedding bands just so I could focus on the proof that it had actually happened.

"Then we dream the same dream, for nothing can take this from us now." I grinned at that. Then we turned to face Dariush as I gathered he wasn't intent on just leaving us here. Wherever here was because this time, it was most definitely real. Which was when it hit me in realization that once upon a time, oh so long ago, a small innocent mortal boy named Judas used to play in this field chasing his mother. I had to say that the sweet knowledge of this made the day even more special. As if a part of her had been with us this day and to know that the flowers surrounding us had inspired his daughter's name, meant that a part of her had also been with us as we made our vows.

It couldn't have been more perfect.

"It has to be said, brother, you are a lucky bastard indeed, and even luckier I presume the sooner I get you both home," Dariush said, handing me back my flowers and shaking his brother's hand before slapping him on the back.

"Indeed, I am," Lucius replied, looking down at my now blushing face. Then his brother turned to me and said,

"Again, my blessings are with you, my sister… oh and a kind reminder that there are no refunds given." At this I burst out laughing before throwing my arms around Lucius and giving him a side hug as if I never wanted to let go. Then I teased,

"I would never return him, not even after I've broken him… which I totally intend to do." At this Dariush burst out laughing just as I felt a big broody Vampire shift his body so as he was now standing behind me. Then I felt his hand collar my neck and pull me back to his towering frame before looking down at me side on, speaking my new name for the first time…

"Oh, is that so, Mrs Septimus?" I couldn't help but grin, one that was so big it actually made my cheeks ache. Then I was suddenly swept off my feet, into his arms, and without taking his eyes from me, Lucius spoke to his brother,

"If you please, Dariush, as I believe I have a wedding to consummate and a new wife to punish." At this he laughed, especially when I smacked him on the shoulder, scolding,

"Lucius!" to which he merely grinned as his brother created a portal, and one that I only hoped led us straight to our marital bed. As for my new husband, he stepped us both through but not after first saying to Dariush,

"Later, Brother." I found this odd but quickly shook it off the moment he started to carry me over the threshold to our room, making me say,

"Why Husband, I didn't know you cared for tradition so much."

"What can I say, I am an old romantic at heart… besides, carrying my new bride to our bed is one tradition I was more than happy to adhere to." I scoffed a laugh at this and said,

"Well, why not, I mean you already took my V card before the wedding day, so we have to stick to at least one tradition." At this he smirked down at me as he lowered me to the bed. Then he held his body caged over me before running his nose up the length of my neck, telling me,

"Yes, but remember, love… there is still one more *V card* I am yet to take, and one I might have saved for such an occasion." At this my mouth dropped and I started to stutter,

"Erh… I… mean… do you…" He started chuckling when hearing my trepidation and clearly enjoying it immensely. I knew this as he confirmed as much when he said,

"As much as I enjoy watching you squirm beneath me… relax, baby, *for I have got you."* Then he kissed me deep and dominated me with his tongue, meaning that all other thoughts flew from my mind.

Well, all but the…

Sinful ones.

CHAPTER 15
NEW DELICIOUS SINS

"*Oh Gods...*" I breathlessly moaned as Lucius kissed his way down my neck, making me arch up into him when he teased over the mounds of my breasts, not yet freeing them from the confines of my clothes.

"I don't mind being your God, sweetheart, but try to remember that there is only one who currently owns this delectable, hot little body of yours... *now turn around,*" he said, but when he added this stern order, I couldn't help but shiver. However, because I was still deep into this sexual haze he had created, I merely lifted my head and questioned breathlessly,

"Huh...? Oh!" This ended on a shocked breath as he suddenly flipped me onto my belly, as clearly he didn't feel like waiting for me to come to my senses. I rose up slightly on my hands so as I could watch him over my shoulder, finding him kneeling up over my legs looking down at my body squirming beneath him. And oh boy, was I glad that I did look or I would have missed the sexy sight of him now taking off his clothes. This started with his jacket, however, before tossing it to the floor like I expected him to do, he first plucked the poppy from his lapel.

I wanted to ask why, but in the end, I didn't need to. As after giving me a grin that was pure bad to the bone, he popped the small ribbon-wrapped length of the stem in between his teeth. This was so as he could use both hands to collect up my long skirt, until it was soon all gathered up by my waist. After this he pulled down my lace panties, doing so enough that my ass was bare, but keeping them just under the curve of my cheeks. Then he then pulled the poppy from between his teeth, keeping it tucked between the backs of his two fingers.

"Mmm, now just look at that beautiful ass," he said, making me blush as he ran the backs of his fingers over the curve causing me to moan. Something that ended in a yelp of shock as he suddenly slapped it. I started to wriggle beneath him just before he started to sooth the sting by caressing over it. This was before framing my cheeks with both hands and kneading his fingers into the flesh. His touch alternated between being tender and forceful, with pain being followed by soothing strokes making me near lose my mind with how long he kept this up. I was so turned on, I was worried I had already left a wet patch on the sheets beneath me.

But every now and again I also felt the slight prick of pain against my flesh whenever the end of the poppy stem struck my skin. One he still held between his fingers and making me wonder if it left small red dots on my ass.

"Please, Lucius," I moaned, feeling myself soaked and saying to hell with any wet patches as I tried to rub myself against the bed just for some relief that never came.

"Ahh and finally she begs me," Lucius said to himself in satisfaction.

"Yesss," I moaned again, making him chuckle.

"Well let's just see how well you can work for it, sweetheart," he replied and I looked behind me, raising up only enough to see him pull the poppy from in between his fingers. My confused frown was enough to get him to grin down at me before I watched as he spread my ass cheeks so as he could tuck the stem in between them, meaning now, only the flower could be seen.

"What are you... Oww!" I cried when he suddenly slapped my ass, telling me in an authoritative tone,

"Silence, my beauty." I swallowed hard as the sound shot another blast of arousal straight to my sex, making my insides flutter. Fuck but I loved it when he got all dominant on me! I swear I was fucking addicted to it and the thrill of what this man could do to me, Gods but I near came from that thought alone.

But then he leaned down over me, his silk tie now falling like a soft caress against my neck, as he whispered,

"Mmm, my dirty girl, my fucking gorgeous wife... I can smell how much you want me... I can scent your arousal... fucking addictive woman." He growled before biting my shoulder without breaking the skin and making me moan in both pain and frustration. I needed to come and so fucking badly, which made it worse, knowing that his essence from biting me would do just that. Something he refused to give me, despite knowing that I was clearly desperate for it.

"Pleeessse," I begged, making him soothe his bite with a lick before gripping my face and turning it toward his mouth so as he could kiss me from behind. It was quick and it was rough and I wanted it to last for so much longer than it did. However, Lucius clearly had other plans.

"Now it's time to show me what a good girl you can be," he whispered, before raising back up from me and telling me,

"Now no matter what, you are to keep that flower

between your ass cheeks... am I understood?" I looked back at him to see he had resumed his earlier position on his knees either side of my legs. I nodded in answer to his demands, making him slap my ass again and I found myself clenching my cheeks tighter just to keep the flower in place like he had ordered me to do.

"You know how I like your words, pretty girl, so what were you missing?" he asked, his tone soft and gentle, something that was a complete contrast to his actions.

"I...I understand," I pushed out in a quiet voice as I swear, I was so near the edge, I was nearly mindless!

"There's my good girl," he praised, and I squeezed my ass together as I shifted up so I could watch him over my shoulder once more. This was to find the droolworthy sight of him undoing the top button of his shirt before tugging his tie loose, all the time keeping his heated gaze to my own. Then after dragging the length of silk through his hands, he snapped it tight, as if he was about to use it to tie me up with. I jumped a little at the sound, making him grin before assuring me,

"Another time for that perhaps." Then he tossed it to the floor before he resumed undressing.

"Like what you see, wife?" he asked as my eyes drank in the sight of him as he revealed his perfect body, each muscle looking as if it had been sculptured by the Gods themselves. I nodded and he paused in his movements, only needing to raise a brow before I quickly added the words he wanted to hear from me.

"I do, very much so," I told him, making him grin before twisting his body in a way so he could remove his shirt, now tossing it to the floor with the rest, and I swear my heart was going to pound its way out of my chest!

Especially when he unbuckled his belt and unzipped his

dress slacks. Then he lowered himself over me, gathering up my dress and after taking the end of the lace bow in between his teeth, he pulled, yanking it hard enough that my body jerked sideways a little. Then he growled down over me,

"Better take this off before I rip the thing to fucking shreds." At this I quickly gathered it up and shimmied my body to allow it to move beneath me so as I still wouldn't lose the flower in my ass from my movements. Then once high enough, I pulled it free of my breasts and up over my head. This left me in just my bra and my panties that were still tucked under my ass and stretched over the backs of my thighs.

Now that I was now mostly naked, I felt him sensually kiss his way down my spine before coming to rest his body stretched out at the bottom of the bed with his head level with my ass. One he had started stroking softly in between kisses. Then his gentle ministrations were soon broken up with sharp slaps, ones I never knew when they were coming. But even as I tried to hold myself tense for it, his soft caresses would continue to lure me into a false sense of security before inflicting another smack of pain when I least expected it.

It was sweet, sweet torture.

"Please Lucius… I need… need…"

"Oh, but I know exactly what you need, wife!" he snarled before suddenly biting into my ass and making me finally come screaming. A release so powerful, I couldn't help but scramble for the sheets, grabbing them so hard that they were soon torn by my fingernails. In fact, had I not been in the throes of such passion, I would have been freaked out when blacken claws started to growl from them, remaining there until I had finished screaming,

"Ahhhh!" Lucius hearing this was only spurred on further as he gripped both cheeks and squeezed hard as he feasted upon my flesh as I continued to orgasm. Doing so until I was shaking and jerking under him as if my body was no longer my own. And all the time, I played the good girl and kept that flower between my cheeks, amazed at my ability and willingness to please him. Although I think Lucius had a big part in this, especially considering he was the one pushing my cheeks together, as if this would help in feeding him as he pushed more of me into his eager mouth.

As soon as Lucius knew my release was spent, he extracted his fangs with a groan of pleasure, licking the small wound closed before suddenly plucking the stem from my ass. After this I found myself abruptly flipped onto my back, making me cry out in surprise.

The sight of Lucius with bloody fangs transported my sex-filled brain back to when he had first fucked me after finding me on his throne. The injection of lust made me sit up about to grab him to me, when suddenly a hand collared my throat and pinned me down to the bed.

"Open!" he demanded on a growl, referring to my mouth as he came to lean over me. He then bit down hard enough on his own lip before opening his mouth above mine, letting his blood drip directly into my own, making me eager to taste him. I swallowed him down, moaning as I did, before pleading,

"More." He grinned at my neediness before lowering enough so as I could kiss him, sucking his bleeding lip deep into my mouth and swallowing what little he drip fed me. However, this only lasted so long before he was taking over the kiss and soon coating both our lips in blood. In fact, I was so lost to his kiss, that I couldn't help but whimper when he pulled back, refusing to give me more of him.

"I fucking love you all needy for me," he growled, placing his forehead to mine before laying a sweet blood-soaked kiss there, letting me feel the wet crimson stain. One I knew he wanted to see remain as his eyes homed in on it the moment he pulled back. Then he tapped on my lips again and commanded once more,

"Open." I did as I was told like a good little submissive, so he could then place the ribbon-covered stem in my mouth, reminding me of the poppy in his hand.

"Keep that between your teeth, no matter what I do to you. I want it to stay there... *understood?"* I nodded, knowing I couldn't answer without dropping it or sounding strange. This sight must have been one he found endearing as it made him rub his nose up my cheek like a loving mate.

"So, fucking lucky to have such a good girl... *my good little wife,"*

he purred, making me sigh happily before he was back up on his knees above me. I was then left to watch the beautiful revealing sight as he made his suit pants disappear, along with his socks and shoes, until he was now gloriously naked. After which, he proceeded to pull my panties down my legs yet strangely, still leaving them at my ankles. After this he grabbed my legs both together and yanked me hard down the bed, making me nearly lose my flower in surprise. He then lifted my legs so far up his body that my ass was off the bed with all my weight rested on my shoulders. Once I was where he wanted me, his arm banded around my thighs, keeping me locked tightly in place as he shifted his hips so as he could line his heavy cock up with my sex.

"Now to make you mine in, *every... single... way,"* he purred each word before thrusting forward and making me cry out as he pushed past my soaked folds and into my sex. A dripping pussy made even tighter due his brutal hold while keeping my legs closed. My ankles were both by his left shoulder as he held onto my legs, using this tight grip on me to hammer his hips forward, and the need to cry out was too much to bear.

"Fuck! So tight, baby... *so fucking perfect!*" he snarled as he thrust even deeper, this time yanking me hard against him to meet his brutal thrust. It was like he was trying to get me to lose the stem, and I could feel myself creating deep bite marks in the ribbon.

He was getting off on my struggle, I knew that, and the knowledge pushed me even quicker, even higher to my next release, for I knew it would only be seconds. It was building like a tidal wave, gaining power and height before it would crash into me.

"You wanna come, baby, you wait for me," he ordered, making me whimper as I started thrashing my head, mindful of my flower.

"Fuck! Gods but this tight pussy... I won't fucking last, baby!" he growled before turning his head and biting my panties, keeping them tight in between his fangs as if he was trying to use the tension to hold himself back from his own release. Then he reached down my body and ripped the lace cup down, tearing the material of my bra and freeing one breast. He squeezed it hard, catching the nipple between his fingers and the pain felt incredible.

"MMHHH!" I moaned, and then around the stem, I pleaded a barely audible,

"Pppeeesssee."

At this he grinned down at me, still with my panties in his teeth before he started going even wilder with his thrusts. Then he shouted,

"COME! COME NOW... AHHHHH!" he roared his own release as I arched my neck, throwing my head back as I screamed, quickly using my hand to cover my face and keeping the flower there through my cries. However, this was when Lucius did something different, and I felt the squirts of cum start to shoot over my body. He had come inside me and pulled out halfway through his release so he could paint my body in his seed.

"Fuck... FUCK, YEAH!" he growled as he fisted his cock, draining it of the last strings of cum, squirting them over me and making it hit higher up my belly, and breasts. Then with his free hand, he reached out and after swiping some of the thick white cum onto his thumb, he used it to rub across my bottom lip and around the abused, bitten stem.

"Fucking beautiful," he whispered, smiling down at me, and I had to wonder why he hadn't yet let go of my legs, making me finally speak his name around the flower,

"L...ucius?" At this his grin turned darker before he told me,

"Looks like I will have to try harder." Then he ripped my panties off my feet, grabbed my hips and dragged me further up his torso. To the point that my shoulder blades were resting against his thighs as I was practically upside down and held prisoner against him. Then he spread me wide, throwing my legs over his shoulders and banding an arm across my belly. This was so he could hold me locked to his face as he buried his head in between my legs, making me cry out as he started to fuck me with his tongue. I was completely upside down now, held against him and his free hand went to my breast, now rubbing his cum into my exposed tit before plucking at the nipple.

"F...UCK!" I screamed around the fucking poppy stem and I felt him grin against my abused sex, knowing how much harder it was for me having to keep this fucking thing in my mouth! It was so dirty, so fucking hot, I was near mindless as he continued to suck, bite, and lick our combined release from me. Feasting on it as if it was a sex craved drug he couldn't get enough of. The growling and possessive snarls he continued making were so intense it was like I was some captured pray he had dragged back to his cave!

Like he was literally trying to feed from me.

But then he started to do something else new, and I was so lost in my pleasure that I only ended up craving more of the taboo feeling. He had gathered up some of his cum dripping down my belly to now use it to circle my untouched, tight little virgin hole. I moaned as he started to push his finger inside the forbidden place, using his release to lubricate it. Then he pulled his mouth back from my swollen pussy and still with this brutal hold, he dipped two fingers inside my sex, fingering me for a moment before pulling the dripping digits free and using this as more lubricant. One of my hands went to my forehead as the feeling overwhelmed me, the new sensation was driving me crazy.

But then the second he breached the now sopping wet hole of my ass with a thick finger, it was no surprise that when my next orgasm erupted out of me, it did so without warning. To the point that my hands slapped to the tops of his thighs and dug my regular human nails in, making him howl like a savage beast.

He continued to finger fuck my ass at the same time rolling my clit in between his teeth before flicking his tongue over it in rabid motion, and one orgasm quickly rolled into the next.

"MMMAAAHHH!" I screamed with my teeth clamped, making him chuckle against me. Then he started to lower my legs to the bed, legs that felt as if they had no power left in them to even move by my own will anymore. Then he flipped me over to my stomach, raised my hips, and while folding his big body over me, he whispered,

"Do you trust me, baby?" I nodded, making him collar my throat at the front and raise my head back.

"Words," he all but snarled.

"Esss," I moaned, making him kiss me on my cheek sweetly.

"Then let's give you an even greater reason to lose that flower." He whispered before I felt him rub his cock in between the soaked folds of my sex, gathering up more of my release to coat himself with. Then after sliding it through my pussy, it paused in a new place it had never been before. I sucked in a quick breath as I felt his cock starting to breach the small hole.

"Ah...ah...ah" I moaned as pain bloomed, even though he was pushing his cock slowly inside.

"Relax, sweetheart... I've got you... I've got you," he said softly, making me do just that, and as soon as he felt me relax he pushed further inside.

"Yes, that's it... fuck you're so tight, baby... you feel fucking incredible... *now take more,"* he said, making me nod my acceptance and the second I did, he gripped my hips in a punishing hold and thrust himself fully inside my ass. Oh, and this time, it was like he had said...

I soon lost my flower.

"AAAAHHH FUCK!" I screamed, making him coo down at me, running a hand down my hair, neck, and spine like I was some good pet of his.

"There's my good girl... so fucking hot... so perfect... Now hold on, my Love," he warned before he started to rock his length deep inside me, and I gripped onto the sheets as he held me locked to him with a bruising hand at my hip. Then his other arm snaked in beneath me, so his forearm soon collared my neck, making me feel completely trapped and locked to his dominant embrace. Then he fucked me even harder once he was assured I was going nowhere. Again, I felt like captured prey and the thought of this predator wrapped around me only managed to drive that sexual intensity higher. It was so raw, so dirty, so taboo, everything made me feel like I was totally owned by this beast and I would let him do whatever he wanted to me.

It was without a doubt the hottest moment of my life and I fucking loved every brutal second of it. But then as he drew closer to his release, I knew he wanted me there too. His hand left my hip and snaked around to the front of my pussy, so he could rub my clit as he fucked me from behind.

The sex was unlike anything I had ever experienced. The pain I felt with every thrust back inside my ass merged with the pleasure of what he was doing with his fingers, and this time, when we came, we both came screaming.

"Oh, Gods yes, Lucius... Lucius, yes... YES FUCK ME!"

"Can't hold it any longer... TOO FUCKING GOOD... FUUCCKKK RRRAAAAHHHH!" He roared like a beast as I felt him explode in my ass, and I continued to jerk and shudder beneath him with an orgasm so powerful, I swear I was seeing stars! In fact, it must have been just as powerful for him also, because he collapsed over my back, now laying his forehead to the bed next to my head. Once there, he panted like he was trying to come down from his unbelievable high and his body shuddered over me, making me bask in the knowledge that fucking me had done that to him.

Of course, he wasn't the only one, as I too felt overwhelmed by the experience. As for Lucius, he was trying to keep his huge bulk from crushing me completely, so after he pulled out, spilling his cum all over my ass, he rolled to the side and then gathered me up in his arms. He cradled me to his chest and kissed my head, my cheeks, my shoulders, his hands caressing me everywhere, soothing my shaking body.

"Gods but I fucking love you, Amelia… So fucking much… fuck but that was…" he said, making me lose count of how many fucks that was and I would have laughed had I the strength. Gods but it sounded as if he couldn't believe how amazing it had been, shocking himself.

"Are you alright, my love?" he asked, gently making me nod in his chest. But then concern took over as he framed my cheeks and made me look up at him.

"I was too rough with you." At this I told him,

"No, no, not at all… well, I mean yeah, you were rough, but I liked it, as well, clearly evidence suggested I did… but I am fine, well, I mean as fine as anyone who just had… erm… their ass… well you know, you were there." I blurted all this out and the amusement grew in his eyes before suddenly, he was laughing and pulling me into him again so he could hug me.

"Then let me tell you a secret, sweetheart." I looked up at him with big eyes and said,

"What is it?" At this he smirked before leaning down to my ear and then admitted the most shocking truth of all…

"It was my first time too."

CHAPTER 16
WEDDING CONFESSIONS

"You know, I have never felt so inclined to frame a flower before in all my life," Lucius said, twirling the poppy stem in between his fingers making me giggle against him. We were currently still lying in bed together and it was only minutes after he had dropped the sexual bombshell on me. One, I confess, I had gotten far too excited about hearing. Literally, I had thrown myself against him and shouted dramatically,

"Oh, thank the Heavens, finally I'm included in a sexual first for you!" At this he chuckled and after kissing me on the forehead, he told me,

"Yeah, I am most definitely certain Heaven had nothing to do with that, but I am glad you're pleased." Of course, I also asked him why he had never done it before, to which he simply shrugged his shoulders and told me,

"I never wanted to claim someone before, so the urge never took me with the driving need to own one's body so completely." This was a good answer, despite making me tease,

"Aww, that should so be on a Valentine's Day card." This

time he threw his head back and laughed, making me snuggle closer to him. After which I felt him reach over and find the discarded flower, complete with teeth marks, which brought us back to the moment he mentioned about framing the thing.

"Well, technically, I think *I* should frame it, seeing as it was more my accomplishment than yours," I said plucking the flower from him, already having a plan forming in my head of what I wanted to do with it. Which was why I reached over and lay it gently down on the bedside table.

"Oh, very well accomplished, indeed," he teased before squeezing me to him. Then, after turning in his arms, I lay on my back with my head rested in the crook of his arm before looking at my rings.

"I can't believe we are married," I said, sighing happily.

"Yeah, and about fucking time," he exclaimed, taking my hand in his and letting me see how well they matched together. Then I ran my fingertip over his, focusing on the tiny red diamond inset flat to the band, prompting him to tell me,

"It represents your soul, a piece you gave me today and this time, one done so freely." At this I couldn't help but grin, before rolling back into his arms so I could face him.

"And what of your soul, Mr Septimus, is that also mine?" I asked in a teasing tone, making him raise his head and meet my lips.

"But of course, Mrs Septimus… *always.*" At this I sighed into his gentle kiss before he rolled me over so that gentle kiss could turn into something more.

I knew this when he said,

"Now, it's time for another first… *now it is time, I make love to my wife.*"

KNIGHTS OF PAST

One shower, two orgasms, and three hours later, I once again found myself standing in front of a mirror, only this time, I was wearing a very different dress. This time it was a long, black, halter-neck dress with a bodice covered in shimmering black sequins, and had a flowing skirt of sparkling tulle edged with black satin ribbon. It cascaded around my legs in waves, making it flare out around me as I moved. It was stunningly elegant and also had me squirming under the keen gaze of who was now my husband.

I don't know why, but I knew the thought would take a lot of getting used to. Like someone who would scrape by financially and saved all their lives only to suddenly find themselves winning the lottery. Yet they still went to the supermarket with a purse full of coupons.

Because I had always wanted Lucius. Ever since my teenage body had become aware of him, twisting into an obsession I had never been able to fully let go of, even after I had told myself that I had, even after he had rejected me, … my heart knew differently.

Which meant always dreaming of him one day being my husband. That had always been the ultimate fantasy. Which was also why it was so difficult to think of this being anything other than a dream, one I never wanted to wake up from. In fact, I kept looking down at my hand and every time I saw the ring, it felt more like a brand against my skin. One I never wanted to wash off.

Of course, this wasn't the only reason I was squirming, and Lucius knew this as he walked up behind me, patted my ass in a playfully patronizing way, and said,

"How are we doing down there?"

I raised a single brow in question, hoping this was enough of an answer. His chuckle told me that my 'I am not impressed with you Mr' expression had not been missed and had delivered its desired effect.

"Are you ready, my dear?" he said, kissing my neck after placing his hands at my shoulders and then pulling me closer to whisper in my ear,

"My wife."

I couldn't help my shivered response, making him grin against my skin knowing exactly what the sound of him calling me his wife did to me. A fact he learned when making love to me and calling me this over and over again in between his passionate kisses. Every time he had called me this while thrusting his cock deeper into my core, had felt like branding, and one I had responded to by calling him mine over and over again in return. Which was why when he felt my body quake in front of him, he knew exactly what he was doing to me by reminding me of this. A reminder he continued to give me every time he whispered my new title in my ear, just like he had done in bed, in the shower, and then once out of it when holding me close in nothing but a towel.

Which was why this next conversation we were about to have made this so much harder.

"So, erm… this party…" I started to say, however, he simply slipped my loose hair from my neck as I had decided to wear it down and straight.

"Umm… yes, Love?" he murmured into the other side of my neck, and I swear it was as though he couldn't get enough of me. Despite this, I pressed on,

"Who exactly is going to be there?" I asked, and when he lifted his head to look at me in the mirror, his face said it all, as he knew exactly why I was asking this.

"Is this you asking me, in a roundabout way, to keep our recent nuptials a secret?" His tone said it all and I winced at this, knowing how bad it sounded.

"I wouldn't have had our wedding any other way, I want you to know that," I told him quickly, now turning around to face him so we were no longer having this conversation in the mirror.

"But?" he asked now folding his arms, making his black shirt tighten around his impressive biceps.

"Honestly, I just know how this is going to go…" I paused before taking the manly stance of my father, wagging a pointed finger at Lucius,

"Oh, Amelia Faith Draven. How could you do this, don't you think that I wanted to walk my only daughter down the aisle… and then my mother will be all like… my only daughter getting married and now I have no need to buy a big hat… and don't even get me started on Pip, who will *freak… the… fuck… out!* I mean, there are crazy people in my family that will have hoped for us to have the biggest wedding of the year… and then there are the gifts and people didn't even know we were engaged and…" At this, he finally pulled me into his arms, chuckling as he did,

"Sweetheart, do you want a big wedding?" he asked, making me tense in his hold before sighing,

"Honestly, it's not really for me but more for my family," I told him, making him tip my face up by hooking his finger under my chin. Then he asked me in a more serious tone,

"Do you want a big wedding, Amelia?"

"Erm… maybe… okay yes, I kinda do… oh Gods, that makes me sound so spoilt, doesn't it!" I shouted, making him laugh before cupping my head and pulling me into him, before telling me,

"Well, it just so happens that wanting to spoil you has become my new favourite hobby… well, *maybe not my favourite,"* he teased, now patting my ass and making me growl playfully. He then took a small step back so he could look at me once more before telling me,

"Amelia, what you gave me today meant everything… meant the world to me… but you have to know that I never expected this to be the only day celebrating our union."

"You didn't?" I asked in surprise.

"I told you, sweetness, if you wanted the big day then I am more than happy to say those vows again, and this time in front of our whole world and everyone dear to us in it. I may be a selfish man when it comes to you, but even I know when I must share. So, I will simply consider myself as twice blessed to become your husband for a second time."

"Oh, Lucius!" I shouted, throwing myself in his arms and hugging him tightly before kissing him passionately. Now grateful that I hadn't yet applied my red lipstick, or we would have both arrived at this party looking like clowns. Then once it became so heated we knew that if we didn't stop we wouldn't get there at all, I finally pulled back.

"And for now?" I asked, looking down at my hand, making him take it in his own before raising it up to his lips to kiss. Then he told me,

"For now, we will tell them nothing."

"And you're really okay with that?" I asked, making him smile down at me.

"Amelia, as much as I want the world to know that I finally claimed you as not only my Queen, but also as my wife, I am not so much of a selfish bastard not to know when to go at my wife's pace. I rushed this wedding because I couldn't wait to make you mine and if now you are simply asking me to wait before telling others… well, just knowing that you are my wife is enough for me right now. So if you wish to hide it a little bit longer, then I will honour and respect that decision." At this, I once again wrapped my arms around him, looking up at him so I could whisper,

"I love you, Husband." To which his sweet reply was spoken like a vow…

"As I love you, Wife."

CHAPTER 17
DRIVING HOME SECRETS

After this matrimonial understanding, we walked hand-in-hand through his home... although, technically it was now *our home* considering we were hitched and all.

Which meant that by the time we reached his batcave garage, I was looking around in awe, as I had never seen it before today. I also decided it would be too much of a wasted opportunity not to tease him. Especially with what looked like a lifetime of passionate car collecting, and something that rivalled that of my father's.

"Mmmm, which one of my newly acquired car collection am I going to drive first, I wonder?" I said, tapping a finger on my lips. Of course, with the horrified look he gave me I just couldn't help it as I burst out laughing.

"Oh my Gods, you should see the look of horror on your face right now," I said, after straightening my body from where I had been bent over I had been laughing that hard.

"Ha, very humorous indeed," he said, making me laugh again before saying,

"No, but seriously, I wonder which one I will take for a test drive first."

"Still not funny the second time round," he commented dryly, making me say,

"Seriously?" I asked as he rounded the vehicle of tonight's choice, another insanely expensive car which was of course, a Lamborghini. This one's name I was trying to remember. Something he helped me out with,

"Well, I would have taken the Vision GT V12 but it's only got one seat and well, I'm a good driver, sweetheart, but with you in my lap, remembering my cock and your ass… fuck, I'm not that good." I tried not to laugh at this but could feel my lips twitching all the same as I fought that grin.

"So, the Lamborghini Terzo Millennio it is," he finished, making me shrug my shoulders and say,

"Well, yeah, it is a nice car."

"That it is," he agreed, making me continue,

"And I bet it's going to drive really well for me." At this he laughed once, doing so in a way as if I must be insane.

"Fuck no, so not happening, Amelia." I nearly sniggered at this.

"Hey, it's only fair, after all, you did just acquire a shitload of Lego," I joked, making him roll his eyes at me before underestimating the power of the small plastic block,

"Yes, and I could probably buy the fucking company for the price of only a few of these cars," he boasted, making me burst out laughing and slap a hand to the window of his precious Terzo Millennio. And again, I giggled when he visibly winced at the sight, as though I had just struck his beloved pet puppy or something.

"Erm, it's a great collection, Lucius, but that company is like worth over forty billion dollars… so as for all this…" I paused to swipe out an arm towards the many, many cars here, and said,

"Yeah, not sure all your pretties here are gonna cut it, baby." He looked thoughtful a moment and said,

"In that case, I think we should start your own car collection. Perhaps you have an affinity like your father for Ferraris." I scoffed at this and said,

"Erm no, I was thinking more VW buses, all those cute little Beetles, like the love bug, Herbie." His frown couldn't have reached deeper levels if he tried.

"I have no idea what you're talking about," he admitted after it looked as though I had just given him a headache, making me giggle.

"I know and really, that's what makes it so much fun," I teased, making him roll his eyes at me for the second time before ordering,

"Get your sweet ass in the car, wife."

"Sure thing, my sexy Hubby," I said, batting my lashes at him and making him groan,

"May the Gods have mercy upon my soul."

"Too late for that now, buddy boy, we're hitched," I said, waggling my ring finger at him and this time, he couldn't pretend any longer not to be amused, losing all power to hold back his grin.

"Ha! You smiled first, which means I win... now hand over the keys, handsome," I said, making him scoff as if I had just told a joke.

"Yeah, that's not happening, sweetheart," he replied before opening his door and slipping inside behind the fancy sporty wheel. I rolled my eyes because... well, he couldn't see me and I could get away with it. Then I raised up the passenger wing, AKA fancy ass door, and slipped in my seat next to him. After this, I huffed dramatically, telling him,

"Fine, but that's blowjob Sundays out the window for you." His response to this was to grant me a bad boy smirk that said it all. He was calling bullshit. In fact, I knew this when he said those exact words.

"I call bullshit."

"Oh yeah, why is that?" I challenged folding my arms and turning his way. Which was when he informed me in an overly smug tone,

"Because, sweetheart… *today is Sunday.*" Of course he had been referring to when I had very recently dropped to my knees and given him a blow job in the shower. Damn him and his knowledge of the calendar.

"Well, obviously my threat starts from next Sunday," I said lamely, making him mock,

"Obviously."

"I am totally serious." *I totally wasn't.*

"Yeah, we'll see about that," he said, calling my bluff yet again. However, when I opened my mouth to argue he purposely started up the engine. This was so my cocky reply was drowned out by the sound of the wind turbines switching on, making the car literally sound like a jet engine, even though the hyper car was all electric.

"I'm sorry, what was that you said, my love? Something about wanting to give me blowjobs every day of the week?"

"No, I said…!" Once again, I never got my words out as he took this opportunity to suddenly race the car out, revving it so that the sound echoed in the colossal space that was his garage. He chuckled when he saw my unimpressed face, and I had to try very, very hard to keep my face straight and maintain the facade of being pissed off.

Fuck, but I loved our banter.

However, after five minutes of silence and finally getting to witness this journey in reverse, I couldn't help but start the conversation I knew we needed as we went speeding down the only single road that connected his castle hideaway to the rest of humanity.

"So, I think that we agree that our giant, mountain size can of worms has truly erupted like Mount Vesuvius now," I said, trying my best to think of the right way to approach this and failing miserably.

"It has indeed, considering you're now my wife," he replied with a raised brow, no doubt wondering where I was going with this.

"Erm well, we never really got around to discussing how it was all going to work."

"Well, sweetheart, when a man loves a woman the natural order of things is they meet, fall in love, get married, and live happily ever after together... in the same house, or castle," he said, adding this part on the end as if this was the bit I was struggling with.

"I think you skipped a step... or in our case, *maybe like a hundred,"* I said wryly. However, he mistook this and said,

"No, I haven't, as that step unfortunately isn't on the cards for us, sweetheart." I couldn't help but tense hearing this, as I knew exactly what he was saying. I bit my lip at what part of our future he was referring to as there was never going to be any pretty little Amelias or handsome little Lucius' running around our mountain home.

I don't know why I was only thinking about this now, as it seemed foolish to only be considering the fact that we wouldn't be having children. Of course, I hadn't been taking the pill and it's not like we had been using contraceptives. But then I remembered this didn't particularly matter before, as a supernatural could withhold that part of himself back so as not to get a mortal pregnant. And well, as for now, well I was no longer mortal so that meant it most definitely wouldn't be on the cards for us. As let's just say that the Fated supernatural baby boom had come and gone thanks to my aunty Ari.

Besides, we'd had enough sex and in turn, I'd had enough periods to know that pregnancy was not in the Fates for us. It wasn't like something magical was going to happen after our wedding night.

"I believe this is one conversation we failed to have," Lucius said, now looking thoughtful and taking my prolonged silence for what it was... *a disappointing realization.* But then, one look at Lucius and I knew that even if I'd had all the facts laid out in front of me, I still wouldn't have changed my decision to be with this man, not for all the world. Which was why I reached across the centre console and took his hand, giving it a squeeze before telling him the truth,

"Even if we had, it would not have changed my answer, nor my decision to spend the rest of my life with you." He gave me a warm, tender smile in return, and I knew he was more than thankful for it. My words had meant a lot to him.

"And well, despite that particular obvious can of worms, it wasn't actually the one I was referring to," I said after the moment had passed between us.

"No?"

"It was actually the conversation of my job," I said, as this had been the one thing burning on my mind.

"Ah, I see."

I had to say, Lucius's answer didn't give me much hope, hence why I told him,

"I need to work, Lucius, even my mother after she married my father worked. Of course, he created the role for her, which she loved doing seeing as it was giving back to the world and taking control of all his charities but still... like her, I will go crazy without my work."

"I know this, Amelia, I have always known this, therefore I would not expect you to sit idly by and do nothing." Okay so this answer definitely gave me hope.

"So, if London is out of the question…" I left that question open ended as I rolled my hand in the air.

"I believe this will be one of those moments, as rare as they may be, that I will be asking you to grace me with time, sweetheart." My eyes widened at this before I started nodding.

"Okay, I can do that."

"Excellent, now, any other concerns?" he asked, making me smirk before saying,

"Nope, I'm good… no other concerns, *my eternal life partner.*"

"Good lord, I really am never going to live that one down, am I?" he asked groaning.

"No, no you're not, and now I'm no longer mortal, then FYI, I have an eternity to tease you about it."

"What fun!" he replied sarcastically, making me giggle, something that always got his attention as his lips twitched trying to fight a grin. I knew he loved being able to make me laugh, as he would always grant me this warm look whenever he did it. Lucius had a surprisingly funny sense of humour too when, of course, it wasn't dry and sarcastic. But I adored every facet of him as it kept our banter going. Meaning that this back-and-forth battle between us continued, and did so all the way to Munich.

Back to Transfusion.

Of course, even for a Sunday, the reopening of the infamous club Transfusion was bound to get a good crowd. Which meant that I wasn't surprised to find long queues leading down the entirety of the building and beyond it, down the street. It seemed as if everyone in the city had missed having the Gothic nightclub open. And despite the reason it had been closed in the first place, well clearly it hadn't had too much of an effect on people to prevent them from coming back.

As for Lucius, he drove us down a side road before we could reach the front of the club, giving me but a glimpse of how busy it was going to be. Then he drove around to what I knew was a back entrance, where there was a gated car park that was reserved only for him, his council and members of his VIP. I knew this because he told me so after punching in the code that allowed us access through the new looking gate. After this, he parked in a reserved space near the back doors that I recognized as being the ones I had once broken into.

Of course, I wasn't the only one with these thoughts as the moment we approached the door, he nodded to the keypad and said,

"Would you like to do the honours, my little thief?" I gave him a pointed look in return and replied,

"Perhaps I should retire my breaking-in skills now, I'm a married woman after all." He scoffed at this.

"Ah yes, because saying vows of marriage in a field of poppies is a sure way to get you to behave," he replied wryly, making me plaster myself to his chest and flutter my eyelashes up at him.

"But of course, after all, being a married woman means I am going to be on my best behaviour." Hearing this he thought to test that lie as he walked me closer to the wall before pinning me against it with his hands at my hips. Then he growled down at me,

"Oh, but I like it when you're naughty… *my unruly little pet.*"

"Call me what you want, Lucius, but the second you bring out a collar with a little bell attached is when I start to bite."

At this, he snapped his fangs at me, making me flinch and in turn, it made him grin. However, after this playful flirting, he took my hand and said,

"Come on, let's get to this party before I end up fucking you against my front door." I laughed and muttered,

"Oh yes, because that will make me want to get to the party quicker."

"I've created a monster," he muttered back, making me beam up at him, now comically swinging his hand back and forth before answering,

"Yes, yes, you have, Mr Septimus." As we walked through the back door, with a faint light casting shadows down on us, it was still enough to see Lucius's knowing grin. After all, he liked me needy, I could tell. But all too soon we were faced with the doors leading into the VIP of Transfusion. And I found myself nervous, knowing I was going to have to lie and tell people we had just got engaged. Thankfully, my ring being as it was, looked as if it had been a part of the design so I knew I could get away without it looking too much like there was a wedding band nestled next to it. We had also already discussed on the way here what Lucius would say about his own ring, agreeing to say it was after my insistence that I made him get his own 'promise ring' to match my own.

Of course the second we stepped inside. I didn't just see the gorgeous transformation that the club had undertaken. No, this was all overshadowed by a sea of people. In fact, it looked as though everyone we jointly knew in the supernatural world was there, with no mortals in sight. Of course, this hadn't been a surprise. However, what was the surprise, was seeing that among these people were hundreds of balloons and banners. One of which was held in between Pip's arms as everyone shouted 'SURPRISE'!

The words were simple and easy to read on each one. Words like 'Congratulations' were natural enough for two people that just got engaged. But the banner that took my brain a moment longer to grasp before panic took over was the one Pip made her husband hold out.

One that read,

'Mr and Mrs Septimus'

I turned to look at Lucius to see it written all over his face. Then I muttered,

"You told Adam!" To which he confirmed by muttering back,

"I told Adam."

We knew this meant that Adam had most likely been coerced by his wife into spilling our secret. Which in turn also meant that our not so secretive wedding was now a well-known fact among our family and friends.

Oh, and speaking of family, the next words out of my mouth were then aimed at the two people stood at the very front, looking at us expectantly,

"Mum, Dad… Yeah, so erm big news to tell… Surprise!" I said, whereas Lucius cut straight to it, pulled me close to his side and stated unapologetically,

"We got married."

CHAPTER 18
TRANSFUSION TAKE TWO

Hearing this, everyone cheered, and the celebration truly began. Or should I say it did for everyone else… as for me, well my parents came up to hug me now wearing the same overly strained grins on their faces as clearly, we were about to put on a show.

"Congratulations, my daughter!" my mum said in an overly dramatic way, which I knew was for everyone else's benefit.

"Thank you, Mother!" I replied in just as weird a tone and the second their joint hug tightened, I muttered so only they could hear,

"Yeah, I'm in big trouble, aren't I?"

"Huge," my mum replied, making me sigh.

"Oh, hey guys, maybe you should come and see something I have to erm… show you… just over here," I said, making my dad roll his eyes and say,

"Your acting is almost as bad as your mother's." At this we both shot my dad an evil glare before I continued to drag them away and out of the door that led into the lobby area. I also noticed Lucius looking concerned, causing me to wave him off, telling him with that one look that all would be fine and he should just entertain the guests. Then as soon as the door closed, my mum and dad both took the same stance and folded their arms in front of me. I placed my back to the doors for a second before taking a step forward, keeping the both doors and a potential quick getaway at my back.

"Okay so I know what you're gonna say," I started.

"Oh really, you do, do you?" my mum said, now with her hands on her hips doing that 'Mum voice' of hers. Which is why I turned my attention to her first and said,

"Yes, you're gonna say how disappointed my father is that he never got to walk his only daughter down the aisle…" I paused to look to my dad and said,

"And then, Dad, you're gonna say how upset my mother is that she never got to see her only daughter on her big day… but before you say all of that and start to make me feel even more guilty than I already do, can I just say my thing first?"

"I think that's all you have…" My father tried, but I quickly interrupted him.

"Yeah, yeah, I know, I have disappointed you both, but just hear me out. Now after everything we have been through, we just needed it to be us. Just one day of utter beauty between Lucius and I, and I know it was selfish, but I don't regret it, because that man in there, is finally my husband. Finally! Finally, I got my fairytale ending, and one I have been dreaming of since the very first day I met him. And I know that seems silly. I was just a teenager who was totally obsessed with him, but it's true…"

"Erm, Amelia," my mum tried to cut in but I carried on,

"…Because today he made me the happiest woman on earth, and I will never apologize for that." At this my dad started to clear his throat, making me hold up my hand and say,

"No, Dad, let me finish. I know you may not approve of the way we did things and I get that, but I would do it all over again in a heartbeat. Because a wedding should be about two people who love each other and it's about making that claim, about making that vow to the only soul that matters and if…" At this my dad stepped up to me, placed a palm to the back of my head and pulled me in so he could kiss me on my forehead before saying,

"Okay, my daughter, you made your point, to us both, and also… *to your new husband who is right behind you and has been this whole time,"* he whispered this last part, making me freeze before my dad let me go. As for my mum, well she was smirking back at me as if enjoying the whole show. I then felt Lucius come to stand behind me and place his hands at my shoulders.

"Keira, Dom, please excuse us, for I need to speak with my wife… *now."* Then I was suddenly up in his arms, making me cry out,

"Lucius!"

However, this had no effect, as he only continued to walk me into his apartment, leaving me with only enough time to shout,

"Erh, okay, so we will finish this later, but just so you know we will have another big wedding and, Mum, if you can help me plan it, that would be great!" Then just before the doors closed, I heard my mum shout,

"YES! Oh, thank God!"

Seconds after this, I was back on my feet and being pushed up against a wall so Lucius could kiss me like he needed my lips as much as he needed his next breath! Needless to say, we didn't arrive back at the party until thirty minutes later, and that was classed as a quickie for Lucius. Which meant that by the time we were walking back inside, he had my hand in his and was free to tease me about what he had overheard... now that the lust part of hearing all this was out of his system.

"So, obsessed, you say." I rolled my eyes and said,

"Yeah, but really, what sixteen-year-old girl doesn't go through the Vampire crush stage and besides, I also had a crush on the Green Giant from the sweetcorn can, but I doubt he wanted to marry me, so I had to pick one and lucky you, you weren't fictional." I then patted him on the arm, making him frown down at me.

"You know I have no idea what most of what you just said means."

"I know, great isn't it... but hey, if you wanna paint yourself green and wear a leaf dress this Halloween, then just saying, you're gonna get lucky." I winked at him and again he looked even more confused, which had me walking through the doors of Transfusion VIP laughing like a loon. Of course, that was until a body of colour came barrelling into me and squealed,

"YEEEEY! WE GET TO PLAN YOUR WEDDING!" I winced as this was screamed in my ear and suddenly, I was being dragged from Lucius by not only Pip, but also my mum and my aunty Sophia. In fact, I looked over their heads to Lucius and mouthed,

'Help me' and thanks to the karma fairy wanting to bite me in the ass, Lucius simply raised his hand to his ear and pretended not to know what I was saying. I glared at him, and he mouthed back,

'Where's your Green Giant now?' Then he pretended to look around and shrugged his shoulders as if my green saviour was nowhere to be seen. My look said it all, which was why he walked toward my father and Adam, chuckling before taking his usual favourite beer. Then he tapped the neck to my father's and to the rest of his council who had joined his man party as they all congratulated him.

As for me, well that was a different story.

"Okay, so I know it's out there even for me, but what about a huge inflatable alter?! Then once they say the I do's, then we all just jump on it and go crazy!" Pip said, making me, Mother, and Sophia groan. Of course, she also was dressed like some warrior Geisha that had been dipped into a rainbow.

"No inflatable... well, any things," my mum said, and because she noticed me taking in Pip's latest mad outfit, she leaned into me and said,

"She's going through a Manga phase." Pip started nodding and twirling her short skirt around like a little girl was happily playing dress up in front of the mirror.

"Now I was thinking roses, or lilies... or some lavish, rooftop garden, saying your vows when the sun is setting," Sophia piped up to say, and I opened my mouth to speak when my mum got in there first,

"Yeah, but what if it rains... no, I really think it needs to be inside, oh I know, but what about Witley Court? I know that's where your father and I got married, but it really was so beautiful and then..." I cut her off by reminding all three of them,

"Okay, well we haven't even planned a date yet so..."

"Oh, make it summer," my mum shouted, clapping her hands in excitement and making her beautiful purple A line strappy dress swish around her knees.

"Oooh, what about a fall wedding? The flowers would be beautiful, all those oranges and reds..." Sophia said, now running her hands down her stunning floor length black gown that was silk and decorated with a cascade of tulle red roses down one side.

"She's going through a flower phase," my mum muttered to me, making me reply silently with a strained smile.

"No, winter for sure! Snow, loads of snow, like even the fake stuff would work, we can get a machine in! Oh and we can hand out candy canes and…" At this I raised my hands and tried to contain them.

"Guys, it's not even…"

"Oh, come on, with how pale Lucius is… what do you want Amelia to look like, that she is marrying the invisible man in the photographs?!" My aunt cried and of course, as for me, my voice trailed off as it was clear they didn't need me in this. Not as the three of them were now arguing the weather and seasons of the year like each was a spokesperson for sunny days, falling leaves or snowball fights. Naturally, I extracted myself from this conversation and made my way over to the bar. One that I certainly couldn't remember being there before the remodel. In fact, hadn't this been where the naked ladies used to dance behind the creepy white screens? That's when I took a longer look at the place to see that now, it had definitely lost a lot of its 'sex club' vibe, making me wonder if this had been more Sophia's choice or Lucius's?

Well, considering Sophia pretty much had her own sex club in her wing of Afterlife, then I was leaning more toward it being Lucius's decision, and I had to wonder if that was because he was now with me. I made a mental note to ask him about this later on but for now, well there was something I needed much more than answers.

"Drink please."

"Which…" the barman started to speak and I held up my hand to stop him, saying truthfully,

"At this point, it doesn't even matter."

A feeling that continued and strengthened every time I looked over at the three quirky hens still pecking at each other's wedding ideas. Which was why thirty minutes later, I was already on my fourth glass of champagne when I felt Lucius come up behind me as I was still watching the 'wedding war' continue. Now it seemed they had moved on from the weather and were now on table settings.

"Well, that looks like fun," he commented dryly, making me reply,

"Yeah, we're totally screwed." Then he chuckled before reminding me,

"It's our wedding, Love."

"Is it though?" I asked in that questioning tone, making him laugh again.

"I mean, at this rate we will be getting married in the same place my parents did, it will be while leaves are falling, saying our vows under an inflatable alter… yeah, don't ask," I said after turning back to face the bar where I had been hiding ever since making my escape.

"Sweetheart, we can do this your way… they are just excited, but I am sure it will calm down…"

"Pip, that's ridiculous! They are not having a petting zoo at their wedding!" my mum shouted, making Pip gasp and as for me, I just glanced back at Lucius.

"I hope you're not allergic to elephants and monkeys… at this rate our ring bearer will be a sloth, but hey, it gives you plenty of time to back out as the little guy makes it way down the aisle… just promise to take me with you," I joked, making him throw his head back and laugh even harder this time. Then he pulled me in closer, grabbed a fresh bottle of bubbly from the bowl of ice and said,

"How about we get out of here right now?" I looked around the room and back at him before whispering,

"Really? You think we can get away with it?" Lucius winked at me and said,

"Well, they are now talking about evening entertainment, so I think we are good for the next hour at least." At this I grinned big and took his hand, ready to run off with him, but stopping just in time to scoot back a few steps to grab an extra bottle, making him laugh when I said…

"Just in case."

CHAPTER 19
NEVER A GOOD TIME FOR A COWBOY

"Okay, so just to be clear, I am admitting it before you comment that yes, that last bottle was a bad idea," I said as my knight in a dashing black suit carried me down from the rooftop after it was clear the champagne had well and truly gone to my head. Although I had to also confess that it had taken me a lot to get me to this point, as I had sneaked down twice to get extra, meaning we had just finished our fourth bottle.

As for the party, well this seemed to have finished as, clearly, we had lasted longer than everyone else. So, the moment we got to the doors to our apartment, I told him to stop. He then allowed me back to my feet so I could sneak over to the double doors that lead back into the club.

"Listen," I said, putting my ear to the doors.

"I don't hear anything, Love." This is when I gave him a cheeky, naughty look and said,

"Exactly!" Then I grabbed his hand and said, "Come on!"

He chuckled at my drunken fun, but let me drag him through into the VIP anyway. As suspected, it was empty, but then, I wasn't surprised considering we had been dancing together on his rooftop until a morning glow was starting to show. We had actually managed to sneak away from the party for most of the night, only going back down every now and again just to show our faces. This became a bit of a game for us, as I started on one side and he on the other and whoever could meet in the middle the quickest after making small talk with people, won.

Of course, now it was empty I could actually see how different it all looked. It was modern but also still managed to maintain that Gothic industrial vibe, with its exposed iron girders on the walls and ceiling, in between bare, exposed brick. New booths had also been added, framing the space with cool twisted-metal frames and deep red leather upholstery. Other seating was also dotted throughout the space, surrounding what now looked like a new charred black wooden dancefloor at the centre. A long bar now replaced where there had once been dancing booths, which had been my first clue that Lucius had tamed down his VIP.

"Oooh, I love what you've done with the place," I said teasingly after letting go of his hand and walking further in the room. Then I turned back to face him, making him raise a brow at me before I said,

"No, seriously, I could hardly see anything when it was full but now you can really tell... it's gothic snazzy." He laughed again before muttering,

"Oh, Gods, please tell me I am in for another drunken dance." I smirked at him over my shoulder before I decided, what the hell... he was due one. So, I sashayed back over to him, flicked his tie once and said,

"I'm hardly dressed for line dancing."

"I've a great imagination, Pet." I chuckled at this before grabbing his tie and using it to lead him to his new sexy 'lord of the club' couch, telling him,

"Come on then, cowboy, what are we waiting for?" Again, he laughed but allowed me to lead him to the centre of the large, curved sectional where he allowed me to push him down into the seat. It was a larger, more lavish version of the booth seating, with thick curls of black iron claws dug deep into the wooden flooring. It looked like some Demonic sea creature was rising up and someone had thrown a padded blanket of dark red leather over the top, meaning the seats were wherever it had settled on the frame.

"Now if I only had music," I said, tapping my lip as he shrugged out of his suit jacket, tossing it to the side. But then as soon as I said this, all it took was a nod from Lucius and a sexy, slow beat started to flow from the stereo system, now filling the VIP with the seductive music.

"Well, I can't line dance to this," I pointed out, making him grin.

"Now that is a shame, especially with you being so good at it. However, maybe I can make the suggestion of a slow dance instead... and I am just throwing ideas out there, but perhaps you can do this while undressing... *slowly.*" I laughed at this before asking,

"And I suppose you want me to throw my clothes at you, huh?" Hips lips twitched, fighting another grin.

"If you insist... after all, I remember it working well the last time."

"Yeah, for who?"

"Oh me... definitely me," he replied assuredly, making me giggle as he never failed to be able to make me laugh. Which is when I started to sway my hips slowly, asking,

"You mean like this?"

"Oh yeah, exactly like that," he said, now loosening his tie and unbuttoning the top part of his shirt.

"And what about this?" I asked as I started to slowly raise

my skirt, making the fabric swish against my stocking covered legs as I raised it higher and higher.

"Mmm... oh yes, that too," he encouraged, and I smirked, feeling very good about myself. Well, until I raised my hands up my chest, and around my neck to where my dress was zipped...

"And what about... erm... okay, so you know what? This is actually really hard to reach on my own, could you just..." I said, now tottering over to him on my heels and making him smirk. Then I turned around so he could unzip me but when he started to pull it too far down, I stopped him.

"Hey, not all the way, or I won't have anything to... you know... tease you with," I said, wiggling my bum in what my drunken mind thought was a sexy, teasing way. Again, he just looked like he was trying very hard not to laugh. In fact, by the time I got back into my position, he had one of his hands covering his lips and his elbow rested to his folded leg, with his eyes glistening with mirth... but I chose to ignore this.

"And what about... oh for God's sake... nope, it's still too high, I just can't..." I said, now trying to reach my arm up my back and looking like I was putting on some really shitty contortionist show. I gave up and walked back over to him as he finally burst out laughing.

"Yeah, yeah, show's over, chuckles..."

"Aww, well that's not fair," he complained, with me now standing with my hands on my hips directly in front of him.

"Oh, you know what, the moment's over, let's just create a new one!" I exclaimed, picking up my shirt and climbing over him so I could straggle his lap.

"You won't hear me complaining, baby," he purred before using his hands up my back so he could easily free me of my halter top, now burying his head to my naked breasts as the dress came with a hidden support and therefore, I had no need for a bra.

"Oh yeah, there he is, my sexy Vamp!" I said, rotating my hips and in my drunken mind, saying something ridiculous,

"Time to ride my cowboy... DAD!" I screamed the second my father raced back inside the club, clearly looking for something.

"OH... Oh fu... whoa, I mean... oh Gods!" At this Lucius grabbed me to him, holding my now naked front to his chest and wrapping his arms around me.

"Gods, Dad, what are you...?"

"I er... Your mother... she... uh... lost and I was found, I mean looking..." He had never sounded as flustered as this in my life.

"Draven, it's okay, I found my purse in... OH MY GOD!" my mum said, now joining the weird ass, awkward as fuck after party where only two had been invited and my parents were never, ever, *ever* going to be on the guest list.

"We thought everyone had gone!" I shouted, with my dad now trying to look at anything other than the two of us.

"Your mother, she thought she forgot her purse... and her phone is in there and..."

"Yes, they get it, Draven, anyway, well this has been... horrifying for us all, and now we are just going to..." my mum spoke as they attempted to make a quick exit.

"Bye, Mum!" I shouted as she grabbed my father, and they both practically ran out the door. I sighed into Lucius's body but then tensed again when I heard the door open slightly so my mum could say,

"Okay, just real quick, Fae, we love you, congratulations, and when you can, you guys must come to dinner... okay, that's all, bye!" I buried my head in Lucius's neck and burst out laughing, making him hold me tighter as I shook in his hold.

"Well, I guess that will teach us for trying to christen the new couch," Lucius said, and at this I lifted my head, shrugged my shoulders and said,

"Hey, I'm still game if you are." At this his bad boy grin said it all. But then as we started getting back into it, He stopped, lifted me up, dumped me on the couch and said,

"Nope, can't do it..."

"Lucius?" I questioned as he started walking away.

"I'm locking all the doors and setting the alarm." I laughed at this as he stormed off and after twirling a piece of my hair in what I liked to think was a seductive way, I said,

"Hurry back, handsome." However, in the end, no amount of Vamp speed would do him any good, as by the time he came back, my drunken self was fast asleep, curled up under his jacket...

Snoring.

CHAPTER 20
WORKING GIRL
THREE MONTHS LATER...

I twisted and turned but still my body continued to sink into the desert sands that were trying to consume me. I knew what was coming. Or should I say, I knew *who* was coming. Because it was every time now. Every time he would only add to the nightmares. Which meant that as soon as I was up to my waist, I would hear his approach before his footsteps turned into armoured feet that came into view. I would look up and the sun behind him would blind me, until he lowered into a crouch. Then only once he was leaning an armour coated arm casually against his thigh would it block out the sun's blinding rays.

"You can't escape me, little queen," he said, making me grit my teeth every time he called me that. But then I would start grinding them together furiously before I felt him grab the lower part of my face, forcefully lifting it up to him. His metal plated hands digging painfully into my cheeks, making my jaw ache and my teeth cut into the inside of my mouth until I tasted blood.

"You carry my curse, which means you carry a piece of me in here," he said, poking at my forehead painfully and with enough force that I still felt his touch long after he had finished.

"I will release them!" I snapped, tearing my face from his hold, despite the added pain it took to do this. Just like I always did as it was like I couldn't help myself, despite knowing it was pointless. Despite knowing that it would only make him grin, with satisfaction at seeing me fight back only making this more thrilling for him.

"And how will you do that, when the door to this realm is lost?" he taunted, making me flinch back from what I knew would be a bruising hold should I let him grab me again, just like he always tried to do a second time. But the bitterness of his words burned in my throat like bile. Because he was right, I had worked tirelessly for months and not even a single clue or a single hint was to be found.

"That's what I thought, woman!" he snarled before standing and signalling the next part of my horror to begin, making me suddenly shout,

"Wait! Just tell me what you want!" Of course, I had tried everything at this point, but the outcome had never changed. I had tried crying out, calling him names, trying to bargain with him, to even the worse one yet... *begging him for mercy*. But every time he simply told me,

"But I want you to suffer. For now, my curse is your curse and that, my dear... *will last an eternity,*" he said before turning his back on me and walking away into the raging sandstorm that surrounded us.

"No! No! Come back here, you asshole!" I screamed as I felt the ground start to rise once more. This now doing so with his commanding actions as he raised up his hands, like he was still the Wraith Master who controlled these lands of the dead.

"NO!" I screamed, but it was no use as hundreds of

bodies started to push their way up through the sand, now caving in around me as I sank deeper and deeper into the dead. Until finally, it became too much, and darkness overtook me as my face was covered over with only my hand reaching up through the death. Reaching up as if someone could still be out there with enough power to break through and save me.

But no one ever did.

"Amelia! Wake up!" I heard shouting but it always came after I had died in my dream. After I had been consumed. It was as if I never made a sound until then. In fact, Lucius had confirmed that it was only ever when I started thrashing in bed that he knew I was having a nightmare. Thankfully, these didn't happen every night but unfortunately, they were definitely becoming more frequent.

I woke with a start, my heart pounding in my chest, and once again, I found my hand outstretched, reaching for a saviour. Then I watched as long, thick fingers intertwined with my own, just like they always did before the comforting voice of his was heard whispering in my ear.

"Ssshh, you're alright now… it was just another dream, sweetheart," he cooed, making me release a heavy weighted sigh, before whispering back,

"Yeah, just another dream." But this was all I managed to say, as the tightness in my chest wouldn't let me say more. Of course, as usual Lucius has more to say about it than I did,

"They are getting more frequent now, it's almost every night."

"I know," I agreed, my tone dejected by the fact.

"Was it the same one?" he asked, as it was only the day after the grand reopening of Transfusion that I admitted to him about my dreams. This was because after he had carried me to bed when finding me passed out under his jacket, a little time later I had woken up screaming.

Which also meant that from that point on, every time I had one, Lucius would ask me about it, until eventually I didn't even need to describe them anymore. Not now, they were all the same. Of course, it didn't take a PhD in psychology to know what they meant. Not considering I was still tied to the Wraiths.

No, now it had just become a constant reminder of the duty my soul was bound to. We both knew it, but neither one of us had yet had the courage to speak it. Lucius was still under the hope and understanding that at some point, my dreams would calm down. However, evidence was suggesting otherwise, and with the frequency of them, it meant that we both knew that his hope was running thin.

"We will get through this, Amelia," Lucius said, taking me in his arms and holding me tight, just like he always did. I released another sigh before rolling over so that I could face him, now running my fingers down the days' old stubble and making him chuckle when I scratched my nails against the scruff on his jawline.

"Is that a not-so-subtle hint for me to shave, Pet?" I smirked playfully before reminding him,

"I don't know, should I allow hair to grow in a certain favourite place of yours just to counteract the feeling?" At this he gave me wry look before grinning.

"Touché, Amelia... I can take the hint."

"And that is why I love you, my husband," I said, knowing that I would never tire of reminding myself of who he now was to me. His eyes heated hearing it, telling me that I wasn't the only one still affected by the title.

"Oh, I think you love me for a lot more than just ability to go down on you and make you come screaming my name." At this I smirked.

"Well, I do love it when you bring me a cup of tea in the morning," I said with a wink, teasing him and making him chuckle.

"Just as I do love the not-so-subtle hints I continually receive from you, my wife." I stretched out like a contented cat and said,

"Excellent… in that case, milk, no sugar, please." This was when he was suddenly over me and caging me is his arms, before running his nose along my jawline all the way to my ear so that he could tell me,

"Yes, sweetheart, I know how my wife likes her tea." Which was when I couldn't resist, reaching down and slapping his ass, making him groan as I said,

"Alright then, handsome, get to it." His response was like a dangerous predator striking. One second he was smiling against my ear and the next, my tender flesh was being held prisoner in his mouth, now caught in between his teeth before he growled like a wild beast.

The sharp sting of pain shot straight to my sex, one he had claimed so thoroughly and now felt deliciously abused from last night. This despite the growing stubble that framed his lips. But then this wasn't surprising as every side of Lucius seemed to be able to make me weep between my legs, and I wondered if there would ever be a time when this man did not affect me the way he did.

"Lucius…" His name left my lips on a breathy sigh, making him release my flesh from the imprisonment of his teeth. Then he sucked and kissed the tender area, now soothing the sting he had made.

"Well look at that, my wife can be tamed after all." Hearing this, I purposely wrapped my legs around his waist so I could lift my hips closer to his morning erection. This made him groan, especially when I grinded my naked pussy, one he had made wet, against him. Then I wrapped my arms around his neck, pulled him down to my lips, so I could now whisper in ear.

"I wouldn't go that far... besides, *I know how much you like me untamed.*" At this, his last growl ended just as his lips crashed into mine, now controlling me with his possessive kiss. Then at the same time his tongue penetrated my mouth, he thrust his cock up inside me, making me cry out as he plundered my holes, dominating them both.

Which also meant that it took a good forty-five minutes before I got that tea.

∽

"You know you don't have to walk me to my office every morning," I said in a light-hearted way, despite loving the fact that he did.

"But then I would miss kissing you goodbye, my working woman," was his sweet reply, making me grin back up at him before walking into my office.

"Yes, but convention dictates that usually the kiss goodbye happens at the front door," I said, making him look back at the door after following me inside.

"Looks like a door to me, sweetheart." I gave said door wry look knowing that he knew what I had meant by front door.

"Besides, we live in a hollowed-out mountain, Amelia, I think we can kiss convention goodbye." Well, I could argue with him there... oh wait, *yes I could.*

"Oh, I don't know about that, Lucius, I mean we did have a Lord of the Rings marathon while eating pizza and junk food last night sitting on the couch and… *it was a Sunday,"* I reminded him.

"Ah yes, another Sunday you failed to enforce your no blow job rule… yes, it was a good day indeed." I couldn't help but laugh at this. Damn his memory!

"Yes, and the start of your man crush with, Legolas," I teased, making him roll his eyes at me, before informing me with an exasperating tone.

"I do not have a man, crush, Amelia."

"Oh really?" I asked, folding my hand over my business suit, one I was only wearing because I had a video call to make today with some curators from Cairo. The Museum of Egyptian Antiquities was the most visited museum in Egypt, as not only was it the biggest, it was also home to over one hundred and twenty thousand ancient Egyptian artefacts. Which meant it basically held the world's largest collection of pharaonic antiquities. So yeah, it was totally a suit wearing day. Which meant this tight, black pencil skirt had also been teasing Lucius all the way here as I swear, every time I looked at him he had been hanging back so he could look at my ass.

In fact, I had been pushed up against the walls twice, with his hands finding their way underneath the material and over my ass. Something that was starting to feel like a new toy to him, as let's just say, it got as much attention now as his other favourite place to hide his dick. Not that I was complaining. I had certainly gotten into the kink myself, sometimes being the one to shake my ass at him like waving fresh meat at a lion and begging it to pounce.

And my big cat pounced every time.

But getting back to elves… the fictional kind this time.

"I simply believed he was the superior fighter," Lucius argued, folding his arms over his own suit, as clearly, I wasn't the only one with meetings today.

"Well, he was certainly more agile than a dwarf, but I always put my money Gimli. Legolas is too pale and serious," I teased, knowing this would do it. And yep, it totally did... Lucius quickly gripped my hips and pulled me into him.

"I thought you liked pale and serious... For you certainly liked it this morning," he growled down at me, not needing to remind me of the most glorious mornings that I woke in Lucius's arms. This before having sex with him, which was always going to be the most perfect way to start any day. Of course, my tease only spurred him on, meaning he was soon walking me further inside my office, now steering me the way he wanted me to go. Oh, and that destination meant my desk, as soon I was feeling my ass hit the edge of it.

"Perhaps you need reminding?" he mumbled, making me chuckle before telling him,

"I'm sorry. I would if I could, but if my boss catches me being late for work, I would get into big, big trouble." His eyes flashed crimson as I knew a big kink for Lucius was hearing the way I always referred to him as my boss. Of course, him being my boss wasn't strictly true, but it was in the game we played. One we both liked playing more often than not.

"Mmm, last I recall, you didn't particularly mind when your boss decided to punish you for your last offence." Images of me being bent over his desk as he spanked with a ruler suddenly flashed in my mind, and a rumbled growl vibrated from his chest as he knew where my thoughts were. Especially when he suddenly scented my arousal. However, the moment he pushed up the sides of my skirt, separated my legs and he stepped into me, the phone rang, making us both groan.

"Leave it," he growled.

"I can't, I'm expecting a call. There is a new shipment coming in and I am, after all, the curator of the… erm, what will we be calling it again… Septimus, something or other," I teased as we had been debating this name for a while now. However, he ignored this quip and growled,

"Fine, but I want your ass on my desk by lunchtime."

I swear I nearly moaned aloud, loving it when he got all bossy and demanding.

"Is that an order from my boss?" I purred, despite the phone that was still ringing. However, he stepped away and was soon at the door. As if he needed to put space between us or he would do something violent again, like break yet another phone of mine. Something that had happened twice before when we were interrupted. But he still hadn't answered me, something he only decided to do the moment I was picking up the receiver and he was opening the door.

"No… *It is an order from your master,"* he said, leaving me with my mouth open, trying to focus on what the person was saying down the other end, but failing miserably as now all I could think about was my kinky husband. I swear I was almost breathless, which made it even harder when I finally had to greet the other person on the phone. However, while on this call, I also didn't miss the distinct sound of a ding at my laptop, making me turn to see he had emailed me only two lines.

The first said…

No underwear.

And as for the second, this made me laugh out loud despite the person on the phone now thinking I was crazy, laughing about the strength of wooden crates.

Because it said…

PS… bring sandwiches ;)

The smiley, winking emoji at the end had me still laughing, even minutes later, and to the point where I had to apologise to the person on the line.

Oh yes, it was going to be…

A good day indeed.

CHAPTER 21
AN INDULGENT HUSBAND

"Mum, seriously, not this again," I said down the phone in a tone of exasperation.

"Yes, this again," my mum replied once again, using her 'Mum tone'.

"I told you, he just doesn't like celebrating Christmas," I reminded her again, when the truth was, I hadn't even asked him. Because despite my family wanting me home for the holidays, we had only been married for a short time and in all honesty, there were other things I was trying to get Lucius to agree too. And right now, Christmas was way down on that list.

"Yes well, he's also over two thousand years old and therefore needs to man up and get over it," was my mum's short reply and I had to admit, she did have a point. But so far, even the talk of Christmas had been met with a raised brow and a pointed look.

"We have only been married for three months, we're still in the honeymoon phase and being in my parents' house, well it's not exactly where I want to spend that phase, if you know what I mean," I said, thinking this was a pretty damn good excuse considering what was now known as the 'unfortunate cowboy' event.

"Yes, I already caught the opening act... *unfortunately*... but, sweetheart, it's a big house, meaning we can give you your own bloody wing if you like as trust me, this phase, is not something we want to think about either... *or ever see again."*

I groaned at this before letting my forehead hit the desk. *"Mum!"*

"I want you home for Christmas, Amelia, is that really too much to ask?"

"No, especially not when you do the 'I know exactly how to guilt, my daughter voice'," I complained, making speech quotations in the air despite her not being able to see this, but it was like she still knew, hence making her chuckle.

"You get that I have a job, right? And what with all the new shipments coming in and..."

"Sweetheart, you're not a heart surgeon and most of the bodies you do come in contact with have been dead for thousands of years... which means they will stay that way and are in no hurry to change that." I couldn't help but giggle at that.

"And what if I was doing life changing research?"

"Okay, answer me this, is anything you're doing right now going to save the world?"

"Well, no," I admitted as it was true, it wasn't affecting the world, just me, and I didn't really want to freak her out with all of that right now.

"Great, then that means you get to hang up your cape for the holidays and come home," she said, making me wish it was that easy.

"Look, Lucius adores you, he loves you, and he will do anything for you... so use that to your advantage."

"Mum!" I shouted, shocked that she would suggest such a thing.

"What? I do it with your father all the time." I had to laugh at this as she was certainly right there, especially considering there was very little my dad ever denied her. Particularly when she reached up on her tiptoes and started whispering in his ear, making his eyes glow purple at whatever it was she was saying... no doubt something I really, really didn't want to know.

"So, what you're saying is that I should strap on a pair of high heels, put on a tight skirt, and march right into his office and demanded he take me home for Christmas before I..." I purposely stopped knowing what was coming next.

"La la, la, la, la... so not listening." I laughed and told her,

"Yes, well consider this payback for all the years I've had to listen to you and Dad flirting and acting like horny teenagers."

"Yes, but that never ended in bloodshed, and your father has way too many weapons to be considered safe, especially listening to you two doing the same, as trust me, three months is no way nearly enough time to erase memories of..." I quickly interrupted her this time, slapping a palm to my forehead.

"Okay! Mum, I got it! And just pointing out, all the more reason not to come home for Christmas." Okay so I thought I had her with this one, but like always, my mother had an answer for everything.

"Yes, but I will also have access to those weapons should you choose not to come home for Christmas, and I will only have one man to blame."

"Okay, good point. Wow, you really are like the Christmas monster," I said, knowing she was only joking as my mother wouldn't hurt a fly. Well, not unless it was trying to hurt her family or friends, then she would turn bat shit crazy on everyone.

"Yes, and this Christmas monster will be released in a fit of rage. One that even Adam will shudder at if I find that you are not home to open your stocking on Christmas morning."

Erm… case in point.

"Okay, but you do get that I'm nearly thirty, right?"

"Are you telling me you don't want a stocking?" she asked, calling my bluff.

"Well… I… I mean not exactly… okay, yes, I want the stocking and the sack of presents and the hot cocoa with a candy cane to stir the sprinkles!" I admitted, because I was weak.

"Hot chocolate, Amelia, we call it hot chocolate."

"Technically, I'm in Germany and here they call it, heiße Schokoladein… sooo…" She scoffed at this before going back to her master plan of manipulation and guilt, now pulling out the big guns.

"Look, I get it, smarty language pants, this is all very new for him and I can be understanding of that. Just like I was understanding about the two of you eloping without telling us, robbing your father the chance to walk his only daughter down the aisle and your mother the chance to buy a ridiculously big hat and play mother of the bride." This time I started rubbing my forehead as if this would help ease the pressure building there.

"I told you, we are planning another wedding… Geez."

"Then this will give you the perfect opportunity to be here with your wedding planners and discuss all the things you would love to have on your big day," she responded, and damn her logic!

"Okay, okay, I will work on Lucius," I said, finally giving

in, and this was when my mother snorted a laugh and muttered,

"Poor bastard."

"I'll see what I can do," I assured her again, now feeling emotionally drained to the point I almost said the same thing about my dad.

"And if you fail, I can simply make it a royal decree that my daughter has to be home with her new husband every Christmas," she said, using her 'posh English' voice making me supress a giggle.

"Great, I would love to see that paperwork," I replied instead.

"I will even use my royal family seal, after all, your father did buy me one and I've not had any need to use it yet." I laughed at this, knowing exactly why she hadn't 'used it'.

"There's no need to be scared of the hot wax, Mum, just pour it on the paper and then press the seal down... easy. It's not rocket science, Mother." She groaned at this and said,

"Yes, but the last time I tried it, I got wax in my hair and then Pip convinced me that peanut butter was the only way to get it out!"

"I'm pretty sure that's for gum," I pointed out unhelpfully.

"Yes, well let's just say that I learned that the hard way and let's also say, that it is not a sexy look to have your husband walk in on you when you have a naughty Imp, wearing a Wookie Onesie, rubbing peanut butter in your hair, picking at it like a monkey and then licking her lips... muttering, oooh, I found another crunchy bit." At this mental image, I couldn't help but burst out laughing, doing so until my belly hurt.

"Alright, Mum, I will see what I can do," I assured her again, making her sigh in relief.

"That's all I ask, my loving daughter," she replied in an overly sweet tone, making me smirk and shake my head at her.

"I better go, a new shipment of artefacts just came in from Lucius's vault in Switzerland. And I've got a backlog of stuff I still need to catalogue."

"And as for me, I have wedding venues to look at," she replied happily, making me roll my eyes, glad that she couldn't see me, as I said,

"Of course, you do."

"I will see you soon, honey!" she said, and I couldn't resist teasing her one last time,

"Oh, and, Mum…"

"Yeah?" she asked, waiting for it.

"…Stay away from the wax seal."

"Ha ha. Comedian, just like your mother," she replied, making me laugh before reminding her,

"I'm pretty sure that's what Dad always says."

"Right, well I'm going now, before I get any more peanut butter jokes. Love you, honey."

"Love you too, Mum."

After this, I put down the phone just as the door opened and another crate was brought inside. My office space could barely be called a room, it was more like some spacious apartment. This was because Lucius had decided to give me what was practically a whole floor dedicated to my work.

I swear I had actually wept for joy when he showed it to me. Because when I had asked him in the car about me working and he had asked me to give him time, this was what he had meant. I knew that the moment he blindfolded me with his hands as he walked me into the space before revealing my dream office.

One we had christened minutes later as I squealed in

delight before throwing myself at him! Then with me still hanging off him like some horny monkey, he walked me around the different rooms, while I raised my head long enough to look before going back to kissing his neck. Needless to say, we ended up back at my fabulously carved oak desk where I got to thank him properly.

As for my 'office' if it could even be called that, there was a storeroom with its own vault space for the more valuable items. There was a large workspace where I could work on the artefacts on multiple workstations, complete with walls full of tools. Most of which I would only ever need if I was planning on some ancient dig or trying to find the lost city of El Dorado. Or if I decided that digging up bones of dinosaurs was now my new hobby. Either one, the wall of tools was awesome, even if it was just to look at!

At the centre, was my huge actual office, and one that was kitted out with every type of technology that made my head spin. There was an x-ray machine, a 3-D printer, a lab space, a library and a sitting room with a kitchenette. Lucius had gone all out, and despite me telling him, this was, way, *way*, too much, the excitement on his face was infectious. Which meant that I decided to just shut up and accept it all as he had gone to extreme lengths to make this possible and I didn't want him thinking I was ungrateful. When really, it was like a work dream come true!

Now there was no more red tape and museum hoops to jump through. It was more like I was my own boss despite the sexual games we liked to play. I knew Lucius just wanted to make me happy and in truth, giving me even half of this stuff would've made me ecstatically so.

But then as the artefacts started rolling in, I found myself not only happy but also excited for the future. Lucius may have created this role for me, but when I started to see the entirety of his collection coming in crate by crate, day by day, it made me realise that he hadn't been exaggerating.

He actually had needed somebody to catalogue everything he owned, as most of the stuff he had forgotten about. I knew this when he would sometimes walk in around lunchtime, pick something out of one of the crates. and tell me,

"Um… I thought I lost this after the Battle of Hastings." I would then run over to him take the thousand-year-old Anglo-Saxon helmet from him that was in remarkable condition. This was with the rest of his collection, with artifacts retrieved from Sutton Hoo in Suffolk. Sutton Hoo was the site of two early medieval cemeteries dating from the 6th to 7th centuries near the English town of Woodbridge. Archaeologists had been excavating the area since 1938, when a previously undisturbed ship burial containing a wealth of Anglo-Saxon artefacts was discovered. Something that he obviously cared little for, as he picked up the next item and started casually tossing the ancient drinking flask between his hands. My reaction of horror and panic made him smirk down at me when I took it out of his hands, only to place it gently back down on my workstation.

Of course, he found my reaction to this highly amusing, which was why he always did it. Especially if the bad boy grin was anything to go by. I was starting to think that Lucius got a kick every time I told him off and scolded him about something, as he still continued to treat his own artefacts this way.

In fact, it was one night as we were having dinner and I had cooked my shredded chilli chicken, (another culinary triumph according to Lucius) that I asked him how he would feel about opening up a museum.

"You have so many rare and incredible artefacts, pieces of the past that people like me would love to see. It's a crime to know that they are just heading their way back to another vault somewhere and most of which, you don't even remember having or get pleasure out of... no, Lucius, not that type of pleasure," I said, laughing when his eyes roamed over my tank top, one, admittedly I had chosen to tease him with... and teasing him was now the main reason I wore yoga sets again too. Although I would have to start working out soon or he was going to catch on.

As for my answer, he simply picked up my hand, nibbled on my fingertips, before looking at me and telling me,

"I will have a think about it, sweetheart." After this, I decided not to push it, even though we both knew that I really, really wanted to. He even teased me about it, especially when that night we were lying in the dark and my mind was going a million miles an hour. Which was when I said,

"It doesn't even have to be a big museum." To which he burst out laughing, pulled me to him, kissed me on the forehead, and said,

"Good night, Amelia."

After this, I finally took the hint... well, *at least for the night.*

But that had been a month ago and I hadn't mentioned anything about it since. Besides, work was keeping me busy and now the idea of going home for Christmas had overwritten all thoughts and dreams of running my own museum... well, *almost.*

So, with this new mission in mind, I grabbed the basket I had prepared, now filled with sandwiches and other goodies, from the kitchenette.

Then, after shimmying out of my underwear, at his order, I made my way to Lucius's office, one, that was purposely not too far away from my own. I knew this was for a few reasons, as clearly, Lucius was in no rush to put too much distance between us. I also think this was the reason he was holding back agreeing to the museum idea.

I knew time was the key to easing his worries, but time worked differently for a vampire over two-thousand-years old. Meaning three months was merely a drop in the Ocean for Lucius, just as it was for my father. Because for them both, they had lived throughout a history I had only ever dreamed about experiencing. A history I had only ever had the pleasure of learning through study and books. Throughout the few stories my father had shared with me, keeping them edited for first, a child's ears, and then for my protection as a mortal.

I suppose knowing how to summon up your grandfather, the King of Lust all from reading the wrong book, wasn't something my father could trust. Hence my limited access to the family library. But that had been when I was thought of solely as being human, and before I married a Vampire King with his own extensive library. One I'd had full access to, which was another thing for me to squeal over the moment Lucius showed me. He had also been making a point to teach me things about my world that I had previously been kept in the dark about.

It started when I had first been brought to Königssee. We had been making our way to Lucius's private space at the centre of the mountain, when I saw the Sigils on the doors. He had started to teach me what each bit meant with the promise of teaching me more. Well, Lucius hadn't forgotten this promise, despite all that had happened after this point.

I found this out when he showed me to his library for the first time, taking out the books and making a pile of the ones he thought would interest me the most. We had spent the whole night in front of the fireplace, sitting reading old texts with Lucius explaining elements of each realm. This along with ancient symbols I didn't recognize and other worldly events I had no idea had even happened. There was a whole hidden world of history that had taken place and I had no clue to any of it.

It was a historical minefield, and one that Lucius seemed only too happy to indulge me in, until the point that I fell asleep in his arms clutching a book of Fae history to my chest. One he had to pry out of my hands before carrying me off to our bed.

I had been like a kid in a candy store ever since, spending half my time studying Lucius's extensive collection of antiquities, and half the time in his library studying a whole new world of knowledge. Of course, that wasn't always to say that we only read in the library, as let's just say, Lucius found my enthusiasm very endearing. And the sounds and noises of pleasure I would make, he often commented that he found very cute.

To the point that his biggest turn on was clearly corrupting his little scholar by pinning her to the thick, *thankfully,* sturdy shelves, fucking me senseless against dusty old books.

And speaking of sex and my hopeful powers of persuasion...

I knocked on his door.

CHAPTER 22
THE DAY BEFORE CHRISTMAS

"*Amelia.*"

"Huh?" The sound of Lucius's voice finally pulled me from my nervous thoughts and where I had been flicking my bookmark in between my thumb and my forefinger for the past twenty minutes. Of course, for the hours before this, I had been fidgeting in different ways and each time I knew Lucius had wanted to comment.

"Why are you so nervous?" he asked from where he was sitting across from me. We were on a flight on our way to Portland, Maine, where my parents were expecting us. Because, of course, Lucius had, yet again, given me what I wanted and I, in turn, had asked Liessa to find me something so as I may say thank you. Which meant that when he walked into the bedroom that night, he did so to find me wearing nothing but a see-through red baby doll and a Santa's hat. His face had been a picture, especially when I said,

"Merry Christmas, baby." His reply came out as a sexy, husky growl as he stalked toward me.

"Merry Christmas, indeed."

This also meant that I made my point after paying special attention to a certain part of his anatomy, practically purring as I swiped the cum from my lips after swallowing most of it down, telling him,

"See, I told you Christmas can be fun." Then I winked at him, making him laugh before dragging me up the length of him and well...

Making it fun for me also.

But that had been a week ago and now here we were, on our private jet, with a plane full of wrapped gifts and enough luggage for the week we planned to be there. And Lucius was right, I was nervous. Yet I lied and said,

"Me? I'm not nervous." Of course, the sound of my bookmark once again flapping nervously in between my fingers named me as a liar. Which is why he reached across the table and took my hands, plucking the bookmark out of my fingertips and setting it on top of my open book. One about lost realms and fallen cites. Oh, and it was also one I had given up reading over an hour ago.

"Now try again, and this time without the lies," he said, reading me better than I had been trying to do with the damn book.

"It's just that it's the first time we're all going to be together as a family," I told him, and his expression told me that he still didn't see what the problem was.

"And?"

"And last time didn't exactly go well," I whispered like this was a secret. Although, who could overhear...? I had no clue, seeing as we were the only ones traveling. I also hated to remind him of the past and of what happened the last time we had set foot in Afterlife. In fact, the only way it would've ended worse, was with Lucius at the end of my father's sword.

"Amelia."

"Honestly, Lucius, you say my name like it holds the answer without actually being an answer. It's very frustrating." At this, he chuckled.

"I say your name that way because the answer is obvious and shouldn't need my words. But seeing as you apparently need them, I will remind you that the last time we were at Afterlife was very different. Your parents didn't even know we were together. Also, I may remind you that you didn't trust me and I didn't trust you with the truth. But I would say we've come a long way since those days, don't you think?" I released a sigh and admitted,

"I guess you have a point."

"Yes, and that point includes a marriage. It also includes your father no longer want to rip my head from my neck," he added.

"Another good point."

"I do have them occasionally," he replied wryly.

"Occasionally," I agreed, making him raise a single brow at me.

"Besides, I will also remind you that this was your idea… it was your choice, sweetheart." I groaned at this, throwing my hands up dramatically, saying,

"I know, I know, I know." I also did this now focusing my attention out of the window, wishing that the sight of land coming in to view held a more comforting sight than it did.

"Amelia, my love, you are overthinking this. Your father and I are on good terms. We are no longer at war with each other. If anything, and I cannot believe I'm about to say this, the only good to come out of our turbulent, *runaway,* past was that we were forced to work together. We were forced back into the alliance we once had and at the centre of that alliance was you." Again I released another sigh before saying,

"See, was that so hard to say?" My response obviously amused him, making him smirk and reply,

"I am just happy that we're doing this without you shooting another pilot and flying the damn plane."

I scoffed at this. "Yes, well after riding a demented Harpy like a damn glider, let's just say I've been put off air travel for quite a while." At this, he started coughing, which alarmingly sounded like he was choking.

"Come... come again?" I shook my head quickly and we both ended up speaking at the same time...

"You don't want to know."

"I don't want to know."

∼

Shortly after this and gaining the assurances I had needed from Lucius that all would be fine, we came into land. And just like last time, there were people to meet us at the airfield. My father's welcome party. However, unlike last time, the Viking we found there was a little less cold toward my vampire companion. Of course, after running into his open arms and failing to make it all the way around the big beast, I pulled back this time to give him a teasing grin.

"Nice sweater, Ragnar, please tell me it lights up." At this he groaned and for the second time today, my comment this was echoed by another, as we both said who the culprit was at the same time...

"My mother."

"Your mother."

You see the thing about my mother was that around this

time of year, she got a little Christmas crazy. Hence why poor Ragnar was now wearing a Gods awful sweater with little knitted gothic Christmas trees and drunken Santas. One that didn't light up, but it sure as shit did sing when he pressed a hidden button, making me howl with laughter.

But that was my mum for you. Ever since I had been born my dad told me he didn't know what happened, but it was as if someone had flipped a switch and BOOM, she was then forever known to all as the Christmas menace. But then, perhaps that's what happened when you had kids, you went bat shit crazy and spent half your time on Pinterest just looking for that perfect Christmas craft idea. Or the very best sugar cookie recipe, so that by the time the day comes, your kid is covered in glitter and doped up on so much sugar, they literally pass out after the presents… but hey, at least you can find them easily, what with all their sparkling skin.

Literally every Williams' family tradition was pulled out of the stocking and thrust upon us all. Of course, being a big fan of Christmas myself, there was very little complaint from my side. Even if I was now sounding a bit like a Scrooge. In all honesty, I think it was more because I was worried about Lucius and what he would think of it all. But usually I enjoyed the fun and embraced my mother's crazy side, even going so far as to encourage it. Especially given the joy at seeing my father being forced to wear a Christmas hat and read aloud quite possibly the worst jokes in history from spilled guts of paper crackers.

But Christmas for my mother was also incredibly special and because of that, the amount of traditions, that yes quite possibly were boarding along the lines of insanity, was basically my mum keeping that part of her humanity alive.

So of course, I was worried about Lucius. I was worried

about what he would think of it all. I was also hoping he would embrace it, if only to indulge me further. But just in case…

I had packed the Santa's hat.

After this we all piled into the convoy of cars, and like last time, Lucius sat next to me. Then he took my hand, laying it on his lap so he could play with my fingers.

"Are you doing that so I won't bite them?" I asked.

"I'm doing this to help you relax, Sweetheart. Besides, this should come a lot easier now that we don't have a naughty Imp about spilling our secrets." I laughed at that, agreeing,

"Well, that's true."

"It will all be fine, Love, and now that your cousin has been found, I hear that she will be spending it in London?" he said, reminding me of these facts and making me sigh, because this had also been another big worry of mine during these last seven weeks. Of course, as per usual for the life of one of the Kings' Chosen, it was complicated and despite how much I had wanted to intervene, I learned my lesson with this after turning up at Jared's club. After that, things had gone from bad to worse and after I had given my cousin Ella a little bit too much information about our Supernatural world, I had promised not to get involved again.

However, when she went missing for a time, well that had been the hardest weeks to endure. Doing nothing had no longer been an option, it just turned out that doing something hadn't helped either. But now she was back and despite how desperate I was to go and see her, Lucius had urged me not to at Jared's request. Things had gotten even more complicated and if I had showed up during this delicate time, then it would have only made matters worse. And for once, I agreed with them, so continued to let Jared play it his way. Which meant that I wouldn't be seeing her at Christmas this year.

"Besides, now that I agreed to partake in this family tradition, I find that I am quite looking forward to experiencing it." Hearing this drew me from my thoughts and made me shout,

"Really?!" Of course, this made him grin at me with that gleam in his eyes he usually got when he found me endearing.

"I am… wait, is that why you are worried, because you think I won't enjoy this?" he guessed, now making me look sheepish.

"Maybe," I admitted, making him say my name in that same way he always did.

"Amelia."

"Yeah?"

"Come here, my Khuba," he said in that soft, affectionate way I adored.

"My joy comes from watching your own, and a sure way of making me experience that is for you to be yourself and enjoy this time with your family. In my eyes, it may be a day like any other, but if it is one that comes with extra smiles and a reason to shower you with gifts, then it will be a day I will enjoy all the more." At this I hugged him tighter and told him,

"Have I told you I love you today?"

"Well, I believe I was between your legs at the time, so it may have been a little muffled." At this I smacked his chest in fake outrage. But then I remembered what he'd said and focused back to that.

"Wait, so does that mean some of those gifts on the plane are for me?" He smirked and said,

"Maybe." At this I threw my arms around him again and said,

"Then here it is unmuffled… I love you, husband." I felt his chuckle as he wrapped his arms around me and said,

"I love you too, my little Claus."

CHAPTER 23
MEMORIES PRESERVED

We were walking through the halls of Afterlife on our way to the sitting room where Ragnar said everyone would be. He had gone on ahead after I had asked for some of his security team to help take in the gifts they had packed in the convoy of cars.

I had also been in the process of telling Lucius that, this year, my mum had assured me that she had toned it all down a bit so as to ease him into the festivities gradually. However, the second we opened the door, I had to wonder if during our short walk here I had somehow managed to be drugged.

"What the…?!"

"Er… you were saying, Pet?" Lucius asked the moment our brains took in the madness. In fact, our eyes both widened in sight of the Christmas wonderland on crack that my family home had been transformed into. It was like a total contrast to how the nightclub looked, as that had been all stylish black trees covered in purple fairy lights and silver ribbons as thick as my waist. It was gothic but elegant, and no doubt was all down to my aunt Sophia.

Now as for this, well it looked like my mum had robbed Macy's entire Christmas selection!

"I know, I know, I might have gone a bit mad this year," my mum admitted when we walked into the large sitting room and my mouth had just dropped. She hugged me to her and when she looked at my casual red dress, I could tell she was already planning which Christmas sweater she would make me wear tomorrow. I bet the damn thing was already laid out on my bed waiting.

"Dear Lord," Lucius muttered next to me before I elbowed him, making him cough before saying,

"Naturally, what I mean to say is it looks lovely, Keira Girl." At this my mother frowned and was about to say something in retaliation, when Zagan looked to be juggling presents.

"I will be right back!"

"Yep, that was smooth," I commented under my breath when my mum was directing another arm full of gifts to be placed under the... one, two, three, four, five... *the sixth Christmas tree!*

"Is it always like...?" he asked, making me interrupt quickly,

"No."

"And does she always do..."

"No," I replied again before my dad came up to embrace me, making me nearly choke on my laugh when he whispered,

"Gods, child, please save me."

"Er... what's with all the extra trees and well, extra *everything*...? Dear Gods, are those life-sized Elves?" I asked as I took in more of my mother's insanity. My father sighed, taking a step back and telling me,

"A store in the mall got closed down and were selling all

their Christmas stock and then your mother got chatting to the woman…"

"Oh no, I can see where this is going," I said, making him continue,

"Yes, well, she found out the store owner's grandmother was sick and she needed the money for medical bills."

"So, Mum bought the whole store!" I shrieked.

"No, she bought all the stock from the *three stores* the woman had, as two were also in Portland… she also bought the woman a dialysis machine."

"Of course, she did," I muttered, making my dad wince when he watched as Ragnar carried a seven-foot Nutcracker soldier into the room, now placing it at the side of the fireplace so it could match the other side were another already stood.

"Well, maybe that's the last of it," I said, patting his arm and making him sigh.

"The only rooms in the house that don't have a damn tree in them are the bathrooms as I was finally able to draw the line," my dad said, making Lucius stifle another laugh, pretending to clear his throat instead.

"I gather that's why Afterlife has only one big tree in it this year."

"Yes, thankfully logic won that argument, as anymore and there would have been no room left for actual people." I laughed at this.

"Isn't this great?!" Pip shouted as she entered the room with Adam, who, like the rest of the men, was also carrying something festive. This time I think it was a giant gingerbread man holding a wreath.

"Yes, it's like Santa and his thousand elves all glitter vomited over the room," I replied dryly, making Lucius laugh next to me as my father smirked. As for Pip, she was currently dressed like someone had decorated her like a Christmas tree as her whole dress was made of red and white striped tinsel and red baubles.

"Yeah, I know, right? I mean, this wasn't even something you could buy, but was in one of the shop window displays... I mean, I have never seen your mum this crazy. I woke this morning thinking she had been snorting crushed up candy canes or something," Pip said, and one look at my mum and I had to agree with her, as I watched as Takeshi took one step in the room, and then as if knowing his fate, turned around and promptly left it again.

"Lucky bastard... she didn't see him," Zagan muttered after coming to stand by us when he had finished doing my mother's bidding.

"No, unfortunately what this is, is your mother trying to prove a point after I told her we wouldn't have room for all this stuff," my dad said, referring back to Pip's comment about snorting candy canes.

"Really... this is Mum trying to prove a point?"

"Unfortunately, yes, and after she reminded me of my expensive car collecting hobby, to which the conversation somehow turned into me being called the Grinch. Something I now know is some strange furry green demon because, of course, we now have one here somewhere." At this I couldn't help but feel sorry for my dad, giving him another hug for good measure. A gesture he seemed pleased about as he patted my back and granted me a warm smile.

"I'm sure she will calm down soon... wait is that a... you know what, never mind," I said, ignoring the pieces of a giant snowman Ragnar now seemed to be trying to juggle by carrying all three snowy balls at once.

"Yes, well, she stormed off muttering about how this year I was getting the ugly sweater... I swear, near thirty years together and I still don't understand women," my dad said, making me say,

"Aww, Dad... you know if you makes you feel any better, I made Lucius put up a tree with me in our living room." Because yeah, once he agreed to Christmas, that was it, he was all in! Of course, this was helped when I bribed him with a bag of left-over icing that I started squirting down myself after making cookies and, well, it made for some sweet fun in the bedroom.

"How many trees?" my dad asked, making Lucius hold up a single finger, unable to help now looking smug. I rolled my eyes and said,

"Yeah, okay, so it was just the one." To which Lucius added,

"And now I know I am a lucky bastard indeed. But I am thinking that in light of all... *well, this*... that perhaps you need a drink?" I don't know what I found more funny, the way Lucius waved a hand at the room as if his eyes were close to burning from all the lights, or my dad's quick and almost desperate reply,

"Gods yes!"

"Er, I wouldn't say no," Zagan added, just as Ragnar had finally made his way over to us after first wrestling with the snowman until it was finally erect... even though it was a little drunk looking.

"Can I get in on that action?" Adam asked, but it was Ragnar that pointed out one crucial flaw.

"We can't all leave together or she will notice," He said, making my father slap him on the back and say,

"It's good to be King." Then he started to walk away, when I grabbed him by the shirt and said,

"Be fair, Father," I said, making him groan. "Look, I've got your back, old man, so you can all go together... Right,

Pip you and me are on diversion duty." She saluted at me and said,

"Lead the way, Captain." As for my father, he pulled me in for another hug and told me,

"It's good to have you home, Honey… oh and make it last at least an hour and I will buy you a pony." I laughed at this and replied,

"Make it the new LEGO Star Wars AT-AT set and we have a deal." Lucius looked at me like I had lost my mind, making me point out,

"I already told you once before, it's epic and has six thousand seven hundred and eight five pieces, and can fit forty mini-figures inside." At this he pulled me in closer so he could kiss me on my forehead before saying in a patronizing tone,

"Okay, sweetheart."

"But it's so I can relive the Battle of Hoth in The Empire Strikes Back!" I shouted, which only prolonged his chuckle as he and my father walked out the door. As for Adam, he kissed Pip quick and said,

"Be good, my little tree."

"Yeah, nice try, like that's ever gonna happen, Pookie bear," she replied, making him wink at her as she shook her baubles at him. However, it was when Zagan and Ragnar were also about to leave that we held them back.

"Don't go until we give you the signal or you will never make it out of this place without tinsel being involved," I warned, making them both reply,

"It's good to have you back, little apple."

"Most definitely, Little Princess."

I winked at them both before turning to Pip and saying,

"Right, Pipinator, we are on." She fist-pumped the air and after gritting her teeth, she growled,

"Yeah, let's do this!"

∽

"Merry Christmas!" I shouted, making my mum groan before putting a hand to her head and saying,

"Not so loud." At this I walked over to where she was sitting on the couch, put my arm around her, and said,

"What's up, Mum, not feeling quite as festive today?" I teased, knowing that she had a hangover. I think whatever part of my mum was still human, it was the part that clearly retained alcohol. This was why Pip's idea for distracting my mum had been to blast cheesy Christmas tunes, break open a bottle of tequila, and start the Christmas party early.

Which also meant that by the time the men eventually did come back last night, they found all four of us surrounded by life-sized Santa's Elves. They found my mum slow dancing with one, Pip gyrating against another, and Sophia swinging an elf hat around her head as she twirled around the one now missing a hat. And as for me, I had one on the couch with me, tapping my shot glass to its lifeless head before downing it. This after first telling it all about how wonderful married life was. Turned out, he was a pretty good listener.

However, the looks on the men's faces had been classic, but it was Ragnar who spoke first,

"Who ate all the food?" I burst out laughing at this, slapping my new friend on his wooden leg. Because Ragnar was right, we had given up waiting for the men to come back and started to devour half the buffet an hour before. It was also one that my mum had ordered in special and had been the first to dig in. I was holding half an eaten cookie in my hand before saying,

"I think there might be some broken gingerbread men

cookies left at the back, but they have no heads, as Pip bit them all off."

"You're damn right I did, those little bastards were giving me the stink eye!" Pip had said as she continued to give it good to her new friend getting its painted face rubbed in her crotch. What made it more disturbing was most definitely the creepy smile it had, although in Pip's defence it looked like it was having a good time at least.

"No, they weren't, I'm just not that good at icing the faces, so they looked a bit..."

"Demonic?" Sophia provided, making my mum scowl.

"I was going to say surly." I snorted a laugh at this as the men had started to walk slowly inside, as if at any minute, we would make them do a dance off or something. As for Lucius, he sat down next to me and I put and arm around the elf and said,

"Lucius, this is Nathaniel... *I know, right, fancy name...* Nathaniel, this is Lucius... *my husband. Sorry, but I did say I was taken,*" I had whispered to my new friend, making Lucius throw his head back and laugh. However, this was seconds before he took one look at me, then must have made a quick decision, as I was soon being pulled from the couch with my hands in his.

"Sorry, Nathaniel, but it's time I get my drunken little wife to bed. Come on, up you get, Sweetheart," he said, making me moan,

"But wait, you haven't had a headless Gingerbread man yet... oh wait, I still have this one," I said, holding it out to him and making him take a big bite with a grin.

"Yummy," he had mocked, making me giggle before I was up in his arms, and he was telling everyone goodnight. Then as I looked over his shoulder as he made his way to the door, I saw Ragnar devouring the food table, before

informing us it was time he went back to his own Fated. Zagan was dancing with Sophia and was wearing the Elf hat. Adam was carrying Pip over his shoulder with the lucky elf tucked under his arm, (something I didn't want to know about).

And as for my parents, they were slow dancing in the middle of the room like they were the only two people in the whole world.

A sight that had made me sigh before whispering to Lucius,

"And now it's Christmas."

Thankfully I had been saved from drinking anymore as Lucius took us both to bed. Although when walking in my room I didn't know what he shook his head at, being back in my Geek room or the fact that my mum had laid out two Christmas sweaters for us to wear. She even made them look like they were holding hands, making me say,

"Aww cute, look, they are in love just like us." He had chuckled at this before dropping me on the bed with a bounce and teased,

"Amelia, how could you? You just crushed their love." I giggled at this and then I twirled a piece of my hair before asking,

"Wanna crush them with me?"

"Fuck yeah!" After this, we crushed them good.

Although I think that Lucius was getting way too much of a kick out of knowing we'd had sex on top of something I was being made to wear for Christmas day. In fact, I know it was the only reason he was wearing his, something admittedly I was shocked to see him do. Or maybe that was the reason he did it, as the sight of my mouth dropping when seeing him put it on was one he soon looked smug about. Mine was naturally Star Trek themed, as it looked like the red uniform with the classic collection of ships in rows with the words, Trek the Halls at the top. As for Lucius's, even he rolled his eyes as it was rows of knitted fangs, bats, coffins, and gravestones with the words, 'have yourself a bloody little Christmas.'

"It has to be said that your mother has a strange sense of humour," he had said on the way to the dining room, and looking at the both of us, I couldn't help but smile and agree,

"Yep, she sure does."

As for my mum, she was now cradling the biggest mug of tea to her chest like it was her miracle cure, and I had to laugh when my dad brought her over a chocolate sprinkled croissant, kissing the top of her head and telling her to eat as it would soak up the alcohol. He then winked at me before going back to get his own from the table where the breakfast had been laid out.

Lucius met my father there and they each took one look at what the other was wearing, my dad in a Grinch sweater and now I knew why. It also warmed my heart when my dad slapped Lucius on the back and said,

"Welcome to the family… oh and I find she usually lets you take it off after dinner."

"Only after the family photos have been taken!" My mum added before taking a huge bite of her buttery goodness, something I started to eye with envy. Well, that was until Lucius brought over my own delicious beauty.

"God, you are such a weird child," my mum joked as she always did when seeing me eat crispy bacon with my chocolate doughnuts.

"Yeah, but it's the maple kind… MMM," I said, taking a huge bite and making her scrunch up her nose in a cute way.

After breakfast, we then found ourselves, all sitting around the biggest tree. As we were making space to accommodate everyone, Lucius and I opted to sit on the floor with his back to Chesterfield foot stool, and me tucked in between his legs with my back to his chest.

Pip and I then played Santa's little helpers as we were the ones who picked the gifts out and delivered them to the right people. I had a pile next to me, everything from bird books, tons of geek stuff and of course, funny T-shirts. But when it came time to exchange gifts between Lucius and I, well I started squealing when opening the very Lego set I had mentioned to my dad last night!

"And you thought I wasn't paying attention," he muttered in my ear when I threw myself at him. Of course, he was referring to the long list I had reeled off months ago, when I had been dusting my geek shelves. In fact, after I had opened my gifts from him, I had enough Lego sets to last me half the year as it looked like he had bought half a shop!

As for my gifts for him, I had of course added in some joke ones, like the flying lessons I had gotten him, mouthing,

'Just in case.'

Thankfully, he laughed about it. This was before he started sounding pretty excited by the idea. This then led into a conversation with my dad as he had been flying his own planes for years. Another present from me was dance lessons, even though we didn't really need them as we managed just fine. As well, thankfully Lucius could dance and I could follow. But it was more symbolic, which was why I was most excited about this last one, knowing that no one would know what it meant other than just the two of us.

"You seem excited about this one, Sweetheart," he commented as I was practically bouncing when I passed it to him, needing both hands as it was heavy in its box.

"I am, so please be quick and open it." However, when he started to tease me by peeling the tape back as slowly as possible, I growled, making him chuckle before tearing it off. Then as he opened the box and took out its contents, he simply stared down at the small clear ball in his hands, dumbstruck. He seemed totally lost for words.

"Oh, Amelia." My name left his lips on a whispered breath before he grabbed me to him and held me tight, as if overcome with emotions.

"Do you like it?" I whispered in his ear, making him answer,

"I love it... it's the most perfect gift anyone has ever given me... *it's our Poppy."* I sighed happily, glad that I had waited to give it to him until now. I'd actually had the idea to preserve it somehow and told Liessa about it, and amazingly she had come up with the perfect solution... *Ruto.*

I was surprised to find that in his spare time he and his husband Keto or as I like to call them, the 'ToTo twins', actually created art with resin. So, I had them set the flower in a resin ball so clear it looked like glass. This had a black obsidian base that his brother Dariush had helped me get from his Realm in Hell as I wanted the black and red to represent us both.

"It's a flower?" Pip said, sticking her head closer and looking for herself as, clearly, her curiosity had gotten too much for her. I looked back at Lucius and answered...

"No... it's our flower."

Lucius

CHAPTER 24
FATHER-IN-LAW WISDOM
LUCIUS

I had to admit, that the thought of celebrating a day that was supposed to represent the birth of Christ had always left a sour note on my tongue. But after recent events and the peace they had awarded me, I found my reasons of distain for the holiday were no more. In fact, just seeing how much Amelia wanted this and had tried to convince me... or should I say, *how easily she had convinced me,* then it made me want to give her this all the more.

As time went on, and I saw her excitement growing, I found it was infectious and I started to enjoy certain elements the season brought immensely. For starters, it didn't come as a surprise that I would relish being able to shop for gifts to give Amelia, knowing what she would like. Now, what had been a surprise was the excited eagerness that would continually build inside me, waiting for the day to come that I could finally to give them to her, knowing of the smiles she would gift me in return.

But it had also been the little things too. Like decorating our home together, watching Christmas themed movies, although, most of which I had lost focus in pretty quickly as they most defiantly lacked any violence. Although, I had enjoyed the one with the kid who defended his home against thieves' and pretty much tortured the poor bastards. Now that had been entertaining.

But there had been something surprisingly serene about our lives together, a sort of comfort of the likes I had never known. Our daily routine suited me very well, when I had never previously believed such a thing could happen to me. Not when I thought back on what my life had been like before her. Because a mundane life as an immortal was a dangerous thing, which was why you were constantly trying to chase the next excitement in life. And yet it was now those mundane things that I found the most exciting. It was like I was experiencing them for the first time and never feeling like I had even lived before there was Amelia. Like I had simply been...

Existing.

As for now, well the girl even had me baking cookies with her, and bizarrely still, I had enjoyed it. Although what I had enjoyed more were the parts where I got to watch her as flour got in her hair, or the way she didn't even realize she had smears of icing on her cheek. The way she would bend every time she checked the oven in those Gods be damned yoga pants of hers! Pants that I knew she only wore to tease me, the vixen! And now that I had finally taken that phenomenal ass of hers... well, for now I knew the sheer erotic pleasure there was to be had in such a place.

All of these things combined led to a blissfully happy marriage that I had quickly become addicted to being a part of. Life was good. Better than good. It was fucking great! Hence why I didn't want a single thing to change that. But this then became my battling thoughts, for there was something that Amelia wanted and it was something that would disrupt this daily bliss. These warring thoughts that pushed against each other until eventually, I knew which one would win. Which was why this last gift I gave her, I knew was going to be the biggest yet, for nothing would beat it. Not even if I bought her every set of Lego ever created.

Although personally, nothing would ever beat the flower she'd had immortalized for me. For that had been like her handing over a piece of her heart. A piece of her soul represented, just like when giving her vows on our wedding day, for nothing could be more special. A gift I would treasure forever.

But now it was time for her gift in return and amazingly, I actually found myself nervous.

"What is it?" she asked like she always did, despite the very reason for wrapping up gifts being the surprise from opening them. However, I had already teased her enough throughout this gift giving ritual and major focus of the day.

"Open it and find out," I said gently, as she looked at the thin rectangular piece of wrapping.

"Is it a very thin book?" she asked, making me laugh,

"Just open it." Seriously, she was killing me here and now I knew what teasing her felt like when I had purposely gone slow at pulling off the paper. I looked around now, glancing at the others who had all finished with their own gifts, now focusing on the two of us. It was as if they all sensed this was a special moment. Like I was giving off a nervous vibe or something. Gods, but I was turning soft and did I fucking care…

Not. One. Fucking. Bit.

"Lucius? What is this?" she asked when finally she was past the paper and now looking down at the folder in her hands.

"Open it, Love," I said softly for the third time, before she did and the moment the architectural drawings came spilling out into her hand, a sudden realization dawned on her.

"Is this… is this really… really what I think it is?" she asked, her voice getting thick with the emotions I could see bubbling up, making her hands actually shake. Fuck but she had wanted this. *No, she had dreamed of this.* Which meant that I now knew that despite not wanting things to change, I had made the right decision. Because she deserved this. Deserved this type of happiness, and damn but it felt so fucking good to be the one able to give that to her.

"It is, wife," I told her with my own voice sounding strained as these new feelings made my chest feel tight.

"You… you… *you got me a museum?*" she asked in a tone that was utterly astonished, and the second I nodded, my own voice failing me as I saw the tears now swimming in her beautiful eyes as she suddenly launched herself in my arms.

"You got me a museum!" she shouted as the papers went everywhere but she didn't care. No, all she cared about in that moment was wrapping her arms around me and crying happy tears into my neck. My skin absorbed every single one like some soothing balm that was still healing the ragged edges of my soul that her leaving me had left behind. But slowly and surely, day by day, I would wake to find her still there with me and it would start to mend, filling me with ease that she was going nowhere.

That she loved me.

That she was still my wife and… *always would be.*

"Amelia, baby," I cooed after needing to clear my throat just so as I could speak past my own emotions, now cradling her head to me and seeing the affectionate looks her family were all giving us.

"You bought me a museum!" she shouted again, and once

more the tears started making me chuckle into her hair before kissing her forehead.

"It's all you asked me for," I told her, making her hiccup a strange sound, before telling me,

"No, I asked for Lego too, and you got me that as well!" she cried again, making me grin against the side of her head.

"Baby, don't cry," I told her, finally making her pull back so as she could look at me. Then she framed my face with her still shaking hands and said,

"You bought me a museum, how can I not cry? It's the best day of my life! Oh… apart from our wedding, so this is second best." I laughed at this and hugged her to me.

"Thank you, Lucius… a million times, thank you."

"You're welcome, my Khuba."

After this sweet, tender moment between us, the rest of the festivities commenced. Even her parents had offered me their thanks for making their daughter so happy. Something I didn't need to hear, but was nice all the same.

But these festivities included a Christmas dinner feast and I had to laugh, as all throughout it, Amelia was still asking me questions about the building I had bought ready to be turned into her museum. A building that was in Munich, meaning that most of our time would now be spent at Transfusion, which she didn't seem to mind at all. It actually helped ease my worry when she told me,

"As long as you are there, I will be happy anywhere." It had been said as such an absolute, such a definite, like this was so very obvious, it took me aback. Especially considering she had been casually eating at the time and my reaction made her drop her fork and knife with a clatter as I took her face in my hands and kissed her before she could take another mouthful. A dinner that, despite being delicious, was even better tasted on Amelia's lips.

Of course, I hadn't cared that this caused everyone to stop mid-conversation, no doubt now questioning what had caused such a reaction from me. I cared for nothing other than my gorgeous, perfect little Khuba, my sun, my Fated... *my wife.*

Fuck me but how I loved to call her this. Like the pinch I needed to remind me that it was all still true. That this wasn't just some perfect dream I would cruelly be woken from. That she was finally mine and nothing could ever change that.

As for her gift, I had shown her the plans I'd had drawn up for the project, telling her that as soon as we were home, we would set up all the meetings so we could get work underway. She would need to speak to the project manager, as well as the building company, the architect and the interior designers who would also be working on the build. She seemed more and more excited the more I talked about it, and not fazed by all the work ahead of her in any way.

Once dinner was over, she took some calls, one to wish her friend, Wendy, a Merry Christmas, promising to see her again soon. The other had been to her uncle Vincent and aunty Ari, who were away from Afterlife at the moment, for reasons unknown to me. But as soon as Amelia was back by my side, I had to laugh at the next question from her mouth.

"What are we going to call it?" At this I pulled her closer to my side and chuckled before kissing her. She was so fucking cute!

Hours after this and when the carved ornate grandfather clock was chiming twelve times, I found myself carrying my exhausted little wife back to her childhood room. My wife who had clearly had too much excitement and too much sugar for one day, as she didn't even stir when I finally laid her down on her ridiculous bed.

I, at the very least, took off her shoes, and covered her with a blanket, knowing that trying to get her naked right now would only wake her up. So, I decided to wait for this until I was joining her, but first I wished to speak with her father on a matter and thought there might not be another time better than now. Not considering his own wife had called it a night moments before I had carried Amelia to her juvenile bedroom. Dom had told her that he would join her soon, which meant I knew exactly where to find him.

"Let me guess, she passed out after too much sugar?" Dom asked the moment I entered his office. I couldn't help but grin when I saw that his office had not managed to escape his wife's Christmas madness as this space was yet another casualty. Even his fucking desk had tinsel around it.

"I take it this happens every year?" I asked in response to what sounded like an educated guess.

"Every year of her life," he replied, making me smirk as he handed me a glass of Cognac, and I recognized the signature bottle. The Louis XIII de Remy Martin, Rare Cask Grande Champagne Cognac, despite having such an annoyingly long name, was well known as being one of the best. It was also one of the most expensive, and the brand could easily boast as being an authority on this type of brandy. For starters, the spirits within this bottle were aged from forty to over hundred years. Meaning it was nice to see him breaking out the good stuff.

"This also happens at home. Thank the Gods she is no longer mortal for I fear that her teeth would not have lasted much beyond forty." He laughed at this before agreeing with me.

"Her mother has the same sweet tooth, and one I confess to indulging in, as well as I did with Amelia when she was a child and even at the fear of enduring Keira's wrath." I scoffed at this.

"I don't blame your apprehension at doing so, not after

witnessing the feared and famed Christmas menace for myself." At this Dom threw his head back and laughed, sipping back his brandy after saying,

"Fuck but how I do love my fearsome wife!"

"As for mine, she is resting peacefully, looking adorably cute." The words were out of my mouth before I could stop them, and I could tell that I had surprised him. However, I just shrugged my shoulders and told him in an unapologetic tone,

"And yes, before you say anything, I am most definitely aware that I am going soft, now ask me if I give a fuck."

"You gave my daughter a museum for Christmas, Luc, trust me, I already know you're going soft, but that is what us Kings do… we finally find our hearts and our humanity." He lifted his glass and made me raise my own, toasting the sentiment.

At this, Dom motioned for me to take a seat opposite his desk before taking his own behind it.

"But this also means I have no need to ask how married life is going, for I know all too well the affliction we Kings suffer willingly when meeting our Chosen Ones." I nodded to the decorated trees in his office and said,

"Indeed." To which he smirked and muttered,

"Still the same cocky bastard." At this, I raise my glass to him and took a sip in silent acknowledgement to that statement.

"But I sense you did not want to speak with me tonight to tell me how good life is." My reply to this was a sigh, before words followed.

"She's been having nightmares." He frowned before questioning,

"Oh?"

"She dreams of the Wraiths, Dom," I added, and when hearing this, Dom set his glass down slowly.

"From what you've told me about her connection with them, and after seeing it for myself when they aided us in battle at her will, then I can't say I'm surprised."

"I don't like it," I admitted feeling my body tense, as her dreams had been getting worse.

"I can quite honestly say, Luc, that I know exactly what you're going through." I raised a brow in question, making him continue,

"Keira's mind has always been so in tune with the future. The weight of the prophecy set against her shoulders was a constant reminder and this manifested in her dreams."

"Yes, but Amelia has fulfilled hers, so why does she still dream?" I asked, already knowing that Amelia had suffered from nightmares before, but it had never been like this… *not nearly every night.*

"Has she though?" he asked, making my frown deepen.

"What, you believe there is more? More for us to fucking endure?" I asked, the disbelief dripping from every word.

"As her father, my answer wants to instantly say, fuck no… like you said, she has endured-enough already. You both have. But as a King in our world, who knows…? But I do know this… only too often have I had to learn of the many paths the Fates do weave, and each one a bitter sting to endure. So, I give you this piece of advice and tell you this as a friend, *prepare yourself for anything."*

"I had a feeling you were going to say that," I said wryly, making him sigh back in his chair and retake his glass.

"I wish I had better news or better advice," Dom said, making me drink back the amber liquid that really needed to be savoured.

"Tell me, in these dreams, is she frightened?" he asked,

making me look down at the glass and swirl the liquid, releasing more of its mouth-watering scent.

"She tells me no, but I don't know for sure… although, if anything, she seems more frustrated," I told him.

"Frustrated?"

"She made a vow to all those trapped, lost souls, and it is one that she fears she will never fulfil. The weight of an entire nation is set up on her shoulders and, well, as Kings of our own kingdoms, we know how that feels." Dominic nodded, there were very few of us that would understand the true meaning of the weight of the world upon your shoulders as being more than just a throw away comment.

"She is young, Lucius, but what makes up for her lack of age is her ability to see beyond past mistakes. When the time is right, she will know what to do." Before I could say anything, he took my look for what it was, and said,

"And yes, I am quite well aware that my tune has changed. But then, after seeing what my daughter became on the battlefield, what she achieved, her strength and courage, her intelligence… Gods, but I will be the first to admit that I foolishly underestimated it."

"I can't argue with that," I said, helping myself to another refill and topping up his own glass while I was at it.

"Yes, well, hence the reason for my second piece of advice, one that is simple enough, for I only advise that you do not do the same… trust her, Lucius, trust in her abilities to do what is right for the future. For if there is a prophecy she is tied to, then it is a fight out of our hands. For if the Fates have taught me anything, it is that sometimes we fight in the shadows of our fear, instead of looking to the light and seeing that there lies the truth."

"And what truth is that, old friend?"

"That our Queens are fearless in the face of fighting for

what is right. They are pure of hearts, and pure of souls, despite what blood runs through their veins. They are the light and like you once told me, old friend…"

"We are but the moths attracted to their…"

"…Eternal flame."

CHAPTER 25
CHOSEN ONE CHOICES
AMELIA

'Aristeas in which you seek, find the Raven behind the door and we will speak…'

I woke with a start the moment I thought I heard the voice, and the name Aristeas was one that lingered in my mind. Now where had I heard of that name before?

"The Book!" I shouted before scrambling up from my bed and frantically looking for my bags. I also noticed that Lucius wasn't here, but I gathered he had been the one to carry me to bed. I hated to admit it, but that made this easier as I didn't have to suddenly explain my manic actions after waking up hearing that name.

"Voila, here it is!" I said the moment I found my oversized handbag that I had thankfully stuffed the book I had been reading on the plane into.

"Amissa regna et lapsus Urbes," I read out loud the title of the book, which was Latin for Lost Realms and Fallen

Cities. I quickly started scrolling through the old pages until seeing that name, one I thought I had recognized.

"It just has his name but nothing else..." I let my verbalized words trail off before I was standing and stuffing my feet back into the converse Lucius had obviously taken off me, having no time to add the socks because I needed to get to the family library before Lucius came back. Of course, to find me missing would no doubt send him into a bit of a panic, so I quickly scribbled down a note.

One that literally said,

'Don't worry, I couldn't sleep and decided to go find a book. Love you, handsome, x'

After this I slipped out and made my way to the library, pausing the second I heard the voice again, knowing this time that it hadn't just been in my dreams after all.

'Aristeas in which you seek, find the Raven behind the door and we will speak...' The moment I felt the voice calling for me, I knew that it would only lead me to answers. Of course, the last time I had been foolish enough to let a voice lead me anywhere, it had led me down into my father's prison. But this voice wasn't panicked or asking for my help. No, it was calm and almost soothing, and the moment it started to lead me into the library I knew my instincts had been right. I would finally find my answers to the biggest question of all.

How to gain access into the Realm of Hyperborea.

Hyperborea was more Greek mythology than anything else,

as all research led to it being half myth and half real. In fact, most of it seemed just like any other story as there was very little evidence to support it ever having existed. Of course, after my very physical experience with the Wraith Master, I know knew differently. For starters, the stories of how Hyperborea crumbled away into ruin were all told of being by a Volcanic eruption. A natural disaster, swallowing up its inhabitants and immortalizing their bodies just like it had at Pompeii.

But very few Supernaturals knew of the truth. That the beginning of the end started with a King driven mad by greed and jealously. The Realm that had been ruled by two brothers, a divided land that had only known peace before madness overtook one of their Kings.

King Theron wanted to be the only ruler and was planning to overthrow his brother's crown. But there was also another reason for this, as it was clear after their first meeting that King Phalaris, Theron's brother, had fallen in love with his wife. The jewel of the land, for it was said that she was the most beautiful woman in all the realm.

One now facing a life locked away as jealous rage filled her husband, becoming the first step taken toward starting a war. Which then ended with him making a deal with some Elemental version of the Devil, selling not only his own soul as payment, but also that of the entirety of his army.

And so, the Wraiths were reborn.

However, despite winning the war, especially seeing as after all Theron's men had all been killed, they simply rose once more and fought the winning side, only this time, they could not be beaten. Which meant that due to the curse, and now having no living ruler, one that would crush all who tried to claim the throne, the Hyperborean people were left to perish. This meant that with no living souls left in the Realm, the gateway closed and crumbled, feeling no life source to keep it open.

Of course, this had been the only information I had learned from endless hours spent studying lost realms. That the power of a gate depended on the life source behind it and seeing as the Wraiths were technically dead, then it seemed impossible. Of course, the Wraith Master had been the only one with the power to cast these lost souls out to different realms. But I learned far too late that this was only for a short time. Meaning that day in King Auberon's office, we had only needed to continue fighting them for a time and eventually they would have disappeared, for their time was limited.

But now I was the new Wraith Master, so I could do the same, having now being burdened with the same curse. What I couldn't do as a living person, was get there and set them free… *Or could I?*

I mean, this was the first time I had heard even a whisper or a hint that there might be something, so maybe the key had been in Afterlife all this time?

Once inside the library, I was thankful that I found it empty. However as soon as I closed the door behind me, I cried out in surprise as a book suddenly flew off one of the shelves and landed on the floor.

"Well, that's no coincidence," I muttered before walking over to it and reading the title aloud.

"Greek Poets? Oh my Gods, Greek Poets! Aristeas! That's where I know that name from," I shouted, only to gasp again as the book suddenly opened and the pages started turning so fast, it was like the book was possessed!

It finally stopped seconds later, now landing on the exact page I needed, making me look around the room in a wary way as if I half expected to find someone there watching me.

But then when no eyes were found spying on me from the ornately carved spiral staircases, I focused back on the page before bending over to retrieve the book.

I then walked over to one of the high wing-backed leather chairs and started to read what it said about Aristeas. It told the tale of him being a legendary Greek Poet dating back from the 7th century BC. A legend clearly not known to many as its only evidence seemed to be written in the Suda. The Suda was an ancient encyclopaedic text, written in Greek. Within this encyclopaedia was written knowledge of the ancient Mediterranean world, previously attributed to an author called Soudas, and held within it roughly thirty thousand entries. One of which was clearly, the story of Aristeas.

Now according to the Suda, it stated that Aristeas, had the power to detach his soul from his physical form and enter a new one. This was said to have first happened after Aristeas had entered a fuller's shop. Moments later and he suddenly dropped dead on the floor, causing the shop owner to shut the shop before telling his family what had happened. The report of the death spread throughout the town, but it was a death that was soon contradicted when a Cyzicenian traveller arrived from Artaca. He said that he had met Aristeas on his road to Cyzicus and had just not long ago spoken with him. The shop owner obviously denied this claim and encouraged the traveller to proceeded to his shop to see the body for themselves. However, the moment the shop was opened, Aristeas' body was nowhere to be found, either dead or alive.

But like I said, this was only the beginning of the story, as seven years later, Aristeas reappeared, and he continued to do so throughout the years. However, it was during one of these reappearances that the book spoke about a poem he had written. One that described in detail of a place known as

Hyperborea. But there were only accounts of it being written as the poem was lost almost as soon ink graced paper. A poem that, if the book was right, held the key I needed, for it spoke of how he entered the realm.

Of course, the book also said that even two hundred and forty years after his death, Aristeas was still reappearing. One example of this was when he was seen in Metapontum, situated in southern Italy. He apparently commanded that a statue of himself be made along with a new altar dedicated to the God Apollo. A God who he had claimed to have been travelling with since his death in the form of a sacred raven.

"A raven," I muttered, and the second I did a curious thing happened as the door to the Janus Temple suddenly opened and the same words were heard once more whispering from beyond it,

'Aristeas in which you seek, find the Raven behind the door and we will speak...'

"Okay, so I will play along," I said to myself as I shut the book, set it aside, and made my way over to the fireplace. I also found myself even more thankful that I was still alone so there was no one around to talk me out of this next chapter of craziness.

But I was getting desperate to rid myself of this curse, so I didn't question it, nor was I going to think back on the last time I did this only to discover how I had been fooled by Lucius's crazed ex-wife.

I also didn't know what it was exactly, but I just had feeling that I was meant to do this. That this was part of the Fates' plan, and that voice now was one I could trust. So, I let it lure me in, as if I was now listening to music from afar and the closer I got, the clearer those notes became. Because foreign words started to replace those that had first drawn me from sleep and to the library. Turning now into the most beautiful melody, and one I couldn't seem to get enough of. Like there was a whole Symphony inside the Temple playing a song that connected directly to my soul. One that could not be ignored.

So, I stepped through the opening inside the fireplace and answered its call with my actions. And just like last time, I was in total awe by the sight that met my eyes. The colossal space filled with endless possibilities behind each doorway, it was truly astounding to know how many realms and hidden worlds there were. How many places each door would lead to. How many prophecies lay in wait of but a single soul to step through the threshold, just like I was about to now.

Despite Lucius wanting to believe my dreams would one day fade away, I knew the truth. Because I had once believed my own prophecy had been fulfilled, but what if I was wrong?

Perhaps this was only the first chapter of a new one. One that started right here and right now. So, I continued on, now following the path that the song led me to. The gentle hum of foreign words I didn't understand like a spell I welcomed to be cast upon me.

I tried not to let myself be distracted by each door I passed. Be it, doors with their shattered glass or nothing but twisted roots reminding me of the Tree of Souls. There were some that didn't even look like doors at all, covered in paper flowers made from the pages of torn books. Ones of jagged metal, or melting plastic, whatever it may be, each told a story without a title I could read.

Because almost all of them held some sort of symbol, whether it be on a keystone above or some hidden symbol forcing my eyes to scan each door to see if I could find them all. It wasn't surprising that I couldn't find every one but nevertheless, it kept my mind occupied as I tried. My father's vault hadn't been too far away from his own door that led straight into Afterlife. But one look back to see how far I had travelled, and I realized it was most likely too far to be safe as I could no longer see it.

Again, this should have frightened me, or at least made me ill at ease, but I wasn't. Maybe it was foolish to trust this feeling so much, but I no longer cared. Because that's what happened when you gained as much power as I had done on that battlefield. You felt more invincible, as though nothing could touch you. Once again, it might have been foolish to believe this but then again, I had always been brave and reckless. Although, now having more power to face my enemies with wasn't ever going to help quell that particular quality in my personality. Much to Lucius's dismay.

However, the moment the magical chanting sound stopped, so did I, knowing this time I was to face the door my trusting footsteps had brought me to.

"Can it be?" I questioned aloud as I looked up at an exquisite white door calved out of what looked like bleached wood... One that held a white raven at its centre. But its origins I instantly recognized and were easy to see after spending time there myself. Which was why I reached out and ran my fingers along the outline of the raven, knowing this was the clue. This action caused the elvish writing adorning the wooden frame to shimmer. Then the words started to glow a brighter white as if my touch had powered them. After this, they started to move, now spinning faster and faster before the light was so bright, I had no choice but to shield my eyes.

However, when I saw the bright glare disappear, I removed my arm and finally was given time to make out more details, as the door had changed into a simple wooden door. It was as if a glamour of some sort had just been lifted.

So, I did the only thing I could think to do, seeing as it was a door without any handles.

I knocked.

"Should I have done it three times?" I asked aloud when nothing happened. However, it was as if I just needed to allow time for someone to answer it. As suddenly the door opened and the very last person I ever expected to see today was now standing there.

This making me shout…

"Vena!"

CHAPTER 26
ANCIENT THREADS TO PULL

"Vena!" I shouted the moment I saw her waiting for me, standing in her own family's library, one that was like something out of a fairytale. And speaking of fairytales, Vena, as usual, was dressed like some fair maiden and was still one of the cutest girls I had ever seen. Her dark, pink coloured, medieval style dress matched her hair perfectly, although it was clear that she had tried to tame the wild mass of dark waves into twists pinned at the back of her head. The point of her ears could be seen poking through the deep purple strands that eventually turned from raspberry red to pastel pinks at the tips.

But her big dark eyes that matched her hair, widened in excitement before she threw herself into my arms.

"Amelia!" she shouted in an emotional voice as it was clear she was happy to see me. I had to try not to laugh when I noticed the coloured splats on her dress as it was clear she had been painting recently.

"I wasn't sure you'd come… I mean, she said you would, and if anybody knew you would then it would be the Oracle of light… I missed you so much, it's been awfully droll here without you! And my brother said that you won the war?" All of this came out in a barrage of words, and I couldn't help but laugh.

"We did win the war, yes, but we have so much to catch up on and I have to say, I'm so glad to see you again, my friend. I have missed you… I have missed our talks," I told her, making her beam at me again, her already rosy cheeks deepening in colour.

"As have I, dear friend."

"The only problem I have is that I don't know how much time I have here," I confessed, knowing that if Lucius found me gone, he would be manic, and I didn't want to do that to him. Not after last time.

"No one knows you have come?" she asked, surprised.

"I fear if they did, they would not have let me," I confessed.

"You, of course, speak of your Vampire," she guessed, making me grin before telling her,

"Yes, who is now my husband." At this her eyes grew wide, before a dreamy sigh escaped her.

"Husband! Congratulations, I am so happy for you, for anyone could see that you loved each other very much." I couldn't help but smile at her childlike innocence, wishing more than anything the same type of love would find her also.

"Thank you."

"I cannot say I am surprised that he would not have allowed you to come, as I fear this place does not hold great memories for either of you," she reminded me, making me repress a shiver at the memory.

"You are the very best memory I have of this place and despite what happened, nothing will ever change that, Vena," I said, making her beam at me.

"Gosh, but I don't know what to say to that."

"As long as it isn't piss pots, then I will take it." At this we both burst out laughing before we heard someone clearing their throat in the background. This was when Vena moved to one side and allowed me to see who I assumed to be the Oracle of light.

"She looks quite different since when she first arrived," Vena added this as a whisper at my back, a whisper I had no doubt the woman in front of me now could still hear. Of course, I had never met her before as Lucius had purposely kept me away. But he had told me of her and also, the state she had been in when she first arrived. Which was no doubt why Vena had thought to mention it, as clearly the wild forest woman Lucius had described was no more.

No, now she looked more like some Grecian goddess only tarnished by old age. A woman who looked to be in her late seventies, with stark white hair twisted back from her face in plaits that had been entwined with pale vines. Her dress was pure white, with a forest green cloak around her shoulders that looked as if it had been made with moss, meaning clearly some wild elements had remained. A headdress of white thorns and small antlers had been entwined together with tiny thin, red roots and a single clear crystal was decorating its centre.

"I have been healed by the grace of our great Goddess Fjörgyn of the Earth," the woman said, bowing her head as if giving her respect to the name.

"But despite being known as the Oracle of Light, the Goddess has bestowed upon me to become once more, you can know me as Elswyth." At this I nodded my head, and replied,

"It is nice to meet you, I am Amelia…"

"Yes, I know who you are, stone bringer."

"Stone bringer?" I asked, making her ignore this and

usher me over to a seating area as I could see she was relying heavily on a stick of twisted root. One that was so white it looked as if it had been bathed in bleach.

"Come, sit, sit, for I may be healed but these old bones won't last forever, and even less should I be made to stand for too long. But of course, I knew you would come, for you still have answers you seek... yes?"

"I do," I replied at the same time taking her arm and helping her sit back into her chair, making her pat my hand and say,

"Kind girl, yes, yes, you have heart and courage enough for it."

"For what?" I asked but before answering me, she looked to my friend.

"Vena, be a sweet girl and fetch me some of that sweet leaf tea, would you?" Vena nodded before bowing and then coming to me to take my hands,

"I will be back, it takes some time to brew, but I will hurry, for despite wishing daily that you could stay longer, I know you most likely won't be able to," she said, and my heart broke for her, wishing our friendship was an easier one, as I couldn't even say when the next time would be that I would see her. But as for right now, I squeezed her hand and told her,

"I will stay for as long as I can." She smiled at this, looking pleased before nodding her head and leaving us alone.

"I wanted to thank you for what you did for me," I said taking my seat opposite her, but at this she raised a brow and told me,

"I believe my thanks will soon be equal, for your journey is not over yet, but you know this, or you would not have followed my call." I had guessed as much that she was behind the whispered words and music I had followed.

"I've been having dreams," I told her.

"Dreams of a lost kingdom, one filled with nothing more than the bones of the dead and trapped souls you are now charged with setting free," she said not having to guess.

"Yes, at first they called to me, and I would wake feeling helpless."

"But then the dreams changed," she said as if knowing all of this, making me wonder if it would be rude to just ask her skip to the end, as I was kind of on a time limit here. She must have guessed where my thoughts were.

"We have time, my dear child, for this realm is vastly different from your own and therefore, by the time you're back in your room of knowledge, it will be mere minutes gone by… so do not fret." Hearing this I visibly relaxed, allowing the tension to leave my shoulders as I sank further back into my seat.

"Yes, the dreams changed, as now my own death haunts me."

"Then he is feeling even more threatened by you," Elswyth said, making me frown in question.

"The Wraith Master?"

"His essence is in you, child, and his memory still locked to that realm, just like the others are." At this I was shocked.

"You mean he will be there still, in that realm?" I asked, knowing now that this complicated things further, as well… the guy utterly terrified me!

"He is also a Wraith like the others and as you know, you cannot kill a Wraith, only set their souls free."

"But I ate his heart and the cut it out of his physical body!" I shouted, making the old woman raise a withered, gnarled hand.

"Yes, you did, but that only took his power over the other Wraiths away, for his body may not remain as it once did, but he will live on as a Wraith as the others do, despite no longer being their King or their master."

"I don't even know how to find them to set them free. Whether the gateway to Hyperborea even still exists?" At this she sighed before telling me,

"There is a way, but it will be far from easy. Its key remains, and always will do, back behind that door." I looked behind me and asked,

"You mean in the Janus Temple, is there a door to Hyperborea?"

"I am afraid that particular realm wanted to remain hidden since the dawn of its time," she replied, making me feel like rubbing my forehead and asking for mercy here.

"So, there is not a door?"

"There never was in there, no…"

"Then I don't understand!" I said, frustrated and irrupting her.

"Just because they never recognized the Fates as being their Gods, it doesn't not mean they weren't watching all the same. For the Temple of Janus may not hold a door, but that isn't to say there wasn't a doorway created." At this I raised my head from where I had let it slump into my hand, with my elbow at the armrest.

"There is still a way?"

"Yes, but like I said, the key to accessing such a door involves not only the Fates, but the God of it all." I sucked in a quick breath at what she could be implying.

"Janus?" She bowed her head once at this before asking me a strange question,

"Tell me of your mother."

"My mother?" I repeated, wondering why she would ask me about my mother.

"Your mother was a prophesized Chosen One, was she not?"

"Yes," I answered in a wary tone.

"And the first of her kind, but certainly not the last," she added, and again her words made me grow cautious.

"What do you mean?"

"A Chosen One's prophecy never really ends, it only holds the threads for others to pull. You, Amelia, are a vessel for the Fates just as I am, and they care greatly about those threads that you bring along for your journey." I started to shake my head at this.

"I don't understand, what are you trying to say exactly?"

"That your mother's prophecy has not finished and neither has yours, but perhaps, this time, three threads have merely been entwined into one."

"You mean two," I corrected, making her grin at me and it was a little unnerving, especially when she said,

"Perhaps not, or perhaps I mean exactly what I say, child." I thought on this for a moment, not knowing what to say. As it stood, the Oracle had a lot left to say.

"Your mother once had a choice. A journey she chose to make and one that undoubtably changed the course of the future, for not only one realm, but for many unseen. I believe now the Fates are putting that same weight upon your shoulders, my dear."

"That's not very reassuring," I muttered, making her smirk.

"Yes, and like your mother, you can also choose to walk away. You can choose to let the souls of Wraiths spend an eternity locked to the curse of their king and you can be your

Vampire's Queen and live your life in peace… it is your choice," she told me, making me shake my head and say,

"Well, I can't do that." At this she grinned and said,

"I didn't think so… but in case you change your mind, know this, if you choose that peaceful life, that will be another path the Fates did not account for and therefore it will affect many branches from that journey onwards." Again, this wasn't reassuring in the slightest, but I understood it all the same, which was why I replied,

"I understand, you're saying that I will be affecting the Fates of others," I said, making her nod, before tapping her fingers on the twisted knot of the stick that looked as if it was missing something inside its rooted cage.

"We are all connected one way or another, and your journey where it may be your end, for others it is just the beginning, but that journey cannot start without the completion of your own." This is when I finally got it, or more to the point, why I was here at all.

"I'm connected to the Elemental realm?" At this her grin grew even bigger.

"You are clever indeed, my girl, but yes, there was a reason that you were led here in the beginning. For if that gate had never opened and you hadn't been pushed in, finding yourself in these lands, then you would have never been tied to the Wraiths, and in turn, an important branch that leads to this realm would not have been made for another Chosen One to walk its path." I thought on this and frowned, as I had to say the weight on my shoulders seemed to be growing by the minute.

"Are you saying that by coming here, I've changed the prophecy in the Elemental realms?"

"I'm saying you pulled on a different thread and now you've got to decide whether to leave it be, leaving us to our own Fate, or to keep pulling, and lead us to where it was perhaps always Fated to be." I swallowed hard, refraining from making jokes or asking how she got the job of being cryptic for a living.

"I know what I must do," I said instead.

"Then I will give you this, for it will aid you on your journey, an important key, and one I believe you have been searching for…" She said before pulling a rolled-up piece of scroll from her long sleeves.

"Is this really what I think it is?" I asked in awe, as I started to unroll it.

"I now know that it was always Fated to be left in our hands."

"This is Aristeas's lost poem… here is his name," I uttered before I started reading it and making sense of the old text.

"It speaks of a stone tablet, one now broken after the fall of Hyperborea, one with three languages known to mortal man and one of a hidden land, now lost to the madness of its king… But three languages, that must be… Gods, it's the Rosetta stone, he speaks of the Rosetta stone!" I shouted, getting excited and making the old lady smile.

"Then it is a thread worth pulling?"

"Yes, but the language is obviously on the missing piece but I… well, nobody knows where the missing piece is," I told her, making her suggest,

"Then maybe you have to work backwards through time."

"Time… *time is the key,*" I said before looking back at the door that led to the Janus Temple.

"The past, the key is in the past," I said again, and she bowed her head for she didn't need to say it for me to figure out myself.

"Then I know where I have to go."

"I believe you do, but know this, child, the past can be a dangerous place, for those you love today may not be there as you know them in the yester year." I knew she was talking about Lucius and the thought made me shudder, because the biggest flaw in this plan was my Husband. Someone who would never let me do something this dangerous and crazy.

"I understand. But I need to know, what of the prophecy of this realm, how will I know what I'm looking for in order to help you?" At this she rose from her seat and came over to stand next to mine. Then she patted my shoulder and told me,

"You will know, for those that choose to walk the path of destiny never miss the guiding light…"

"Illuminating their way."

CHAPTER 27
A NEW PATH

The moment I stepped back inside the Temple I could already start to feel its pull, as if it wanted me to find its core. The one gate that powered it all. Especially now I knew...

That the Fates weren't finished with me quite yet.

So, after an emotional goodbye to Vena, who I had at least managed to get to spend a little time with, I was now making my way back to the door that would lead me home. Because as much as the Janus Gate was trying to pull me further toward its rabbit hole, I knew there were things I needed to do first.

I even found nervous laughter bubbling up out of me at the thought of what I was planning to do. Because as a historian and somebody who had dedicated their life to history, I couldn't help but be excited by the idea. But then I also knew that I would be foolish not to be also terrified by it. However, the overruling emotion that I did have, was the one thought I kept coming back to...

Lucius.

I loathed the thought of keeping anything from him,

especially something as huge as this. After all, our secrets had been the reason for most of the mistakes we had both made in the past. But then again, hadn't those secrets also led us down a path to a future where the outcome had been in our favour? Because I had to question, what would have happened had I never stepped through the Tree of Souls portal and gone into Hell?

I thought about how many people's lives it had affected in a positive light. The McBain brothers had their souls returned to them for the part they played. Nero had become an elevated member of Lucius's council, despite her decision to stay in Hell for the time being.

But even this meant that she was now considered as being under the protection of the crown. As for Carn'reau, he had been reunited with his brother and after being in their Realm, I had started the potential path for their own prophecy. A war that I knew they still needed to win, and one Lucius and I had vowed to aid them in whenever the time came. And really, what better way to aid them now than to continue along my journey and potentially find this key the Oracle of Light had spoken of.

I even thought about Lucius's brother, as he had finally stepped out of the shadows and had the freedom to join our family by Lucius's side, now known as more than just his second in command in Hell. The blood of the Devil and a King in his own right. But mainly I had to think what would still be happening now if I hadn't taken that first step down what I knew at the time would be a dangerous path. Would the Tree of Souls still weep, losing its leaves as each soul became infected? Would his brother still be creating an army to defeat not only Lucius, but one with the power to take over all of Hell?

Would Lucius have lost the war?

All of these things happened in the wake of what had first been assumed to be a mistake made on my part. Meaning everything you did in life you could be put down to simple coincidence or you could convince yourself it all would have happened the way it was meant to, regardless of what you did. But I didn't believe in that, not after everything that had transpired due to reckless mistakes made. Because throughout history, some of the biggest mistakes ended up becoming a serendipitous event. Our mistakes didn't define us, they simply made us stronger to face the destiny that sometimes those mistakes are forged by.

I knew I had a choice. I could trust Lucius with knowing the journey I was about to undertake and risk the potential outcome. This of course being me locked away in a tower and prevented from stepping foot in this temple ever again. Or I could simply make the journey without his knowledge, in hopes that I would get back to my own time with the proof that I needed that it was all prophecy after all.

That it was all simply meant to be.

After all, sometimes as a Chosen One it was easier to ask for forgiveness than for permission and my mother knew this better than most. I released a heavy sigh as I made it back to the bookcase, stepping through and releasing my next heavy sigh for a very different reason. This in the wake of hearing my mother shout,

"See! I told you, my dreams don't lie!" This was aimed at Pip and Sophia, who were still dressed as they had been for Christmas day. Whereas my mother was in her Christmas pyjamas and those jolly little Santa's might have looked happy, but my mother certainly wasn't. As I now had some explaining to do. Hence why I started off by saying quickly,

"I can explain." However, the moment I said this, three female family members all faced me and folded their arms at the same time. Of course, Pip was slightly more naughty looking with it, as she had a hip cocked out and was wearing a black T-shirt she'd bought herself as a present, that I admit looked a bit tame for Pip as it simple said,

'I'm Peace'

Of course, she wore this with leggings that were the same pattern you would get on a Christmas sweater, making them look knitted. With this she also had on a pair of mad boots that looked like Santa's snowy workshop was making its way up her leg and the heels were actual little Santa's.

My mother, however, unfolded her arms so she could take a different stance, now mirroring Pip and cocking out a hip, placing a hand to it.

"Let me guess, it didn't have anything to do with your father's vault this time," my mum said, making me wince.

"Ooh, ooh, if we are playing the guessing game, can I go…? I am going to guess that you found a door," Pip said after clapping and making one of her miniature candy canes she had glued to her fingernails spring off and go flying off somewhere in the room. She watched it land and then just shrugged her shoulders.

"Really, Pip, that's what you've got, she's just come from a literal Temple of doors!" my auntie Sophia said, who was still wearing a gorgeous green velvet dress that flared at the skirt and had a belt of black ribbon high at the waist. Naturally, her comment made me smirk.

"Okay fine, but my other guess was really out there, I mean it's not like she wants to go back in time or anything… Ooooh… erm… *her bad?*" At this my mother's eyes grew wide, shooting first a look of horror to Pip and then back to me.

"Oh no, please tell me my dream wasn't true," my mum said.

"Er, that depends, what did you dream?"

"I dreamed of you going through a door that looked like it belonged in a Lord of the Rings movie, meeting a pretty girl with raspberry hair…"

"Oooh Rad… sound like a cool chi… erm, sorry, please continue," Pip said before my mum did in fact continue,

"Then there was an old lady wearing a garden lawn around her shoulders, with a crown of twigs and you were both talking about going back into the past." It was at this point that I released a sigh, walked over to take her hand, and then I said,

"Mum, I think it's time you sit down."

"Well, that's never a good sign," Pip muttered, and my only thought was… no, no it never was.

∽

A little time later…

I had just finished telling Sophia, Pip, and my mum all there was to know about my dreams, the Wraith Master, and now about what the Oracle of Light had just told me. Naturally, this was a lot to take in. Hence why my mum started chanting,

"No no, no, no… please tell me this is not what you have in mind?" my mother asked, making me sigh as Pip leaned in and said,

"Sorry, Toots, but that sigh isn't a good sign either." My mother shot her a look over her shoulder and Pip held up her hands, doing so quick enough that she lost two more candy canes this time.

"I have no choice, Mum, surely you can understand that?"

"That's where you're wrong, you always have a choice," she argued, making me throw logic of her own double past back in her face,

"And you, Mum, did you have a choice when you stepped through that fountain?" Hearing this and she flinched, and I knew that I had her trapped in her own argument.

"Oh come on, Keira, did you really expect her not to use that one?" my aunt said, coming to my defence.

"Okay, so that's not helping... and you, young lady, it's not the same thing, Amelia," my mum said.

I knew she was only worried about me and considering she had experience in this past jumping department, then I couldn't say that I blamed her.

"But you're wrong. You had a duty, just like I do."

"I was prophecy bound," she threw back, making me scoff,

"And you think I'm not?" At this Pip and Sophia started to look slightly awkwardly toward one another.

"Maybe we should just leave you two to..." My aunt Sophia tried to say, only she was quickly stopped in her tracks,

"Oh no, you two are not going anywhere. You are having my back on this." At this Sophia and Pip once more looked at each other, making me frown.

"Okay, so what am I missing here?" Sophia sighed and scooted her chair closer to my mum, so she could place her hand over my mother's before telling her,

"Amelia is right, the prophecy isn't finished. It isn't finished for either of you."

"What?!" My mother's disbelief was easy to read in that one screeched word alone.

"What are you not telling me, Sophia?" my mum accused, shooting eyes to Pip who put her hands behind her back and started whistling, now focusing on anything but my mother. This meant that it was then left up to Sophia to explain.

"Pythia, may have mentioned something like this might happen."

"What?!" Again, my mother was gaining a higher pitch each time she shouted this.

"Okay, so the time she spoke of us being back in time… it kind of didn't… I mean it wasn't so much…" My mum rolled her eyes and said,

"Spit it out, Sophia."

"We thought the Oracle made a mistake or you did when we went through that gate and ended up in the desert, when she said it was all like fields of green and knights with big swords, et cetera, et cetera… what, I cracked okay," Pip aimed this last part to Sophia who was holding the bridge of her nose like my father did when he was frustrated. Oh, and all of this was after delivering this information bomb.

"Are you serious… I got the date wrong?" she questioned, shaking her head as if she couldn't understand it.

"I'm sure it can happen to anyone," Pip said in a sweet, endearing way.

"Yeah, but this isn't like forgetting your anniversary," my mum argued.

"Aww has he still not forgiven you, because that was like once and ten years ago," Pip said, patting my mum's back making her sigh,

"No, he has… wait, so not important right now… why didn't you two tell me?" This time it was my aunt Sophia who answered.

"Because we won the war, we beat the bad guys, and the time we went back to worked. We just figured that if anything else popped up after that, we would tell you."

"Which brings us to now," Pip said, sticking her head in between them both and whispering this obvious part.

"So, what? You're now saying I have to go back to the past, that me and Amelia have always been destined to do this?" At this I took my mum's hand and gave it a reassuring squeeze.

"It will be fine, Mum, we will be together."

"Er excuse me, aren't you forgetting somebody?"

"Yeah, like two bodacious time traveling babes," Pip added to this cry of outrage by Sophia, now shaking a thumb in between the two of them.

"Wait, what are you saying?" I asked in a confused tone. This is when Sophia stood and seeing as Pip was already bouncing on her feet, it made and me and my mum both stand with them. Then Sophia placed a hand on each of our shoulders and said,

"What? You didn't really think we'd let you guys go alone, did you?" I looked to my aunties and then to my mum, who released a big heavy sigh.

"Okay fine, I'm in, but only because Amelia is and not because any Oracle told me to."

"She's not gonna let this wrong date thing go, is she?" Pip muttered to Sophia, who was shaking her head and only stopped again when my mum looked back at her no longer giving Pip a glare.

"So, we are really doing this… we are going back in the past?" I said as I looked at the four of us, wondering how the Hell we were gonna pull this shit off.

"Great, anyone have any idea what time period we're going back to…? God, please let there be a toilet and toothbrushes." I laughed at this, secretly wishing the same thing as my mum.

"If you'd have asked me an hour ago, I would never have

been able to guess but now…" I paused, handing over the poem the Oracle of Light had given me.

"…now I'm thinking it has something to do with the Rosetta stone." Sophia granted a look to my mother.

"What…? Oh come on, what am I missing now?" I asked, making my mother sigh.

"I've been dreaming of a stone cracking, pieces of it being used as foundation, light forming around it. I haven't wanted to tell your father but, well… let's just say now I'm not surprised why."

"Er, on that cheery marital note, so about our husbands?" Pip said, rolling her hand around.

"Oh shit, yeah, we're not telling them," Sophia said.

"No way," I replied.

"Yeah, definitely not," came my mum's reply.

"Okay cool, so all on the same page then… Gotcha. Well I would say girly road trip but…" Pip said, making my mum and me raise a finger to her and say at the same time,

"Don't go there, Pip."

"Oh yeah, say it, Pip." As the major movie Geek in the house, of course I was the one encouraging this.

"Oh I sooo am gonna, my friend… '*cause where we're going, we don't need roads…*' What? I'm sorry, okay, Toots? It just had to be done… I mean, there's gonna be a lot of Back to the Future references here so it would be best if we all just get used to it now, okay?" Pip said, making the other two groan as I just high fived her.

"So, we're really going to do this then, we're really gonna go back in time?" I asked, needing them to be absolutely sure about this.

"We are not letting you do this alone… so yeah, I guess we are," Sophia replied, whereas my mum hugged me to her and said,

"You're definitely not alone."

"Woohoo and the time travelling boobateers are back in business!"

"Yeah, I'm so not going if she's going to do that the whole time," Sophia said in response to Pip's excitement and really, I had no idea who the Boobateers were.

"Are they like, a band or something?" I asked, making my mum shake her head at me from behind Pip.

"What? I mean, it won't be the same without big, bummed beauty Ari," Pip added, thankfully missing my question about it being a band.

"Wait, aunty Ari went with you last time?" At this my mum sighed, took my hand and said,

"It's a long, long, long... like the longest story in history... and clearly, it's still going on and apparently never wants to end. It is literally, the never-ending story," my mum said dramatically, making me say,

"Okay, Mum, I get the idea."

"So, we're all in agreement we say nothing to the husbands?" I iterated, thinking it was best we were concrete on this fact.

"Oh shit, they're gonna be so mad when we get back."

"Pip, that shouldn't make you look happy," Sophia pointed out.

"Hey, I don't know about your husbands, but my husband when I'm naughty well, let's just say stuff can get pretty interesting, and when I say interesting, I mean kinky shit... like a whole sex shop of kinky, like suspended ropes and tools, and not even the type that you'd think would work but they totally do... like a whisk, you would be surprised at what else you can do with a whisk," Pip said, making us all groan.

"Okay please stop with the kinky talking now, we get it,

you're kinkier than shit and like the kinkiest Imp in all the land," Sophia said, making her pluck her fingers at her T-shirt with both hands and say in a cocky proud voice,

"Yes, yes I am."

"So just to be clear, and getting back to this poem. We need to go back before the Rosetta stone was even moved, before it got broken... right?" I nodded at Sophia's question.

"Yeah, and when was that exactly?" my mum asked, making Pip quickly shake her fingers at me and said,

"And if you could say it like Doc Brown does in the movie, that would be great." I released a sigh and did as she asked...

"Back to the year, 1202."

CHAPTER 28
PAINFUL GOODBYE

"Are we interrupting something?" the sound of my father's voice the second the door opened made all four of us turn and instantly look guilty.

Because that was the problem with our family, there was only one of us that held the title as being cool, calm, and collected when it came to lying. Meaning that three of us instantly made the mistake of looking toward Sophia. It was as if we all knew who to rely on in this tense moment. I swear she was most likely in half a mind to roll her eyes before that cool facade swept over her features like a veil. Then she causally rose from her seat, walked gracefully up to my father, and then after patting his chest, simply told him,

"We might have been having girl talk, and it might have included our men… Speaking of which, after all the deliciously naughty things we have just spoken about, I'm in mind to go and find mine. Ladies, until our next talk." Then she granted us a wink and walked out the room. My mother and I both released a sigh of relief whereas Pip giggled and skipped to Adam. Of course, the second I saw his T-shirt it dawned on me, as his own matched Pip but his words read…

'I come in Peace.'

"Oh, right, I get it now," I said, making her wink back at me before wagging her brows at her husband and saying,

"The T-shirts have spoken." Then she turned to face us, threw her hands up in the air and gave us some devil horns with her fingers in a rock symbol before saying,

"Later, me biatches!" After this my mother and I both looked at each other, laughed and then looked to our two brooding husbands as they strode toward us with purpose.

"Amelia," Lucius breathed my name into my cheek, before hooking an arm around my back and guiding me up and out of the chair into his arms, now growling down at me,

"What have I told you about not finding you where I left you, Pet?"

"Most likely what I have told you about not being a fan of you leaving me in bed alone," I countered, making him run the backs of his fingers down my cheek and said a soft,

"Touché, Sweetheart."

"I woke up and you weren't there. So what else was a girl to do?"

"…but come to a library," he finished off for me, making me also point out,

"Besides, I did leave you a note this time, so you have to give me brownie points for that and well, it was rather the library or starting my next Lego set. But then I feared falling asleep halfway through and then you waking me up when you howl in agony after stepping on the pieces making your way back to the bed. So really, I was just being incredibly thoughtful…" I paused at this point, now getting up on my tip toes so I could reach his face and walk my fingers up his chest before then whispering over his lips,

"You're welcome."

I knew he couldn't stay angry any longer as his lips twitched before forming a definite grin.

"How very thoughtful indeed."

"Whoa!" I shouted out when he swept me up into his arms and turned to my parents who were having their own flirty conversation.

"If you'll excuse us, I believe it's time I get my wife to…"

"Yes, yes, she's still my daughter, Luc, which means I don't want to hear any statement that ends with the word bed," my father said, flicking his hand out as if hoping we would leave before any more mental images infected his mind. He already had one memory he had no doubt tried very hard to forget, we didn't want to give him any reminders of it.

"In that case, we will simply say good night," Lucius said with a bow of his head, making me shout just as we walked through the door,

"…and go to bed!" I could hear my mum's laughter after I had teased my father, chuckling when I heard him groan. However, it was when we were walking down the corridor that Lucius also joined in this merriment and chuckled, making me ask,

"And just what do you find so amusing, Mr Septimus?"

"Your father is currently blaming your mother for your inherited humour." I laughed.

"But of course he would… sucks that your hearing is better than mine," I muttered, grumbling and making him grin down at me. Then he continued to carry me to bed just like he said he would and for one of us, it would be the last time in I don't know how long. Which was why as soon as he stepped through my door, I placed my palm to his cheek and whispered,

"Make love to me." He seemed taken aback a moment but whatever his thoughts were on this request, he kept them

silenced so that he could grant my wish. Meaning this was also the sweetest torture as he laid me down and slowly stripped me of my clothes, his actions now gentle and tender.

And were exactly what I needed in that moment.

Which was also why after we had finished making love, finding our joint release while looking into each other's eyes, I had to fight my tears when he placed his forehead to mine and whispered,

"Merry Christmas, my wife."

That night I had gone to sleep silently crying, being careful not to wake Lucius with my tears. I let the guilt carry me through the night knowing that in only a few hours, I would be leaving him, and I didn't even know for how long. I hated having to do this to him, knowing he would find out as soon as I got back. Because I would have never been able to keep such a thing from him.

But our time apart for him would only seem like minutes whereas for me, well... like I said, *I just didn't know.* So, what he hadn't known when saying goodnight to him and telling him I loved him, just like I did every night, was actually also my...

Painful goodbye.

～

A little time later and when it was still dark out, I took one last look at Lucius, resisting the urge to reach out and touch him. Resisting the urge to place my lips to his for one last kiss. But I couldn't dare chance it, so I slipped out of bed, knowing the others would be doing the same. We decided this was the only opportunity we would likely have and if caught, we could just say that we were going to get a drink of water or something.

We were to meet back in the library and so as Lucius didn't stir, I gathered up my clothes and stepped out, getting changed in the hallway. Thankfully, it was empty, or someone might have wondered why I was naked and slowly putting my jeans on like I was expecting my clothes to start biting me or something.

I then hurried to the library, meeting my mother on the way. She was also wearing a pair of jeans and a long-sleeve black T-shirt, just like I was. Although we had managed to make some plans last night, one of which was what we would wear and what we could get away with taking. Naturally, Pip and Sophia had been on costume duty, seeing as we didn't have anything suitable for where, or should I say when, we were going.

"I am starting to think this really is Fated as your father never sleeps this deep," my mother said, voicing her fears that she thought she was going to get caught. I then patted her hand in silent encouragement, knowing that all four of us were going to find this part hard. The guilt weighed on us all.

"Let's go," I said, opening the door and finding Pip and Sophia already inside.

"I just hope good old Fatey man is feeling generous with what we are allowed to take through," Pip said, throwing a long gown around her shoulders and adding a black wig to cover up her green and red hair, which she had dyed specially for Christmas day.

"That reminds me, I found a pair of your extra glasses, although the prescription might be a bit weaker but hopefully you don't need them and here's an unopen pack of contacts, with your case and a bottle of solution and..." I laughed before taking the stuff from her,

"Mum, it's okay, my eyes are fine now, remember?" This was when my mum gave me a strange look and said,

"Please, just take them, okay? It's just in case." I nodded knowing it would make her feel better, so I created a bundle with the dress Pip handed me, placing the stuff inside and now using it as a bag after tying the sleeves.

"Here, I brought us these... okay so they were left over from last year's Halloween party, but they will help us fit in and fight off the weather... *wherever we end up,"* Sophia said, muttering this last part, and my mum gave her wry look in return as she took two of the long black cloaks that were hooded and made from thick polyester with a satin lining. Meaning Sophia was right, they would work well to keep us hidden and against whatever weather we might encounter.

Pip and Sophia put on theirs and we started to look like we about to join some cult.

"Well, it is believed to have been on display at a temple at Sais," I said, as my mum struggled with getting her cloak tied.

"Sais was the capital of Egypt in about six hundred and sixty-four to five hundred and twenty-five BC..."

"Seriously, how does she remember this stuff?" Pip commented as I carried on,

"It's located is on the western Rashid Branch of the Nile, halfway between Cairo and Alexandria."

"Erm, so Egypt then?" my mum clarified with a smirk.

"Yeah, Egypt, and we have to go back before the Mamluk period, as that's what new evidence suggests is when it was moved... and yes, before you ask, that's how I got the right date," I replied, making my mum do her class hand raise and 'I was just asking' look.

"But it was found in Fort Julien, right?" Sophia was tightening her boots, as we had all agreed good footwear was a must until we needed to ditch them to fit in. Of course, after she said this, Pip whistled, making Sophia roll her eyes and say,

"I do remember most things, and besides, I was around for most of this shit… older than the lot of you, remember?" This was when she smirked and pointed a finger at all of us.

"It was eventually used as building material in the construction of Fort Julien near the town of Rashid, which was also known as Rosetta, in the Nile Delta. It was discovered in July 1799 by French officer Pierre-François Bouchard during the Napoleonic campaign in Egypt. Okay, okay history lesson over. Jeez, it's not like I am gonna make you guys take a test or anything…besides, Sophia would clearly beat you two." At this I high fived Sophia when she held her hand high to me, making me smirk. Of course, Pip and my mum faked their outrage.

"We better go, after all, I don't know how long those chains will last," Pip said, making all three of us groan,

"Seriously?"

"Again, Pip?" my mum and Sophia said at the same time, making her shrug her shoulders as she removed as many of her piercings as she could.

"What? He was our greatest threat to waking up and now, this has bought us some more time in case he does, problem solved… simples," she said this last part like the cute yet surprisingly disturbing Meercat in the TV commercial advertising insurance.

"Yeah, and he will also disturb the whole house when his beast wakes up with him, instead of just Adam, who would have most likely just calmly come looking for you," Sophia said, pointing out the major flaw in this logic.

"Oh right… in that case, we better hurry," Pip admitted, making me groan as we walked through the fireplace,

"The Fates are so screwed."

Moments later and we were all standing next to the Janus Gate which was a magnificent fountain that could have fit a bus inside the circle of water. But this wasn't all, as the water didn't flow down like gravity would dictate it should, but instead it flowed straight up to the ceiling, disappearing to somewhere above and I had no clue where.

Of course, I was nervous, as it was said that if your cause was not worthy in the eyes of Janus, then just touching the water could kill you. Which was when my mum took my hand and said,

"It's okay, me and Janus are tight... plus, I've done this once before and survived, so what could go wrong, right?" At that very moment, the thing that could go wrong just showed up and shockingly in the form of my cousin.

"Amelia!" she shouted, and I thought for a minute I was hallucinating.

"Ella?" I spoke her name in question before seeing it was true, as there she was. Of course, all thoughts of what we were about to do fled me and emotion took over as I started running toward her.

"ELLA!" I shouted as I threw myself in her arms seeing as she was ready for me.

"What happened to you? Why are you here, did something happen?" I asked quickly, now looking around and expecting Jared to walk in here following her... which would have been bad... *very bad.* But then as soon as I asked this, her face fell and unshed tears made her green eyes glisten.

"Oh Fae, it's... it's a mess... there was a raid on Jared's club, he was sucked into some kind of portal and..." I looked back at my mum who looked torn, and I knew the feeling. But then she made the tough choice when telling her,

"I'm sorry, Ella, we can help, I promise you we will, but right now... Fae honey, I'm sorry but we don't have much time." I tensed at this, nodding to my mother who was trying to express so much in just that one look alone. If any one of our husbands woke, it would be game over. Meaning it was now or never. So, after taking a deep breath, I made my decision. Meaning I turned back to my cousin and told her,

"Ella, listen to me, I know what I am going to say won't make much sense. I have to go, but I promise I won't be long." She frowned back at me, shaking her head a little and making my guilt double when she asked,

"What do you mean?"

"Okay so…" I was about to speak when my mum warned,

"Fae don't…" and I knew why. She wanted to protect her, and I couldn't blame her, but I had to give her something. I couldn't just let her think we were all abandoning her in her time of need.

"I have to! I can't just leave her here to think the worst…" I told my mum making her sigh before nodding in agreement.

"What's going on, please tell me?" Ella pleaded and again, I owed her that much.

"Okay, so you have to trust me here. What you see will seem impossible." She scoffed at this and told me wryly,

"Trust me, after today, that ship has fucking sailed." I wanted to ask her more about what had happened, but seeing as I was unable to help, I knew there wouldn't be much point.

"Fae, we have two minutes." This time it was my aunty Sophia who warned me of this, as if she could sense something coming. Perhaps one of the men had woken up and she could feel their emotions rising. She was quite in tune like that with her brothers, and I knew it was because they were triplet souls. Gods, but I really hoped my dad hadn't just woken up.

"Okay, so super quick version, that fountain is something

we are going to step into, but in no time at all we will be stepping back through it. Where we go, I can't tell you..." She heard the word portal and focused on that as she shouted,

"Wait, is it a portal, could it lead me to Jared?!" I released a weighted sigh, wishing it could but telling her the truth before she got any dangerous ideas.

"No, Ella, it's... it's a way for us to step back in time." Not surprisingly, she gasped at this.

"That's... but that's impossible... isn't it?"

"Yes and no... mainly yes. But only for those with the most worthy of causes and those brave enough to allow themselves to be judged by the God Janus. The timekeeper of all our realms," I told her, hearing my mum whispering my name and I knew my time was up... literally.

"But I don't understand..."

"I can't explain more, I wish I could, as ironically, I am out of time but please trust me. If we aren't back in less than five minutes, use the door, the one with..." She interrupted me, raising a hand and telling me,

"The one with the books, yeah I know." She sounded so dejected and I hated it. Hated that I couldn't do more. I wanted to tell her how sorry I was. How much I missed her. There were so many things but in the end, I only had time to tell her the important stuff,

"Good, and do me a favour, if we aren't back, tell them we are sorry... that we failed... that we..." I had to stop before the tears fell, now grabbing her hand and holding it tight.

"Fae, if you still want to do this, it's now or never," my mum said, looking more nervous by the second as if any minute my dad was going to burst through the bookcase and run straight for us. I released another sigh and told her,

"...Tell them we love them." Then I squeezed her hand and said,

"I loved you like a sister." At hearing this I watched as a tear escaped before she nodded, telling me,

"Me too." After this I let her go and ran back over to my time traveling gang.

"Love you, Ella, and for the past, I am sorry," my mum said, saying her own sorry and her own version of goodbye, but Ella looked confused by this, as she was now frowning.

"I don't understand," we heard her say, just as we each held hands and started to step into the fountain. Then something strange came over me and I felt compelled to speak, like a message from the Fates themselves that she needed to hear,

"Time isn't beyond us all, Ella... Remember that." Then I took the last step, holding my breath, until I watched in horror as now Ella was running toward us.

"NO!" I screamed, but it was too late, as the last thing I saw before the time consumed us, was Ella…

Following us into the past.

CHAPTER 29
TIME UNRAVELED

"Ella!" I shouted my cousin's name in desperation, despite knowing the truth. Because as I looked around, I knew that it was pointless. Hopeless. Useless.

Ella was gone.

"What happened?!" I continued to look around, still searching despite my mother's voice asking me what was wrong. Because she obviously hadn't seen what I had. I felt her grab my arm to get my attention.

"Amelia, what happened, what did you see?" I turned to her with wide eyes filled with tears of panic, then I told her the awful truth.

"Ella... she... I couldn't stop her. *I couldn't stop her, Mum,"* I said quietly this time as the tears rolled down my cheek, making my mother swiped them away with her thumbs before pulling me in to her embrace. Then I cried with my head to the crook of her neck, just like I always did when I was upset.

"It will be okay, Fae... it will be okay... *it has to be,"* she reassured me, but even I knew not to ignore the worry in her tone.

"She's a Chosen One, which means the gate would have allowed her access, and as the God of Fate, he would not have harmed a prophesized one."

"How can you be so sure?" I asked in a small voice, hoping and praying that my mother was right.

"Because everything happens for a reason for us, which means everything happens for a reason for her," my mother answered as Sophia approached, now putting a gentle hand on my shoulder,

"Your mother is right. Janus wouldn't have allowed her to pass if it wasn't her destiny to do so." I released a held breath before asking,

"Then why isn't she here with us?"

"I don't know, but all I do know is that she will be where the Fates have decided she needs to be, for her own future. She mentioned something about Jared and a portal, perhaps she has a King to save and the only way to do that, is in the past," my mum said, making hope bloom bright in my chest.

"I hope so… I just hope I did the right thing… maybe if I hadn't said anything, then maybe she would have…" This was when my mother framed my face and told me,

"No, Fae, don't go there… don't do that to yourself. None of this was your fault. She made a choice, just like we all did." I released a sigh and nodded, knowing my mum was right, there was no turning back now. We just had to hope that wherever she was, she was safe. Like my mum had said…

She just had to be.

"Speaking of which, where are we?" my mother asked, looking around and taking in our surroundings like I just had. Because this was about as far away from Egypt as you could get. No, if anything…

"Is this England?" I looked to Sophia because if anyone would know, it was likely to be her. She looked around and we both watched as recognition sparked in her eyes.

"Could it be…?" she murmured, as she took in the rolling green hills looking bleak thanks to the rain and the very early morning light. In fact, it was still mostly dark, but the slight glow in the distance suggested it wouldn't be too long before the sun was up.

"What is it, where are we?" I asked, taking in the countryside and not a shit load of sand like I had been expecting. However, this question was forgotten the second I started to look around for the fourth member of our group.

"PIP!" I shouted, making the others do the same.

"Oh Gods… Pip!" I shouted the second I heard a groan in the undergrowth. I raced over to where I heard the sound coming from a Hedgerow.

"So yeah, not in Kansas anymore," she said as we helped her up and I straightened her wig and pulled some twigs and leaves out of it.

"No, we most definitely are not. Come on, we better get moving and try and find shelter out of this rain," Sophia said, lifting the hood of her cloak and becoming the voice of reason. Yet, there was something in her tone that worried me. It was like she knew exactly where we were and because of it, she was worried.

"I think I can see a cottage, come on, let's hope they have a barn so we can get shelter in there," Sophia said obviously seeing what I couldn't as it was strange, like with every step I took I started to feel different. But in the end, I put my growing fatigue and blurry eyes down to our situation.

We all trudged on through the thick mud as it appeared we had stumbled across a dirt road, making me wonder what year we had actually travelled back to.

"It looks like a cottage, but I don't see any lights on, or should I say candles," my mum said with a shrug of her shoulders.

"How did you do this last time?" I asked, thinking this was most likely useful information to know.

"Two thousand years in the past? My ass just kind of landed in the desert. And let's just say going to the toilet wasn't exactly a delight," my mum muttered sarcastically as we continued up the road toward the house.

The faint sounds of tinkering reminded me of wind chimes tapping in the wind, which certainly made for an eerie sound combined with the squelching of our feet. In fact, walking in the thick mud was making me glad I wore flat boots, despite knowing I would most likely have to do without them at some point if I wanted to fit in.

Although I wasn't so sure, seeing as we weren't exactly in Egypt. No, from the looks of the stone house, we were definitely in Europe, perhaps France or even Italy as Sophia hadn't actually told us yet.

However, despite these many possibilities, I still couldn't help the feeling that we were in England somewhere. I then had to wonder if Ella was also somewhere in this time and if maybe by her coming through with us, it had somehow thrown us off course and out of timelines.

As we got closer to the building, I could see that it was simple in its design, thankfully seeing a stone cobble house and not a less sturdy wooden Tudor house. Did that mean we were well past a medieval age? We were most definitely before electricity, that was to be sure as there was nothing around to suggest that this could possibly be modern day or even close to it.

"Is anyone gonna knock?" my mum said as we

approached the door, all looking at each other as if waiting for one of us to come up with the answer. Of course, the three of us groaned the second Pip joined us and happily was the first to knock on the door before opening it and saying,

"Yoo Hoo, hello in there, four little wet Goldilocks standing out here in the rain hoping the bears aren't home?"

"Really, Pip?" my mum asked smirking.

"Oh, come on, can you really blame me? I mean look at this place, it's like something right out of a creepy fairy tale." I shuddered at this as Pip wasn't wrong.

"Yeah, well forget bears, I'm just hoping there are no witches in there wanting to eat us," I added, now poking my head inside.

"Nah, look, there's nothing sweet about this house, trust me... come on, Gretel, it looks empty," Pip added with a wink, now inviting us all in with a roll of her outstretched arm.

"Yeah, well it doesn't mean it'll stay that way for long," my mother muttered as she took my hand before stepping inside.

"It's also filthy," Sophia complained, being a total germaphobe and now looking at everything with utter distain. The four of us took a moment to take in our surroundings, seeing that Pip was right, it may have been creepy, but at least it was empty... *for now.*

There wasn't much in the way of furniture, as everything seem to centre around a rickety table with two dusty chairs either side. There was a stone fireplace, a side table that looked to be used as a kitchen area, and some earth ware pots and bowls left on the side, with some tankards hanging on hooks over a stone sink.

"Well, first things first," Sophia said, walking up to the

fireplace and after rubbing her hands together, creating fireball in her palm before throwing it toward the kindling. However, it was at this point that Pip gasped, making us all turn to see a horrified expression to the window. This was also just in time to see a man's shocked face disappear from sight, as he started running after witnessing Sophia's power.

"Oh dear, well that's one way to scare the locals," Pip said, and I had to agree with her, as he had definitely started crossing himself and praying to God while he legged it. As if God could save him from the wickedness inside that was four wet women in need of a fire. However, this was the least of our issues as I turned to my mum when realization hit.

"I didn't hear him… did you?" She shook her head, now looking thoughtful.

"And I thought my eyes were just tired, but the more we have walked the less I have been able to see without it all going blurry." She released a deep sigh and I had to say, it was not a happy sound.

"What is it?"

"I probably should have mentioned this before we decided to time travel," my mum answered, making me suddenly realise why she had insisted on me taking my glasses and contacts.

"Oh no… are we…?"

"We're both back to being mortal," she replied solemnly, making me gasp as I took a step back in shock.

"We are? But how, why… I mean I didn't feel any change at first but now I'm really tired and starting to feel different," I admitted and I had to say, my mum looked even worse, as she was fully leaning her weight against the back of a chair now.

"It happened the last time… it was as if… I was stripped of everything that had ever happened to me. As if I had never met your father which makes sense it happening now, as neither of us has even been born yet."

"Which means no powers," I concluded in what I knew was a dejected tone.

"Exactly… we're going to have to be careful, Fae." I nodded in a disheartened way, knowing that this complicated things somewhat. Hell, it complicated things a lot, as I was kind of relying on my invincibility to get me through this without getting me killed. It made me wonder about Lucius and if he did find out I had left before I managed to get back and tell him… would he would know about this too? Something that would only be harder for him and give him more to worry about.

However, I was at least comforted to know that in all probability, he wouldn't have to wait long. My mother had already told me that the last time she did this, it was only minutes that she seemed gone for. Meaning that if we did get back to our own time, for Lucius it would be no time at all. That thought did bring me some bit of comfort at least, despite our dire circumstances.

"Do you think that was the guy who lived here?" Pip asked now picking up a pot, lifting its corked lid and smelling inside before making a gagging face.

"It doesn't exactly seem like there's a woman's touch here," Sophia said dryly, still clearly not wanting to touch anything.

"And what exactly would a woman's touch look like in this time period? One I will remind everyone, that we have no idea which one we are even stuck in?" I said, making a point to which Pip shrugged her shoulders and made her own point,

"Wildflowers in a vase."

I said nothing to this, but instead looked to my aunty Sophia, who looked as if she had a lot on her mind and was now currently staring out the window. I walked over to her and placed my hand at her arm, making her flinch.

"Hey, are you okay?" I asked, and I watched as it took seconds before the mask slipped into place and veiled her worry.

"I'm fine," she said tensely.

"We are all fine," my mother added in more of an encouraging tone.

"Look, we are all together, that is the main thing," she said again when no one else filled the void of silence.

"Why, what happened last time… did you not all arrive together?"

"Let's just say that it took a while for us all to find each other again," my mum replied, trying to see the best in our situation. And well, considering what she just said, I had to agree with her, at least none of us were alone in this. But then I felt guilty even being thankful for this, knowing that Ella was no doubt all alone and scared out of her mind. I mean, I knew my cousin was tough but this… well this was something else.

"The sun won't be up for a few hours yet, so there's no point going out there again until we have daylight on our side and not until the rain has lightened at least… and even though Pip and I can see better in the… well, never mind about all that…" my auntie Sophia said, not needing to finish that sentence, hence why she didn't. Because they wouldn't have needed to worry about getting cold or sick, or falling over in the dark breaking an ankle. However, now they had two mortals to worry about. Both me and my mother looked at each other, nodding our heads as we both thought the same thing.

We would need to be careful.

"There looks to be a level up there for sleeping in, why

don't we take it in shifts," my mum nodded and pushed me toward the ladder.

"You go first, sweetheart." I nodded as it had been a long walk to find this house and I had to admit now I was mortal again, I was feeling the exhaustion a lot quicker than I had gotten used too. Being stripped of that side of me felt far too familiar. But then again, I had only had months to adapt to my new power. Which was why when I looked to my mother to see her shoulders sag again, I realized that for her it had been nearly thirty years since she had experienced being mortal. It was why I first nodded to Sophia and then jerked my head toward my mum, trying to silently get this across to her without making it obvious. Thankfully my aunt took the hint, now coming over to my mother and putting her arms around her shoulders. She then started to lead her to the ladder, telling her,

"Pip and I have got this, go lie with your daughter. We will be fine." My mum agreed silently with a nod of her head as she was looking more exhausted by the minute. I pulled myself up first to the sleeping platform and started to unbundle my dress that I had purposely kept under the cloak out of the rain. As for my cloak, we had all taken these off so they might have chance to dry in front of the fire.

I took out my glasses ready for when I woke up and set the thin black frames aside. Then when I was ready to lie down and cover myself with my dress, I looked down at my mum to find her already fast asleep, curled on her side. So, I used my dress and covered us both, thankful for its thick material and long skirt. I then put my arm around my mum and cuddled in close, knowing it would help keep her warm. The only evidence that she wasn't passed out cold was I felt her squeeze my hand, making me smile in the dark.

The next time I opened my eyes I had no idea how much

time had passed, only that I felt sluggish. It was as if a sound had stirred me from my sleep and I was being forced to wake. That was when I realized that I no longer had my mum's hand in mine.

"Mum?" I spoke to the darkness, before raising my head, looking to see if she had moved from the platform.

"Ssshh," I heard her hushed whisper before finding her shadow by the ladder. I reached for my glasses as I sat up, then I asked her,

"What is it?" Her answer came just as I was scooting off the musty mound of bedding and shifting closer to her.

"Pip and Sophia heard horses approach, they've gone to check it out." I frowned thinking this was a bad sign. It was even worse when my mother started to slip her legs over the edge, making me grab for her arm.

"Shouldn't we stay up here, hidden?"

"It will be fine… I'm just going to see if I can see them through the window." I opened my mouth to argue, but she quickly cut me off with a reassuring smile.

"But, Mum…"

"It will be fine, Fae. Stay here," she said before climbing down the ladder and going out of sight. But, in the end I lasted for only a minute before I couldn't stand it any longer. So, I followed her down and I found her looking out the window. But then when she heard me approach with the floorboards creaking beneath my feet, she moved away from the window and came toward me.

"I told you to stay up there."

"I know but… Mum, look out!" I shouted the second I saw a figure emerged from the shadows and grab her from behind. Then just as I was about to react, pain erupted from behind me, as somebody had knocked me on the side of my head. I fell to the floor instantly, hearing my mother's scream.

"Should we take this one too?" a man's voice asked who was now standing over me.

As I started to flitter out of consciousness the last thing I heard was,

"No, we will be quicker with one... besides..."

"He only wants the blonde."

CHAPTER 30
HISTORICALLY COMPLICATED

"Amelia!" The sound of my aunt Sophia shouting my name roused me from my own unconsciousness before I felt them trying to pick me off the floor.

"What... what happened?" I asked, trying to scramble for answers, yet something in the back of my mind was screaming at me, before I suddenly shouted,

"Mum!" That's when it came flooding back to me as I bolted up from the chair they had put me in, only to stagger into my aunt Sophia's arms.

"Whoa... easy now... we found you unconscious on the floor, where's Keira, where's your mum, Fae?" Sophia asked, looking more concerned by the minute.

"I woke up... there... there was a noise, one minute she was looking out the window and the next..." I groaned, as the pain in my head intensified,

"Take your time, Sweetheart," Pip said, leading me back to the chair and making me sit again before I fell down. That's when I felt the side of my face was wet and I reached up, feeling the cut I had there making me hiss in pain as it stung.

"There was a man… one behind my mum who grabbed her but before I could stop him, I felt pain… another guy must have been hiding and struck me from behind. Did they…?" Oh God, I couldn't bring myself to say it,

"We couldn't find her, so they must have taken her with them," Sophia informed me, which was when my memories started to slot further into place.

"Wait… I think I remember something… one of them saying something, like they asked if they should take me too, and a voice answered that he only wanted the blonde… what does that mean, who would know that my mother was here?" At this Sophia's features tensed, making me grab her hand and squeeze it tight.

"What aren't you telling me, Sophia?" She released a heavy sigh, before surprising me.

"I think I know where they have taken her, come on… I have something to show you." She put an arm around me and helped me to stand. Pip was now climbing back down the ladder, with my dress bundled under her arm.

"Let's be quick and get ready to leave," Sophia said, prompting me to put my dress over my clothes, as they did the same. Then I swapped my glasses for my fresh contacts that I knew would at the very least last me a month. Gods, I hope we weren't here for that long. Thankfully, the case I had for them had a little mirror in the lid so I could at least see what I was doing. I was also glad the dress had hidden pockets in the skirt, so I didn't have to carry the contact solution and my glasses in my hand. I then took the cloak from Pip who handed it to me with a wink, no doubt trying to make me feel better.

After this we made our way out of the cottage and now that the sun was up, it was easier to see the beautiful countryside that surrounded us. Rolling hills full of trees encircled the flat lands of farming fields and as far as the eye could see was a vista of lush green landscape.

"We tried to track them, but with all this rain and then being on horseback... I'm sorry, but we lost them," Pip said after a time, obviously feeling guilty that they had managed to get away with my mother. I reached for her hand and squeezed it tight before telling her,

"We will get her back." After this she took in the sight of me and anger twisted her usual cute, endearing features,

"But they hurt our little bean!" she said before fussing over me in a motherly way, now trying to wipe the blood from my cheek that had dripped down from the cut I obviously had on my forehead.

We continued to follow the same path we had last night, walking in the same direction we had been doing when we spotted the cottage. Thankfully, it was an easier journey, as for one, I could see now thanks to my contacts and also it was morning. Although I didn't have high hopes for the weather as those dark grey clouds overhead looked thunderous and menacing.

However, after following a bend in the road that curved around a copse of trees, the landscape opened up even more, making me gasp at the sight. Even more fields rolled out in front of us like a blanket with a snake of water winding through it, making it look silver under the sun. But it was the sight that sat up on a hill that was surrounded by thick forest, that interested me more.

It was a castle.

"What is this place?" I asked after we had walked for an hour or two.

"It's what I feared it would be as we didn't just come back to the wrong time, Fae, but we are in the wrong place entirely for I thought I recognized the shield on the guards. I had a feeling last night but wanted to be sure before I said anything..." Sophia said all this with a solemn expression, making me turn away from the sight of the castle and face her,

"Sophia?" she winced before answering me.

"The man at the window, he must have seen what I was doing... in his fear he must have thought of only one place to go." Again she refrained from telling me what I really wanted to know, which was why I came right out and asked her,

"Sophia... who owns that castle?" Of course, I already had a feeling I knew the answer, which meant I wasn't surprised when she turned to me and said,

"It's your father's castle." I couldn't understand her tone of dread, which was why I asked,

"But that's good, isn't it?" Sophia first looked to Pip who also seemed to have the same look of dread on her face.

"No, this is bad, this is very, very bad," she said, and Pip nodded before adding,

"Yeah, and when we say bad, we mean the shit has not only hit the fan but destroyed the spinney little bugger." I shook my head, feeling the pain when I did, meaning I regretted it instantly. Therefore, I narrowed my eyes and winced before asking,

"I feel like the answer to this should have been something I had known before stepping through the Janus Gate, but I will ask it now... so, tell me why is this bad."

"Because your father just kidnapped your mother, and trust me when I tell you, he is not going to let her go... *as in, never.*" I looked toward the castle with wide eyes and said the first thing that came to mind,

"Oh shit."

"Yeah, now she gets it," Pip said with a sigh.

"What are we going to do? I mean it's not like I can just

walk up to the door, give it a knock and say, him Dad, I'm your long-lost daughter from hundreds of years in the future... hey, don't suppose you can give my mum back, could you? I mean, do we even know what time period this is?" I aimed this last part at Sophia.

"It must be the late 1700s, as this wasn't our main home, just more like... well, like a holiday home," she replied, making me mutter,

"Of course it is... only the Dravens would have a castle as a holiday home, where's home exactly, Buckingham palace... don't answer that?" I said the second I saw her face, it told me everything.

"So where are we exactly?" I thought best to ask next.

"We're in the Lake District."

"The Lake District... Gods, but how could this have gone so wrong so quickly?" I complained.

"Well, the last time we went back in time, your mother found herself with a knife held to her throat by your father... so hopefully it's not that bad," Pip said as if forgetting herself.

"What?!" I screeched.

"Pip!" Sophia also shouted.

"Hey, no biggie, I mean it all turned out okay, I mean sort of... he did make her part of his harem, so that part was fun... well until that bitch tried to... okay, shutting up now." I started to rub my forehead in exasperation before this started to hurt so I stopped before I made my head bleed again.

"Dear Gods, this really is bad."

"Unfortunately, it gets worse," Sophia added when I said this and I quickly wondered how much more of this I could take.

"How so? Because seriously, how could this get any worse, Sophia?"

"The last time we went back in time, Pip was close enough to Keira that she was able to mask who she was to your father." I shook my head at this, forgetting myself again and pushing through the pain this time enough to ask,

"What do you mean?"

"My brother was attracted to her, yes, and most definitely drawn to her and despite thinking it was forbidden, he even fell in love with her."

"Okay, so that doesn't sound so bad," I said still not seeing her point, although this account didn't exactly match up with Pip's knife story.

"Yes, but this was despite not knowing that she was his Chosen One." I looked to Pip again, my eyes wide and questioning,

"You can do that?" She shrugged her little shoulders.

"Yeah, I can do that."

"But why? I don't understand, wouldn't it be easier if he knew?" I asked, feeling like I was missing the bigger picture here and really wishing I had learned all this before we left on this crazy journey… although, when we would have had the time to do that, I wasn't sure.

"Your father, like most of the kings, doesn't exactly like to share, nor do they like to let go of their possessions. But when finding your Chosen One, the one soul Fated to be yours from the very Gods… well, let's just say my brother can take possessive to a whole other level. Whereas, back in your time, the act of taking a Chosen One prisoner would be known as nothing more than being barbaric, here to the King of Kings, well let's just say he would feel it within his right to do so and not be questioned by anyone." At this my mouth dropped open,

"But… But that's… that's insane!" I cried.

"No, to a king, it is simply his right."

"So, you're telling me that my father has likely taken my mother as his prisoner, one he intends to marry… do I have that right?"

"Yep, pretty much a nutshell situation," Pip answered, patting me on the back.

"Come on, we'd best get moving if we are going to reach it before the storm hits," Sophia said and started walking.

"But wait, what are we going to do when we get there?" At this she smirked back at me and said,

"What do you think we're gonna do… we're going to break your mum out of my brother's prison."

"His prison!" I shrieked again, this time loud enough to frighten wildlife as a few birds took flight.

"Not the sentence you thought you were going to hear today, eh…? But don't worry, little bean, when she says prison, what she means is his bedroom, as trust me, the only place he'd want to be keeping her right now is…"

"Okay, I get it, this is already enough to have me needing therapy, Pip, I don't need any added visuals." She laughed when I said this, now skipping along the road that I knew would be a muddy nightmare again when that storm hit.

"So, other than the plan being to break my mother out from my father's castle, hundreds of years in the past, I might add, and one where he doesn't even know he has a daughter… never thought I'd be saying that sentence either…" I muttered this last part making Pip shoot back,

"Really, like not even a little bit, considering we're in the past and all." I shot Pip a single look that was enough of an answer before continuing with my rant,

"… how are we planning on doing this?" I asked as we continued on, this time veering off the road and taking what I assumed was a shortcut across the fields.

"Thankfully, I know this place and I know it well enough

to make it inside, I'm just hoping I've got the year right," Sophia said, making me catch up to her as I was lagging behind.

"Why?" I asked.

"I spent quite a few years around this time with Zagan in Italy. So hopefully I'm still there and there's no... doppelganger mix ups this time." She shot a look to Pip who held up her hands and said,

"Hey, the trunk option was all I had." I decided not to ask.

After this we made good time getting across the fields and closer to a road that obviously wound around the back of the hill and toward the other side of the castle. Thankfully, the heavens opened just as we had made it to the sweeping mud road as my legs felt like they were filled with iron weights as trudging across the muddy countryside wasn't exactly easy. Not now my body was back to being mortal. This also meant that I was clearly the one that kept lagging behind. Meaning my two aunties had to keep on stopping for me to catch my breath. But one look and they understood, so there was no complaint on their part.

"So, my dad, please tell me he wasn't some badass tyrant in this time period." Sophia's expression didn't exactly incite confidence in me.

"Let's just say he's a bit of a broody bastard," Sophia said making Pip snort, like this was a huge understatement.

"But he wouldn't have hurt my mum, right?"

"Gods no! No king would ever hurt his Chosen One... now chain her to his bed, then yeah, most likely, but he wouldn't have hurt her. No, my brother would sooner hurt himself than he would your mother. You can trust me on that, Keira is safe," she assured me, and I relaxed at the knowledge.

"Well, that's something at least."

"Now, as for how he's going to react to her being broken out of his castle and snatched away from him, well that's where things are gonna get tricky," Sophia added, making me realize that this historical adventure had just got even more complicated really quickly.

As soon as the full glory of the castle came into view, I found myself breathless. Although modest in size, it stood proud and majestic against the open vista of the countryside it looked to have dominated. Its stone seemed to change colour in the light, being pale grey with hints of red in the stone that only came out when touched by the sun. It was all square in its shape with sharp corners and no round towers To speak of. It also had a rough charm and I could see why my father liked it. It was less the type you'd have expected in a fairytale and more the type where you expected to see armour clad warriors running out of its doors.

Sophia suddenly pulled me behind a wall as servants scurried past carrying armfuls of the flowers in beautiful bouquets.

"What's going on?" I asked in hushed tones,

"It looks like my brother must be holding a ball… it must be a celebration for finding his Chosen One."

"Oh shit… this soon? He's known her for all of a day?" Sophia shrugged her shoulders and said,

"My brother works fast… but I actually think this is perfect."

"How?" I asked, making Pip agree,

"Yeah, I am with little bean on this one, how is this good?"

"Whenever you throw a ball or celebration, we enlist more help from nearby villages as more servants are needed, some of them you won't even recognize… come on, I have an idea," Sophia said when the coast was clear.

"She walked us up a cobbled path toward what looked like stables.

"We can hide in here until then." We walked under the arch of stone and into a cobbled stable yard that was surrounded by not only stables but small buildings where they kept supplies and housed the stable staff. It was in one of these building we slipped inside and hid behind some bales of hay.

"Pip, do you think you could get us a couple of outfits."

"Gotcha!" Pip answered, winking before slipping out of our hiding place and making her move.

"What exactly is your plan, Sophia?" This is when she gave me a naughty grin and told me,

"It is time we go to a ball."

CHAPTER 31
ACTING THE PART

"This isn't exactly what I had in mind when you said we were going to a ball," I said now looking down at my maid's uniform that I gathered was typical for this era. It was black woollen dress with a white linen apron pinned into position at the front. Sophia had twisted my hair back in plaits and pinned it under my maid cap that was embarrassingly frilly around the edges.

"Yeah, I kind of feel like me and little bean have drawn the short straw here," Pip added as we both looked down at our servant outfits and then looked to Sophia who was dressed in all her beautiful finery.

She wore a low-necked gown of blue silk with large flowers shimmering thanks to the silver thread. This was worn over a pale blue petticoat with a skirt that was opened at front to show the petticoat beneath. The bodice of the gown was also open at the front and filled in with a decorative stomacher, one pinned to the gown over the laces. Of course, she had need help getting into this and, man, wasn't that a complicated process.

Close-fitting sleeves just past the elbow were trimmed

with frills and fine linen was tacked to the inside of the gown's sleeves. The neckline was trimmed with a lace ruffle the same colour as her petticoat and voila, she was fit for royalty.

"Yes, well out of the three of us, I'm the one that's going to get recognized and I think my brother would wonder why I decided to turn up to his party to celebrate finding his Chosen One, dressed like a commoner." Okay, so I had to admit that she had a good point. Of course, I hadn't wanted to know where Pip had managed to snag these outfits from. But I had a strong suspicion that there was most likely three mortals that were currently unconscious somewhere and dumped in the bushes.

The sun was already setting early, telling me it was as I suspected it to be and we were still winter, just as he had been in our time. It also meant we didn't have to wait long before the festivities began as the guests had already started to arrive in their carriages.

"Right, you both will have to slip through the servants' quarters as I will arrive with the rest," Sophia said, reminding us of the plan.

"And you're sure your other self won't turn up?" I asked despite feeling like this was an obvious question and one she would have already thought about.

"Yeah, because no offense, the last time I met past you, you were a bit of a bitch," Pip added, making my eyes widen at this, trying not to laugh when my aunt argued,

"I was not!"

"You tried to poison Toots…"

"You what!?" I interjected, making Sophia rub her forehead as if a headache was coming on before saying,

"You might not want to share everything that happened in

the past, Pip, and anyway, future me saved her, so it's a moot point."

"Okay, so there was a lot you guys have not told me," I said, again feeling like we would have needed a week to prepare me for all of this.

"Oh, you have no idea," Sophia muttered before Pip nodded like a madman.

"Yeah, remember the time we all got locked in the underground prison together…? Fun times."

"Okay yeah, I take it back, I don't want to know." My auntie Sophia tapped me a few times on the cheek and said,

"Smart choice that, my niece." Then she walked out of sight, no doubt waiting until the right time to make her move. As for me and Pip, we had no choice but to play our own parts, starting with making our way into the servant quarters. Something that was surprisingly easy to get into. Although considering we were dressed the way we were, I don't know why I was surprised. Because after only a few minutes of being inside and we were quickly having orders barked at us.

This meant that the first sight I got of the inside of my father's castle was while I was holding a silver tray of white wine glasses. The room was filled with people all dressed in their decadent finery, just as Sophia was, creating a sea of luxury fabrics.

It was like suddenly waking up and discovering you were now part of some historical period drama. The lavish room boasted so many antiques and pieces of wealth that it was hard to pinpoint just one thing, as my eyes scanned the grand but modestly sized ballroom. Like I said, the castle wasn't the biggest I had seen, no doubt why it was only classed as a holiday home. But what it lacked in size, it made up for in opulence and rich, elegant splendour.

However, the moment the room parted I could finally see what I had been looking for...

My mother.

The room separated to allow for my aunt Sophia to make her arrival like the royalty she was, and at the end of that partition were my parents. They were both sitting upon carved wooden thrones gilded gold and if seen in any other setting, I would have said they looked gaudy and ostentatious. However, with my parents gracing the seats, they looked exactly who they were to my father's world...

A King and his Queen.

Both were wearing my father's colour, meaning he looked gallant and strikingly handsome, in his knee-length purple and black jacket, knee breeches, a long waistcoat underneath to match. My mother's dress was very similar to Sophia's in style, with only the material and colour being different. Long lengths of luxurious deep purple silk that I could see ruffled into a long train at her back.

I decided to try and get closer, so I could hear what was being said, offering people drinks as I went and giving me the perfect excuse to move around the room.

"Sophia, what are you doing here, I had believed you were in Italy," my father said, making me tense.

"Word travels fast, brother," she replied in that cool manner of hers.

"And sisters even faster," Was his quick-witted reply.

"In truth I was already on my way here, when I happened to hear about this beautiful young lady who you have taken as your betrothed, is this true?" she asked, making my poor mum look awkward trying to play the part of said beauty.

"It is, for her name is Catherine, *my golden fleece.*" My father said this in a way that was an obvious compliment making my mother blush. Naturally, Sophia continued to play her own part by looking surprised as I knew this 'golden fleece' comment was a sure way for his sister to understand that he had finally found his Fated.

"Then I really do have to offer you my congratulations, for she is a rare creature indeed." My father beamed at this.

"Catherine, may I introduce, Mrs Sophia Draven, my sister." Hearing this my mother tried to stand, no doubt so she could continue to act and do a curtsy. However, my possessive father showed his true colours quite quickly as he placed her hand over hers and prevented her from standing. This meant Sophie was left to curtsy alone. In all honesty, it was in that moment that I had never witnessed my mum being forced to act so much like the Queen my father had always claimed her to be.

I knew that my father was making a point by doing this, letting everyone in the room know exactly who my mother was to him. Which was why he used his sister to do so, in a calculated act of possessiveness. As was usual with my mother, she blushed easily and started to bite her bottom lip as the embarrassment was getting to her. My father watched this with heated eyes before leaning over and whispering something in her ear, making her blush even more.

"I must impose upon you, Sophia, to stay… yes, stay and become my betrothed's companion, for strangely she knows no one here," he said in a way as he didn't believe her story on how she came to be. And well, my mother wasn't known for her acting skills any more than she was known for being a good liar. Something I had a feeling my father was getting a taste of and no doubt calling her on her bluff often.

"No one?" Sophia asked, clearly knowing this would have been strange if she hadn't.

"Yes, my little beauty here, came to be in my possession by strange means indeed, but that conversation is for another time, I dare say." My father said making my mother look as if she wanted to shrink down into her seat and let it swallow her whole.

"Very well, let us speak no more about it, for it is a joyous occasion and one needed not celebrated with jolts of the past." The way Sophia said this I could tell she was trying to let my mother know in a subtle way, that she was the Sophia my mother knew. And thankfully, it worked. I could tell this by the way my mother released a relieved sigh. Although unfortunately it was also one my father hadn't missed. Not when he now raised a questioning brow down at her, before frowning back at Sophia.

Sophia knowing that she might have gone too far, simply curtseyed to them one more time, before speaking,

"If you'll excuse me, the journey was arduous, and I would like to freshen up before the festivities are to fully begin." My father bowed his head, clearly relieving Sophia of her being there. As for my mother, she took another drink from a servant who held a tray next to her, and started drinking down the wine quickly, no doubt needing it. However, she also looked like she was about to choke on it when my father leaned forward and whispered (Gods but I do not wish to ever know) in her ear before placing possessive hand on her leg.

I knew then that Sophia had not been exaggerating, as trying to get my mother free of my father's clutches was going to be more complicated than I had allowed myself to believe.

However, it seemed that complicated was most definitely in the cards for us all, as my tray was empty and I had no choice but to go back into the kitchen.

And it was a complication that arose on my way there, as I caught sight of something that made me stop dead.

Because now I knew that my father wasn't the only King here.

However, unlike my father who was currently kissing his Chosen One, this particular King was kissing somebody else.

And was why in the end, my pained little cry came out by speaking his name in utter shock…

"Lucius."

Acknowledgments

Well first and foremost my love goes out to all the people who deserve the most thanks which is you the FANS!

Without you wonderful people in my life, I would most likely still be serving burgers and writing in my spare time like some dirty little secret, with no chance to share my stories with the world.

You enable me to continue living out my dreams every day and for that I will be eternally grateful to each and every one of you!

Your support is never ending. Your trust in me and the story is never failing. But more than that, your love for me and all who you consider your 'Afterlife family' is to be commended, treasured and admired. Thank you just doesn't seem enough, so one day I hope to meet you all and buy you all a drink! ;)

To my family…

To my crazy mother, who had believed in me since the beginning and doesn't think that some"thing great should be hidden from the world. I would like to thank you for all the hard work you put into my books and the endless hours spent caring about my words and making sure it is the best it can be for everyone to enjoy. You, along with the Hudson Indie Ink team make Afterlife shine.

To my crazy father who is and always has been my hero in life.Your strength astonishes me, even to this day! The love and care you hold for your family is a gift you give to the Hudson name.

To my lovely sister,

If Peter Pan had a female version, it would be you and Wendy combined. You have always been my big, little sister and another person in my life that has always believed me capable of doing great things. You were the one who gave Afterlife its first identity and I am honoured to say that you continue to do so even today. We always dreamed of being able to work together and I am thrilled that we made it happen when you agreed to work as a designer at Hudson Indie Ink.

To my children, my wonderful daughter"Ava…who yes, is named after a cool, kick-ass demonic "bird and my sons, Jack who is a little hero and Halen

And last but not least, to the man that I consider my soul mate. The man who taught me about real love and makes me not only want to be a better person but makes me feel I am too. The amount of support you have given me since we met has been incredible and the greatest feeling was finding out you wanted to spend the rest of your life with me when you asked me to marry you.

All my love to my dear husband and my own personal Draven… Mr Blake Hudson.

To My Team…

I am so fortunate enough to rightly state the claim that I have the best team in the world!

It is a rare thing indeed to say that not a single person that works for Hudson Indie Ink doesn't feel like family, but there you have it. We are a Family.

Sarah your editing is a stroke of genius and you, like others in my team, work incredibly hard to make the Afterlife world what it was always meant to be. But your personality is an utter joy to experience and getting to be a part of your crazy feels like a gift.

Sloane, it is an honour to call you friend and have you working for Hudson Indie Ink. Your formatting is flawless and makes the authors books look perfect.

Xen, your artwork is always a masterpiece that blows me away and again, I am lucky to have you not only a valued member of my team but also as another talented Author represented by Hudson Indie Ink.

Lisa, my social media butterfly and count down Queen! I was so happy when you accepted to work with us, as I knew you would fit in perfectly with our family! Please know you are a dear friend to me and are a such an asset to the team. Plus, your backward dancing is the stuff of legends!

Libby, as our newest member of the team but someone I consider one of my oldest and dearest friends, you came in like a whirlwind of ideas and totally blew me away with your level of energy! You fit in instantly and I honestly don't know what Hudson Indie Ink would do without you. What you have achieved in such a short time is utterly incredible and want you to know you are such "a short time is utterly incredible and want you to know you are such an asset to the team!

And last but by certainly not least is the wonderful Claire, my right-hand woman! I honestly have nightmares about waking one day "and finding you not working for Hudson Indie Ink. You are the backbone of the company and without you and all your dedicated, hard work, there would honestly be no Hudson Indie Ink!

You have stuck by me for years, starting as a fan and quickly becoming one of my best friends. You have supported me for years and without fail have had my back through thick and thin, the ups and the downs. I could quite honestly write a book on how much you do and how lost I would be without you in my life!

I love you honey x

Thanks to all of my team for the hard work and devotion to the saga and myself. And always going that extra mile, pushing Afterlife into the spotlight you think it deserves. Basically helping me achieve my secret goal of world domination one day…evil laugh time… Mwahaha! Joking of course ;)

Another personal thank you goes to my dear friend Caroline Fairbairn and her wonderful family that have embraced my brand of crazy into their lives and given it a hug when most needed.

For their friendship I will forever be eternally grateful.

As before, a big shout has to go to all my wonderful fans who make it their mission to spread the Afterlife word and always go the extra mile. Those that have remained my fans all these years and supported me, my Afterlife family, you also meant the world to me.

All my eternal love and gratitude,
Stephanie x

About the Author

Stephanie Hudson has dreamed of being a writer ever since her obsession with reading books at an early age. What first became a quest to overcome the boundaries set against her in the form of dyslexia has turned into a life's dream. She first started writing in the form of poetry and soon found a taste for horror and romance. Afterlife is her first book in the series of twelve, with the story of Keira and Draven becoming ever more complicated in a world that sets them miles apart.

When not writing, Stephanie enjoys spending time with her loving family and friends, chatting for hours with her biggest fan, her sister Cathy who is utterly obsessed with one gorgeous Dominic Draven. And of course, spending as much time with her supportive partner and personal muse, Blake who is there for her no matter what.

Author's words.

My love and devotion is to all my wonderful fans that keep me going into the wee hours of the night but foremost to my wonderful daughter Ava...who yes, is named after a cool, kick-ass, Demonic bird and my sons, Jack, who is a little hero and Baby Halen, who yes, keeps me up at night but it's okay because he is named after a Guitar legend!

Keep updated with all new release news & more on my website

www.afterlifesaga.com
Never miss out, sign up to the
mailing list at the website.

Also, please feel free to join myself and other Dravenites on my Facebook group
Afterlife Saga Official Fan
Interact with me and other fans. Can't wait to see you there!

facebook.com/AfterlifeSaga
twitter.com/afterlifesaga
instagram.com/theafterlifesaga

Also by Stephanie Hudson

Afterlife Saga

Afterlife

The Two Kings

The Triple Goddess

The Quarter Moon

The Pentagram Child /Part 1

The Pentagram Child /Part 2

The Cult of the Hexad

Sacrifice of the Septimus /Part 1

Sacrifice of the Septimus /Part 2

Blood of the Infinity War

Happy Ever Afterlife /Part 1

Happy Ever Afterlife / Part 2

The Forbidden Chapters

*

Transfusion Saga

Transfusion

Venom of God

Blood of Kings

Rise of Ashes

Map of Sorrows

Tree of Souls

Kingdoms of Hell

Eyes of Crimson

Roots of Rage

Heart of Darkness

Wraith of Fire

Queen of Sins

Knights of Past

*

The HellBeast King Series

The Hellbeast King

The Hellbeast Fight

The Hellbeast's Mistake

The Hellbeast's Claim

The Hellbeast's Prisoner

The Hellbeast's Sacrifice

*

The Shadow Imp Series

Imp and the Beast

Beast and the Imp

*

King of Kings

Dravens Afterlife

Dravens Electus

*

Kings of Afterlife

Vincent's Immortal Curse

*

Afterlife Academy: (Young Adult Series)

The Glass Dagger

The Hells Ring

The Reapers Book

*

Stephanie Hudson and Blake Hudson

The Devil in Me

OTHER WORKS FROM HUDSON INDIE INK

Paranormal Romance/Urban Fantasy

Stephanie Hudson

Xen Randell

C. L. Monaghan

Sorcha Dawn

Harper Phoenix

Crime/Action

Blake Hudson

Jack Walker

Contemporary Romance

Gemma Weir

Nikki Ashton

Anna Bloom

Tatum Rayne

Ingram Content Group UK Ltd.
Milton Keynes UK
UKHW011046020623
422771UK00001B/22